BLANCO CANYON

DAVID E. WADDELL

Copyright © 2024 David E. Waddell
All rights reserved
First Edition

Fulton Books
Meadville, PA

Published by Fulton Books 2024

Blanco Canyon is a work of fiction. Any references to historical events, real people, or real locales are used fictitiously. Other names, characters, places, and incidents are the product of the author's imagination, and any resemblance to actual events or locales or persons, living or dead, is entirely coincidental. The views expressed by characters in this book are not necessarily those of the author.

ISBN 979-8-89427-040-1 (paperback)
ISBN 979-8-89427-041-8 (digital)

Printed in the United States of America

Also by David E. Waddell

Apache War Cry
The Lawless Land
Escape from Pandemonium
A Divided Family
Ransom
Canyon Station
Big Medicine
Old Washington

To Charlotte, Allyson, and Reagan

Be forewarned if the Comanches catch you near Blanco Canyon, you'll be tortured first and then roasted alive.

1

Arrows flew by Cooper McCaw while he was riding his horse at a fast gallop. Four Comanche warriors who were looking forward to taking his scalp were pursuing him. He drew his Winchester lever-action repeating rifle from its saddle scabbard before spinning his horse around. He cocked the lever on his rifle, aimed it at one of the Comanche warriors, and pulled its trigger. The bullet ripped into the warrior's chest knocking him off his horse.

Cooper cocked the lever on his rifle before picking out another Comanche to shoot at. He squeezed his rifle's trigger and watched his bullet kill the Comanche he was aiming at. He then slid his rifle back into its scabbard and drew his revolver from its leather holster. He kicked his horse into a fast gallop with the heels of his boots and charged toward the two remaining Comanche warriors.

The two Comanche warriors continued shooting arrows at Cooper while galloping their horses toward him. Cooper targeted one of the Comanches and pulled his revolver's trigger. His bullet smashed into the warrior's left shoulder. While the warrior was falling off his horse, Cooper shot him again. The warrior died before his body hit the ground.

Cooper turned his attention toward the last Comanche attacking him. He aimed his revolver at the Comanche and then squeezed its trigger twice. Two bullets ripped into the Comanche's chest while the Comanche was nocking his arrow. The Comanche dropped his bow and arrow before falling off his horse. He landed on his back and died a few moments later.

Cooper pulled back on his horse's reins to slow it down to a walk. He slid his revolver back into its holster, then spun his horse around and headed toward a small trading post called Dusty's. He was tired, needed a bath, and was running low on food and ammunition. His horse was exhausted and needed to be fed, watered, groomed; and its horseshoes needed to be replaced. He was also looking forward to drinking a shot or two of whiskey, and he knew Dusty's would have all that he needed.

He rode his horse for two hours before reaching Dusty's Trading Post. He rode his horse up to the hitching rail in front of the one-story adobe building, dismounted, and wrapped his horse's reins around the hitching rail. He walked into the building and saw Dusty Lange standing behind a counter wearing a smile on his face.

"Hello, Cooper," Dusty said. "It's been a while since I've seen you."

"It sure has," Cooper replied.

"What have you been up to these past two months?"

"Drifting here and there."

"Soldiers from Fort Concho have been stopping in here once a week looking for you."

"Did they say what they wanted?" a curious Cooper asked.

"They said their commanding officer needed to talk to you about something, but they wouldn't tell me what," Dusty replied.

"I'll ride to the fort in a few days and find out what its commanding officer wants, but right now, I need a bath and my horse could use some food, water, and a good grooming."

"I'll have one of my men take care of your horse while I'll go get your bath ready for you."

"My horse could use some new horseshoes too," Cooper suggested.

"No problem. I'll make sure your horse is taken care of."

"Thanks," Cooper said.

Dusty poured Cooper a shot of whiskey and handed it to him. Dusty placed the bottle of whiskey in front of Cooper and said, "Enjoy the whiskey while I go get the bathtub ready for you."

"I sure will," a grateful Cooper said while wearing a wide smile on his face.

*****

Cooper climbed out of the bathtub, dried his naked body off with a towel, and then shaved his face with a razor Dusty had left for him. He then walked over to a table where Dusty had left him a new pair of long johns, trousers, a shirt, and a pair of socks. After he put his new clothes on, he looked around the room for his worn-out cowboy boots. He smiled when he saw a new pair of boots on the floor near the door. He walked over to them and picked them up.

Cooper slipped his new boots on and then walked around the room. *Boy do these feel comfortable*, he thought as he continued walking around the room. He saw his gun belt lying on table and walked toward it. He reached for it and then buckled it around his waist. He drew his revolver and made sure it was fully loaded before sliding it back into its leather holster.

He then opened the door, walked through the doorway, and shut the door behind him.

Cooper felt refreshed and looked forward to having a beer and playing some cards with his old friend Dusty and a couple of his hired hands. He stopped dead in his tracks when he saw two of Dusty's hired hands lying on the floor moaning loudly from their injuries; they both had suffered.

Cooper looked up when he heard Dusty yelling. His lower jaw dropped open when he saw two large buffalo hunters pushing Dusty around.

"Get out of my trading post!" Dusty yelled at the two buffalo hunters pushing him around.

"Not before we break your neck!" a buffalo hunter named Asher shouted back.

"And your arms and legs too!" the other buffalo hunter named Jasper added.

Asher and Jasper kept pushing Dusty backward until Dusty's back was up against the bar. Dusty felt his body trembling with fear while the two buffalo hunters stared at him. He knew both men intended to cause him physical harm and could decide to kill him. He saw his life flash in front of him when both buffalo hunters drew their bowie knives from their leather sheaths.

"We changed our minds about breaking your neck, arms, and legs," Asher said wearing an evil smile on his face. "We're going to slice you up instead."

"After we cut your body up, we'll take your scalp just like a Comanche or Kiowa Injun would!" Jasper said with a threatening voice.

"Please don't," Dusty pleaded.

"Too late, we've already made our minds up," Asher said as he and Jasper both pointed their large knife blades at Dusty.

"I'm going to enjoy cutting your tongue off," Jasper said as he took a step toward Dusty.

"You'll never get the chance to," Cooper interrupted.

Both buffalo hunters froze when they heard Cooper's voice coming from behind them. Asher and Jasper spun around and saw a familiar face glaring at them.

"Stay out of this, or we'll kill you too!" Asher warned.

"Drop your knives," Cooper ordered.

"We take no orders from a coward!" Jasper exclaimed.

"I said drop your knives!" Cooper said in a stern voice while drawing his revolver from its holster.

"Get out of here before we decide to slice you up!" Asher exclaimed as he and Jasper each took a step toward Cooper.

"If either of you take another step toward me, I'll start shooting my revolver at you," Cooper warned.

"We'll slice you up before you get a chance to," Jasper said and then lunged at Cooper.

Cooper sidestepped out of the way and watched Jasper stumble past him. He then saw Asher's knife slicing at him and took a few steps backward as he pulled his revolver's trigger. Asher dropped his knife after a bullet ripped into his chest. He fell down onto his knees and gasped for air. He saw his knife lying on the floor next to him.

While reaching for it, he lost consciousness, fell face forward, and died when his face slammed into the floor.

"You killed my friend!" Jasper yelled.

Cooper spun around and saw Jasper charging toward him. Jasper attacked Cooper with his knife. He sliced his knife violently at Cooper but kept missing as Cooper kept ducking out of the way. Jasper heard gunfire and felt a hot burning bullet enter his abdomen. He looked down and saw blood seeping through his shirt.

Jasper's stomach felt like it was on fire. He moaned out loud before looking back up at Cooper. A second later, he saw a muzzle flash coming from Cooper's revolver. Cooper's bullet smashed into the middle of Jasper's forehead killing him instantly. Cooper watched Jasper's lifeless body fall to the ground as he slid his revolver back into its holster.

"You saved my life!" Dusty exclaimed as he came walking up to Dusty. "They were going to kill me."

"What did you do that made them want to kill you?" a curious Cooper asked.

"I just asked them to pay me their tab they've been running up the past few months."

"How much was it?"

"A lot and they told me they didn't have it," Dusty replied. "When I refused to serve them unless they paid up, they attacked me and my men."

"You won't have to worry about them anymore," Cooper said as he looked down at the two dead buffalo hunters. He then looked over at Dusty's two injured hired hands and said, "Let's help your two hired hands out. They got beat up pretty bad."

"They sure did," Dusty concurred before following Cooper over to his two injured employees.

Dusty and Cooper lifted the two men named Chuck and Austin and helped them over to a nearby table with four chairs around it. Cooper and Dusty helped Chuck and Austin sit down in two of the chairs before walking back over to the bar.

"They have some cuts and bruises, but nothing looks broken," Dusty said.

"They were lucky," Cooper said. "I knew those two men, and they were evil men."

"I hope they both rot in hell," Dusty said while pouring himself and then Cooper a shot of whiskey.

"They're probably there already, my friend," Cooper said and then downed his shot of whiskey.

Cooper set his empty shot glass down on the bar, looked at Dusty who had just chugged his shot of whiskey, and said, "Let's take a bottle of this snake medicine over to the table and share it with your two hired hands. The sooner they drink some of this, the sooner they'll feel better."

"It's what my doctor always prescribes," Dusty said, wearing a wide smile on his face.

"Mine too!" Cooper stated.

2

"He likes you!" Katherine White exclaimed.

"Who likes me?" Lillie Spencer asked.

"You know who!"

"Brett?"

"Yes, Brett!"

"I'm not sure I like him though," Lillie replied.

"There's no better-looking man in the whole wagon train," Jennie Farmer said as she joined in the conversation.

"Jennie's right. He's the best looking," Katherine said. "There's no one else that's even close."

"Looks aren't everything," Lillie said. "Kindness is more important to me than looks."

"Not me," Jennie said.

"It will be dark soon," Lillie warned. "We better get back to the wagons before everyone starts worrying about us."

"Lillie's right," Katherine said. "The sun has set."

"You look worried," Jennie said when she saw a concerned look on Lillie's face.

"I am worried," Lillie admitted. "The wagon master warned us not to venture too far from the wagons, and it looks like we have."

"We'll be okay," Jennie said. "We should make it back before it gets dark if we leave now."

The three young women started walking back to the wagon train. They walked as fast as they could. They were all warned not to venture far from the wagon train, but they didn't listen to the wagon master's warning.

"Why was the wagon master so concerned that we didn't venture far from camp?" a curious Katherine asked.

"He thought Indians could be nearby," Jennie replied.

"Friendly or hostile?" Katherine asked.

"Hostile," Jennie answered.

"Don't worry," Lillie said. "The wagon train is on the other side of that small hill up ahead. We don't need to worry about running into Indians anymore."

"Thank God, I was starting to get—"

Katherine stopped in midsentence when she saw ten Indians run out from behind a group of trees.

"Don't move!" Lillie warned as she, Katherine, and Jennie stopped dead in their tracks when they saw the ten male American Indians standing in front of them.

"We need to make a break for it," Jennie said.

"There's too many of them," Lillie said after she looked behind her and saw ten more Indians walking toward them.

"Maybe they're friendly Indians," Jennie suggested.

"They don't look friendly," Katherine said.

"What should we do?" Jennie asked as she felt her body trembling with fear.

"Pray," Lillie suggested.

*****

"Is your daughter, Lillie, and her two friends back yet?" the wagon master named Lloyd Mullen asked.

"Not yet," a concerned Ollie Spencer replied.

"We better mount up and go looking for them then," Lloyd suggested.

"Should we go get Katherine and Jennie's fathers too?"

"There's no reason to get them worried too. Plus they'll slow us up because they cannot ride horses as well as we can."

"You're right about that. They're lousy riders," Ollie concurred.

"Fetch your horse and meet me over there," Lloyd said as he pointed toward a large boulder.

"Okay, I'll meet you over there in a few minutes," Ollie said before walking away.

Ollie and Lloyd met at the prearranged location, mounted their horses, and then rode away from the large wagon train. They searched the area around the wagon train and found no trace of the missing three women. They widen the area of their search and halted their horses when they came across three dresses and three pairs of shoes lying on the ground. They quickly dismounted their horses and walked over to the dresses and shoes.

"Was your daughter wearing one of these dresses?" Lloyd asked.

"She was wearing this one," a sad-looking Ollie replied after he picked up a yellow cotton dress.

"These other two dresses must have belonged to Jennie Farmer and Katherine White."

"Why would they take their dresses and shoes off?" Ollie asked.

"They didn't take their dresses off," Lloyd replied. "They were torn off their bodies. These dresses are ripped up pretty good."

"They sure are," Ollie concurred as he examined his daughter's dress. He then looked toward Lloyd and asked, "What do you think happened to my daughter and her two friends?"

"They were kidnapped?"

"By whom?"

"Comanches or Kiowas," Lloyd replied.

Lloyd dropped the two dresses he was holding when some movement in the distance caught his attention. He then looked over at Ollie and said, "Mount up."

"What's wrong?" Ollie asked.

"We're being watched," Lloyd replied.

"By who?"

"Injuns," Lloyd replied.

An arrow flew past Lloyd as he remounted his horse. He drew his revolver from its holster and then kicked his horse into a gallop. While Ollie was mounting his horse, he felt a sharp pain in his right leg. He looked down and saw an arrow shaft sticking out of his knee. He ignored the pain and kicked his horse into a gallop and chased after Lloyd.

Lloyd saw two Indians riding their horses at a fast gallop toward him. He aimed his revolver at one of the Indians and then pulled its trigger. He watched his bullet slam into the Indian's chest. The Indian fell off his horse, landed on his back, and gasped for air. While Lloyd was turning his attention toward the other Indian, he felt an arrowhead penetrate his right shoulder. He tried to pull his revolver's trigger, but his right hand went numb. He frowned while watching his revolver fall out of his hand.

Lloyd's lower jaw dropped open when he saw the Indian nocking another arrow. He saw his life flash in front of him when the Indian pulled back his bowstring and aimed his arrow at him. While pulling back on his horse's reins with his left hand, Lloyd heard gunfire behind him. He felt relieved when he saw the Indian drop his bow and arrow. The Indian slumped over for a few moments before falling off his horse. Lloyd rode his horse up to Indian and watched the Indian take his last breath of air.

"Are you alright?" Ollie asked after he rode his horse up to Lloyd.

"I will be after this arrowhead is taken out of my right shoulder," Lloyd replied.

"I have one in my right knee," Ollie said while pointing at the arrow shaft. He then looked down at the dead Indian and asked, "Are the two Injuns we just killed Comanche or Kiowa?"

"Comanche," Lloyd said.

"So the Comanches kidnapped Lillie and her two friends?"

"Most likely."

"Will they kill them?" Ollie asked.

"I'm not sure," Lloyd said. "I've read stories about the Comanches. They love torturing their captives. If you're a male captive, you're tortured first and then roasted alive. Female captives are tortured for a while before becoming a warrior's squaw, sold into slavery or killed. Children are either killed instantly, sold into slavery, or adopted into a Comanche tribe."

"We need to find my daughter and her two friends before the Comanches decide their fate."

"We'll be killed before we can get close to them," Ollie warned. He looked at all the unshod hoofprints around the area where the torn dresses were found before saying, "Twenty or more Comanche warriors kidnapped your daughter and her two friends."

"We'll never see them again if we don't try to rescue them," Ollie said.

"Neither one of us will be able to pursue them for long with these arrowheads inside us," Lloyd said. "We need to ride back to the wagon train and get these arrowheads out of our bodies before they claim our lives. Once we get back to the wagon train, we can send someone to the nearest fort or town and get the cavalry or Texas Rangers looking for your daughter and her two friends. They know this territory like the back of their hands and will be able to track where the Comanches have taken your daughter and her two friends and then try to rescue them."

"Why didn't the Comanches let my daughter and her friends keep their clothes and shoes?" Ollie asked.

"They want to shame them in front of their entire tribe when they take them back to their village," Lloyd said. "The Comanche squaws will beat and torture your daughter and her two friends until their bodies are covered with cuts and bruises. Comanche warriors will then take turns raping them."

An upset-looking Ollie asked, "What will happen to them after that?"

"If they're lucky, some Comanche warriors will take them as their squaws," Lloyd replied.

"And if they're unlucky?"

"They'll be sold into slavery or killed!"

"I'm not letting those savages hurt my daughter," Ollie said. "I'm going to try to rescue my daughter and her two friends now."

"You'll be killed," Lloyd warned.

"I have to try and save my daughter," an angry-looking Ollie said and then used the heels of his boots to kick his horse into a fast gallop.

Lloyd frowned as he watched Ollie ride his horse away knowing he would never see Ollie alive again. He tried to warn Ollie not to go after his daughter, but Ollie wouldn't listened to him. Lloyd spun his horse around and headed back to the wagon train.

Lloyd felt a burning sensation inside his right shoulder coming from the arrowhead lodged inside it. After he rode his horse for a few minutes, he heard sounds of gunfire coming from a far distance behind him. He then felt tears running down his cheeks knowing the Comanches had just killed his good friend, Ollie.

3

Cooper McCaw rode his horse through the gates of Fort Concho. He was returning to the fort where he was stripped of his rank, dishonorably discharged, and branded a coward. A few soldiers started harassing Cooper when they saw him ride his horse up to the fort's headquarters.

Cooper ignored those soldiers harassing him and dismounted his horse. He wrapped his horse's reins around a nearby hitching rail before walking toward the fort's headquarters. Two soldiers that Cooper recognized blocked the entrance to the fort's headquarters and wouldn't move out of the way after Cooper said, "Excuse me."

"What are you doing back here?" Sergeant Otto Black asked.

"Major Cooney asked me to come."

"Turn around and leave before you get hurt," Corporal Luther Decker warned.

"I'm not going anywhere until I see Major Cooney," Cooper responded.

"You're a coward, and no one wants you here!" Sergeant Black yelled.

"You heard the sergeant! Leave before you get hurt!" Corporal Decker said in a threatening tone.

"Let me by before the two of you get hurt," Cooper warned as he took a step forward.

Cooper's movement toward Sergeant Black and Corporal Decker triggered the two soldiers into action. The sergeant threw a punch, but Cooper blocked it with his right forearm. Before the sergeant could swing again, Cooper hit the sergeant with an uppercut that landed underneath the sergeant's jaw. The force of the blow lifted the sergeant off the ground. He fell backward through the headquarters doorway and landed hard on his back. He tried to push himself up off the floor but lacked the strength to do so and then passed out.

"You knocked Sergeant Black out!" Corporal Decker exclaimed. "You'll pay for that!"

The corporal lunged at Cooper, but he was too slow. Cooper sidestepped out of the way and watched the corporal fly by him. The corporal lost his balance and fell flat on his face. He pushed himself up off the ground and charged toward Cooper who was waiting for him. Cooper threw a quick combination of punches, which all landed on the corporal's face. The punches stunned the corporal. He stumbled forward, fell to his knees, and then looked up at Cooper.

"You may see the major now," Corporal Decker said before falling forward and landing on the right side of his face.

"You just knocked out two of my best men," Major Kevin Cooney said as he stood underneath the doorway of his headquarters. "Come inside to my office. We need to talk." Major Cooney then turned around and walked back into his headquarters.

Cooper stepped over the bodies of Sergeant Black and Corporal Decker and followed Major Cooney into the headquarters of Fort Concho. The major led Cooper back to his office and motioned for him to sit down in one of the chairs across from his desk. Cooper sat down in one of the chairs, watched the major sit down in his high back chair, and then waited for the major to speak.

"It's good to see you, Cooper," Major Cooney said.

"I wish I could say the same to you, but I can't," Cooper said.

"I don't blame you. If I were you, I would never have even come back here."

"I was curious why you summoned me here since we used to be friends, so I decided to come."

"I'm glad you did," Major Cooney said. "You were once an outstanding cavalry officer until your command was massacred in the Battle of White River inside Blanco Canyon. Somehow you survived while all the soldiers you were commanding were wiped out. You were tried and convicted by a Military Court here at the fort and then were stripped of your rank, dishonorably discharged, and branded a coward. Now I'm going to give you a chance to be reinstated into the United States Cavalry with your old rank, and you will no longer be branded a coward."

"And what will I have to do to be reinstated into the cavalry?" a curious Cooper asked.

"Kidnap a Comanche warrior named White Buffalo," Major Cooney replied.

"What's so important about this Comanche warrior named White Buffalo?"

"He's the son of General Clayton Fitzpatrick who now commands the Fourth United States Cavalry, which includes all the soldiers within this fort. He'll be arriving here in a month. The general asked me to inquire if you would be willing to try to rescue his son from the Comanches. If you bring his son safely back to this fort, the general will make sure everything you were accused and convicted of in your past would be forgiven."

"Does the general have the authority to reinstate me back into the cavalry at my prior rank?"

"He sure does," Major Cooney replied.

"How did the general's son end up being a Comanche warrior?"

"His son was kidnapped by the Comanches when he was ten years old and had been living with them for the last fifteen years."

"Why hasn't the general tried to rescue his son before now?"

"The general tried to rescue his son fifteen years ago, but his rescue attempt failed. He also hired men in the past to rescue his son, but they all failed in their attempts."

"I saw a white man with long hair and a painted face fighting with the Comanches at the Battle of White River," Cooper said. "If that was White Buffalo, he won't want to come back to Fort Concho with me. After living with the Comanches for fifteen years, he's no longer a civilized white man he's now a full-blooded Comanche and will try to kill any white man who crosses his path."

"General Fitzpatrick believes you along two handpicked soldiers from this fort can sneak into Blanco Canyon, locate his son, and then forcibly bring him back to Fort Concho. He personally requested you to lead the rescue mission."

"It's not a rescue mission," Cooper said. "It's a suicide mission."

"You're the general's last hope, and he's willing to reinstate you back into the cavalry at your former rank if you succeed in bringing back his son to him."

"Let me think about it for a while."

"There's no time," Major Cooney said. "The general will be here in one month, and he wants his son here waiting for him when he arrives."

"Even if I can bring him back here without losing my scalp, he'll try to break out of here as soon as he arrives."

"Once you deliver him here to Fort Concho, he becomes the general's problem so you won't have to worry about that." The major paused for a moment before asking Cooper, "Aren't you tired of being called a coward when you're not?"

"So you believed me when I told you that I didn't desert my men during the Battle of White River?"

"Of course I did."

"Then why didn't you testify for me at my trial?"

"How could I when I wasn't there?"

"Good point," Cooper said.

"So will you risk your life and try to kidnap White Buffalo and then try to bring him back alive?"

Before answering the major's question, Cooper walked over to a map hanging on a wall inside the major's office. He pointed to dark line on the map leading from Fort Concho to Blanco Canyon. "This trail here is called Tomahawk Trail. It's the only way to the area inside Blanco Canyon where the Comanche Nation is now camped. The Comanche watch this trail all the time. Any white man caught traveling down Tomahawk Trail toward Blanco Canyon loses their scalp."

"That's what I hear," Major Cooney confirmed before standing up. The major joined Cooper in front of the map and said, "I know it's a suicide mission. The general knows it is too, but he begged me to ask you to try to rescue his son. The general is getting old and wants to reunite with his son before he's forced to retire. He knows you know the area around and inside Blanco Canyon better than any other soldier or civilian.

"That's what people tell me," Cooper said while staring at the map.

"You're the only man I know who might be able to make it Blanco Canyon, rescue the general's son, and bring him back here to Fort Concho without losing your life."

"I won't be rescuing him," Cooper said as he turned away from the map and faced the major. "I'll be kidnapping the general's son from a Comanche camp located inside Blanco Canyon at the end of Tomahawk Trial. It's a suicide mission!"

"I know it is and the general does too," Major Cooney said. The major put his right hand on top of Cooper's left shoulder before and said, "That's why he's promising to reinstate you into the Fourth Cavalry at your previous rank if you bring his son back to Fort Concho alive."

Cooper turned away from the major and looked back at the map and studied it. After a few seconds passed by, Major Cooney asked, "Will you take two soldiers with you down Tomahawk Trail then proceed into Blanco Canyon and try to rescue the general's son?"

Cooper continued staring at the map for a few more moments before answering, "I'll try."

"Good," Major Cooney said while wearing a smile on his face. "General Fitzpatrick will be happy when he hears that you're willing to try to rescue his son."

"You said that two soldiers from this fort would accompany me on this suicide mission I'm going on?"

"Yes, I did, and you may pick the two soldiers since you know most of the soldiers in this fort."

"I want Sergeant Otto Black and Corporal Luther Decker to accompany me," Cooper said.

"You want the two soldiers that you just beat up for calling you a coward to go with you?" a stunned Major Cooney asked.

"Yes, I do," Cooper replied. He then said, "I know they hate me, but they're the two best soldiers you have here at Fort Concho."

"Yes, they are," Major Cooney concurred. The major then reached into his desk drawer and pulled out a piece of paper and handed it to Cooper. He then said, "Take this note to the quartermaster, and he'll give you all the supplies you need for your rescue mission."

"I want some civilian clothes for Sergeant Black and Corporal Decker."

"Why?"

"Because if the Comanches think we're ranchers looking for stray cattle, they might not kill us if they spot us near or inside Blanco Canyon. If they see Black and Decker wearing their uniforms, they'll try to kill us for sure."

"I'll take them into town and get them some clothes, boots, and two wide-brimmed hats to wear while you go to the quartermaster and get the rest of the supplies you'll need," Major Cooney promised.

"Can you get them two Henry leverage-action repeating rifles, two gun belts with two navy colt revolvers, and plenty of ammunition too?"

"Sure," Major Cooney said. "I'll make sure they have everything they need to pass as ranchers instead of soldiers."

"Thanks," Cooper said before leaving Major Cooney's office.

*****

Cooper grinned when he saw Sergeant Black and Corporal Decker wearing clothes a rancher would wear instead of their uniforms. Both men were proud cavalrymen and hated wearing anything beside their uniforms. He motioned to Black and Decker to mount their horses before mounting his own. The three men then rode their horses through the gates of Fort Concho and then headed toward Blanco Canyon.

All three men kept to themselves as they rode their horses. Black and Decker didn't like Cooper, and Cooper didn't like them. Cooper could have picked any two soldiers from Fort Concho that he wanted to and chose the two that hated him the most. He knew most of the cavalrymen killed during the Battle of White River had been friends with the two men that were now accompanying him. He also knew both men held him personally liable for their deaths.

As they rode their horses down Tomahawk Trail toward Blanco Canyon, Cooper kept his right hand near his revolver's holster just in case the sergeant or corporal tried to attack him. He didn't want to kill either man because he needed both of them to help him kidnap White Buffalo and then bring the captured Comanche warrior back to Fort Concho alive. Cooper was tired of being branded a coward and wanted his reputation restored. He knew the odds were stacked against him bringing White Buffalo back to Fort Concho alive, but he didn't care. He would try anything to get reinstated back into the cavalry, get his good reputation back, and no longer be branded a coward.

4

"Do you hear gunfire?" Captain Josh Stephens of the Texas Rangers asked after he and his small company of Texas Rangers halted their horses.

"I sure do," a Texas Ranger named Chester Taylor replied.

"It's coming from that direction," Josh said as he pointed to the north. He then looked back at the fifteen Texas Rangers riding with him and yelled, "Follow me, men!" Josh and the fifteen rangers accompanying him kicked their horses into a fast gallop and rode toward the sounds of the gunfire they were hearing.

The Texas Rangers rode their horses to the top of a small hill and halted when they saw a small band of Comanche warriors chasing after a Wells Fargo stagecoach. Josh and his men drew their revolvers and then rode their horses at a fast gallop toward the stagecoach. When the Comanches saw the small company of Texas Rangers approaching, they broke off attacking the stagecoach and charged their horses toward Captain Josh Stephens and his men.

Josh aimed his revolver at one of the Comanches and then pulled its trigger. He watched his bullet slam into the Comanche. The impact of his bullet knocked the warrior off his horse. The Comanche died moments later lying on his back. Josh saw another Comanche bearing down on him and quickly aimed his revolver at him. He pulled his revolver's trigger twice. His two bullets ripped into the Comanche's chest killing him instantly.

Captain Josh Stephens and his Texas Rangers were fighting courageously against the Comanche warriors. They used their revolvers and lever-action repeating rifles while attacking the Comanches. The

Comanches fought back bravely using rifles, bows and arrows, tomahawks, and their hunting knives.

Josh saw four Comanche warriors bearing down on one of his men. He drew his Henry lever-action repeating rifle from its saddle scabbard, cocked its lever, and then aimed it at one of the Comanche warriors. Josh squeezed his rifle's trigger and watched the Comanche warrior fall off his horse after a bullet smashed into his chest. He cocked his rifle's lever and then targeted another Comanche.

When Josh was sure he wouldn't miss, he pulled his rifle's trigger and watched his bullet hit and kill the Comanche he was targeting. He slid his rifle back into its leather scabbard then drew his revolver from its holster. He kicked his horse into a fast gallop and charged toward the two remaining Comanches that were attacking a Texas Ranger named Johnny Nelson. He saw Johnny shoot and kill one of the Comanches but then watched in horror another Comanche shoot an arrow right into the middle of Johnny's chest.

Josh saw the Comanche nocking an arrow and aimed his revolver at the Comanche. He pulled his revolver's trigger and watched his bullet rip through the Comanche's throat. The Comanche dropped his bow and arrow as he fell off his horse gasping for air. Josh returned his attention to Johnny Nelson and frowned when he saw Johnny falling off his horse.

Josh rode his horse over to Johnny then dismounted his horse He knelt down next to Johnny and saw his fellow Texas Ranger take his last breath and then close his eyes. Josh felt a tear running down his right cheek as he remounted his horse. He wiped the tear from his cheek with the right sleeve of his shirt then kicked his horse into a gallop and rejoined the battle.

Josh saw a Comanche charging toward him. He aimed his revolver at him and then pulled its trigger twice. He watched two bullets smash into the Comanche's abdomen. The warrior dropped his rifle, slid off his horse, and died moments later after his body landed on the ground. Josh spun his horse around and rode toward the rest of his men who were engaging the enemy.

A Texas Ranger named David Smith saw Josh riding up to him and asked in a loud voice, "Hey, Captain, did we pull all the Comanches away from the stagecoach?"

"We sure did," Josh replied as he rode up alongside David's horse.

"Good, because I was—"

Josh was stunned momentarily after he saw a tomahawk land with a thud in the middle of David's chest. David had a shock expression on his face as he fell backward off his horse. Josh drew his revolver from its holster and aimed it at the Comanche who threw his tomahawk at David. He pulled his revolver's trigger and watched the bullet slam into the middle of the Comanche's forehead.

A bullet whistled past Josh's left ear while he was looking back at the lifeless body belonging to David Smith. He spun back around and saw a Comanche warrior aiming his rifle at him. He quickly aimed his revolver at the Comanche and then pulled its trigger. The bullet fired from Josh's revolver penetrated the Comanche's left shoulder. Josh targeted the same Comanche again and pulled his revolver's trigger. This time his bullet struck the Comanche underneath his left eye killing him instantly.

Josh joined the rest of his men and continued fighting the Comanches. He saw two more of his men lying dead on the ground. When he saw two Comanches trying to take their scalps, he drew his Henry lever-action repeating rifle from its leather saddle scabbard and then shot and killed both Comanche warriors before they could scalp his two fallen comrades.

"They're breaking off the attack!" a jubilant Texas Ranger named Jonah Buchanan exclaimed.

Josh and the surviving Texas Rangers all breathed a sigh of relief while they watched the Comanche warriors ride their horses away. Dead bodies belonging to four Texas Rangers and dozens of Comanche warriors were scattered all over the ground. A few more Comanches were mortally wounded and would drift off to their spirit world soon.

Josh looked at his men and then ordered them to bury their fallen comrades. Once the four dead Texas Rangers were buried and prayers were completed, Captain Josh Stephens and his men mounted their horses and chased after the Wells Fargo coach.

*****

"How many rangers were killed?" Major Noah Higgins asked.

"Four, sir," Captain Josh Stephens replied.

"You were lucky. You could have lost more."

"Yes, we could of," Josh concurred. "We were outnumbered three to one."

"Texas Rangers are always outnumbered, but we're used to it, aren't we?"

"We sure are, sir," Josh replied.

"You and your company of rangers deserve some rest, but unfortunately, it's going to have to wait," Major Higgins said. "I need you and your men to leave tomorrow morning on a rescue mission."

"Who needs rescuing?" a curious Josh asked.

"Three young women."

"Who kidnapped them? Was it outlaws, Comacheros, Kiowas, or the Comanches?"

"The Comanches," Major Higgins replied. "The three women wondered a little too far from their wagon train and that's when the Comanches took them. Their names are Katherine White, Lillie Spencer, and Jennie Farmer."

"Do you know where the Comanches took the women?" Josh asked.

"An Indian scout for the cavalry spotted three white women on Tomahawk Trail with a war party of Comanches. They were heading toward Blanco Canyon," Major Higgins replied.

"Someone once told me, 'Be forewarned if the Comanches catch you near Blanco Canyon, you'll be tortured first and then roasted alive.'"

"Whoever told you that was right, so be careful! If you and your men don't spot three young white women inside the Comanche village that's located inside Blanco Canyon, get out of the canyon as fast as you can. If you find the three women alive, try to bring them back here safely. I wish I could send more men with you, but as usual, we're shorthanded."

"We'll try our best to bring them back alive," Josh said.

"That's what I told their families," Major Higgins said and then shook Josh's right hand. He then said, "Make sure no Comanche takes your scalp. The young ladies in this town will never forgive me if you get killed."

"I'll try my best, sir," Josh said, wearing a grin on his face. He then left Major Higgin's office thinking about the mission the major was sending him and his men on.

Josh was familiar with Tomahawk Trail and the area surrounding Blanco Canyon, but he had never ventured inside the canyon knowing if he did, he probably never return out of that canyon alive. Now he was ordered to venture inside it to locate and rescue three young women whom the Comanches had kidnapped. He knew even if he and his men were successful in locating and sneaking the women out of the Comanche village located inside Blanco Canyon the odds of them getting out of that canyon alive were slim. But he and his men were Texas Rangers, and they were used to risking their lives for others who decided to settle in or travel through the great state of Texas.

5

The three young women who were kidnapped by the Comanches lay naked on their backs inside a tepee. Their naked bodies were covered with bruises and cuts from the torture they all suffered during their journey to the Comanche village inside Blanco Canyon. All three of them had been raped several times by the Comanche warriors who kidnapped them, and now they all lay naked on their backs with their wrists and ankles bound with leather straps not knowing what their futures would be and what types of torture they would all face during their captivity inside this Comanche village.

All three women heard stories of settlers being captured by Indians and how few were ever rescued. All three had kept their faith in God and prayed to him daily asking him to save them from the savages who held them in captivity. Their journey to the Comanche village had been long and brutal, and their bodies ached with pain. They felt dirty on the inside and outside of their bodies, and their lives had been changed forever. None of the three young women knew what their futures would be, but they all knew it would be full of more horrors and pain both physically and mentally.

All three women gasped with fear when they saw the buffalo hide covering the tepee's entrance pulled back. A Comanche squaw walked into the tepee carrying three deerskin dresses in her arms. She set the three dresses on the ground and then cut the leather straps that bound the three captives' wrists and ankles. She then introduced herself to the three young women.

"My name is Sun Flower, and I learned to speak English from other white captives that were living inside this village over the years."

"My name is Katherine, and their names are Lillie and Jennie," Katherine said as she pointed at her two friends.

"Please put on these three dresses, and I'll go get you each a pair of moccasins," Sun Flower said before she left the tepee.

"She seemed friendly," Lillie said as she, Katherine, and Jennie slipped on the deerskin dresses that Sun Flower had brought them.

"She's the first friendly face we've seen since being kidnapped," Jennie said.

The buffalo hide covering the front entrance to the tepee was pulled back again, and all three captives smiled when they saw Sun Flower return. She wore a friendly smile on her face and handed Katherine, Lillie, and Jennie each a pair of moccasins. She then said, "Put these on and the bottom of your feet will feel better when you walk."

"Thank you for your kindness," Katherine said as she took a pair of moccasins from Sun Flower.

"You three have been through a lot since being captured. You deserve a little kindness."

"When will the men of your village quit torturing us?" Jennie asked.

"You won't have to worry about our warriors torturing you anymore," Sun Flower said. "Now it's the Comanche squaws turn, and they are just as bad."

"You're kidding us, right?" Lillie said.

"I'm afraid not," Sun Flower replied. "Unless some warriors here in this camp take interest in the three of you, the squaws in this village will make your life a living hell."

"So if I marry a Comanche warrior, I'll be treated like any other squaw in this village?" Katherine asked.

"Yes," Sun Flower replied.

"What happens if no warriors in your village takes a liking to us?" a worried Lillie asked.

"You'll be tortured some more and then traded to some white men and Mexicans that call themselves Comancheros," Sun Flower warned.

"What can we be traded for?" Jennie asked.

"Rifles and ammunition, which can be used to keep the white-eyes off our land," Sun Flower said.

"What will the Comancheros do with us if your village trade us to them?" Katherine asked.

"I'm not sure, but I hear stories that it's not good," Sun Flower replied. She then changed the subject and said, "Come with me now. I need to teach the three of you how to work like a squaw."

Sun Flower motioned to the three young white female captives to follow her, and they obeyed. The Comanche squaw took them outside and showed them how to do some chores around the village that they would be required to do every day. As they were learning how to do the chores, they saw many Comanche warriors, squaws, and children staring at them. Some of the Comanche children threw rocks at the three white female captives while they worked on their chores.

"Even the children inside this village hate us," Lillie said after a small rock hit her in the middle of her back.

"We have to ignore their hatred of us," Katherine said.

"How can we when they make it so obvious they don't want us here?" Lille asked.

"We need to learn how to do all the chores they want us to do and learn them well," Katherine replied. "If they think we're worthless, they will trade us to the Comancheros."

"So what if they trade us to the Comancheros?" Lillie said. "Living with the Comancheros can't be any worse than living with these savages."

"Yes, it is," Jennie said as she joined in the conversation. "I've heard many stories about the Comancheros and what they do to their captives. They torture their female captives then rape them over and over again."

"The Comanches have already done that to us," Lillie said.

"Yes, they have, but we're still alive. And as long as we stay here in this village, there's a chance we'll be rescued," Jennie said. "Once the Comancheros are done torturing and raping their female captives, they either kill them or trade them away to someone who will continue torturing them and then those female captives are never heard of again."

"The best chance of us not being traded to the Comancheros is for us to work hard here and have three of the warriors inside this village marry us," Katherine suggested.

"Marry us?" Lillie asked as she became more and more appalled by the memories of being raped by the Comanche warriors that Katherine was now suggesting they marry.

"Yes, that is what I said," Katherine replied.

"There is no way I'm going to marry one of those savages who raped us!" Lillie exclaimed.

"If you don't, you'll become property of the Comancheros, and then you'll never have a chance of being rescued again," Katherine replied.

"If I remain trapped here in this Comanche village or traded away to the Comancheros, it doesn't matter to me anymore," Lillie said. "God hasn't heard our prayers, and no one is ever going to rescue us."

"You can't give up!" Jennie said with a stern voice.

"It's too late. I already have," Lille said and then ran as fast as she could toward a group of horses she saw grazing on tallgrass.

Two Comanche warriors saw Lillie running toward the horses. They watched her mount one of the horses as they nocked the end of their arrows against their bowstrings. They pulled back their bowstrings and aimed their arrows at Lillie as she spun her horse around. Before she could kick her horse into a gallop, the two Comanche warriors let go of their bowstrings and then watched their arrows fly toward Lillie.

The two warriors' arrows struck Lillie's chest and became embedded deep in her heart. She fell off her horse and landed on her back gasping for air. Katherine and Jennie both cried out when they saw their dear friend lying on the ground with two arrow shafts sticking out of her chest. They both tried to run toward their fallen friend but were stopped by Sun Flower and several other Comanche squaws.

"If you run to her, you may be killed too," Sun Flower warned as she and several other squaws held back Jennie and Katherine.

"Let us go!" Jennie demanded.

"No!" Sun Flower responded. She then looked at the other squaws holding on to the two white female captives and said, "Take them back to their tepee and then tie their wrists and ankles up."

The squaws all nodded and then dragged Jennie and Katherine back to the tepee where they had been held captive in since arriving in the Comanche village. After the squaws tied up Katherine and Jennie, they left the two white female captives lying on their backs mourning over the death of their dear friend Lillie. As they both mourned, they wondered if they would ever be rescued from this hellhole they were living in.

6

Cooper McCaw pulled back on his horse's reins when he saw six Indians sitting tall on their horses on top of a small hill two hundred yards in front of them. He looked back over his left shoulder and used his left hand to signal Sergeant Otto Black and Corporal Luther Decker to halt their horses.

"Why are we stopping?" a curious Sergeant Black asked as he and Corporal Decker halted their horses next to Cooper.

"We have company," Cooper replied and then pointed at the six Indians.

"Are they Comanche or Kiowa?" Sergeant Black asked.

Cooper took his binoculars out of his saddlebag and looked through them at the six Indians. He then lowered his binoculars and replied, "Comanches."

"Should we try to get away from them?" Corporal Decker asked.

"No," Cooper replied. "We have to kill them all so they can't warn their village about us."

"They outnumber us two to one," Sergeant Black warned.

"So what if they do?" Cooper said. He then drew his revolver from its leather gun belt and said to Sergeant Black and Corporal Decker, "Draw your revolver and follow me." He then used the heels of his boots and kicked his horse into a gallop.

"Wasn't he branded a coward?" Corporal Decker said as he drew his revolver from its holster.

"He was!" Sergeant Black exclaimed as he drew his revolver.

"He sure isn't acting like a coward right now," Corporal Decker said and then kicked his horse into a gallop and chased after Cooper.

"No, he isn't," Sergeant Black mumbled underneath his breath before kicking his horse into a fast gallop and chasing after Cooper and Corporal Decker.

*****

The six Comanche warriors pulled back on their bowstrings and aimed their arrows at Cooper, Sergeant Black, and Corporal Decker. They waited patiently until their enemies drew nearer before they let go of their bowstrings. They quickly nocked their arrows and aimed their arrows at their enemies again.

Cooper signaled to his two men to separate from him after he saw the Comanche warriors aiming their arrows at them. Arrows flew by them as they separated their horses from each other. Cooper waved his revolver at Sergeant Black and then Corporal Decker and signaled both of them to attack the Comanche warriors on their flanks. While Black and Decker attacked the Comanche warriors on their flanks, Cooper rode his horse at a fast gallop straight toward the Comanche warriors.

Cooper picked out a Comanche warrior to aim his revolver at and then targeted that warrior. He pulled his revolver's trigger and watched his bullet slam into the Comanche's chest. The impact of the bullet knocked the Comanche off his horse. The Comanche warrior died moments later after he landed on his back.

An arrow whizzed over Cooper's head as he targeted another Comanche warrior. He pulled his revolver's trigger twice and watched his two bullets kill the warrior. He then turned his attention to Sergeant Black and Corporal Decker to see how they were holding up in attacking the remaining four Comanche warriors.

Sergeant Black heard an arrow whiz by his right ear just before he pulled his revolver's trigger. His bullet hit the Comanche warrior he was aiming at. The warrior felt a bullet burning inside his abdomen as he tried to nock an arrow to his bowstring. He lost control of the arrow and watched it fall to the ground. His stomach felt like it was on fire as he reached for another arrow from his quiver. Before he could draw another arrow from his quiver, another bullet struck and killed him.

Sergeant Black turned his attention toward another Comanche warrior and aimed his revolver at him. He saw the warrior nocking an arrow as he aimed his revolver at the warrior. He then pulled his revolver's trigger and frown soon afterward when he realized his bullet had missed hitting the warrior. He watched the warrior pull his bowstring back while aiming the arrow at him.

Just before the Comanche let go of his bowstring, a bullet shot from Cooper's revolver and struck the middle of the Comanche's forehead killing him instantly. Cooper halted his horse next to Sergeant Black and asked, "Are you all right?"

"I am now thanks to you," a very relieved Sergeant Black replied.

"Let's go help Corporal Decker," Cooper ordered and then kicked his horse into a fast gallop.

Sergeant Black slid his empty revolver into its holster and then drew his lever-action repeating rifle from its saddle scabbard. He then used the heels of his boots and kicked his horse into a fast gallop and chased after Cooper.

*****

Corporal Decker heard his horse squeal and felt it stumble forward. He let go of his horse's reins and jumped off his horse. Miraculously, he landed on his feet, turned around, and saw his horse lying on its side. As he was running toward his horse, he noticed two arrow shafts sticking out of his horse's body. One stuck out of the horse's ribs and the other protruded from its left shoulder.

When Corporal Decker reached his horse's carcass, he dove behind it. He tried to draw his lever-action repeating rifle from its saddle scabbard, but it wouldn't budge. He then realized that his horse's dead weight was trapping his rifle. He then peeped over his horse's carcass and saw two Comanche warriors galloping their horses toward him. He reached for his revolver and felt chills running down his spine when he felt an empty leather holster on his right hip. He then remembered dropping his revolver by accident when he jumped off his horse.

As the two Comanche warriors charged toward him, Corporal Decker drew his hunting knife from his leather sheath. He knew his knife was no match against two Comanche warriors' bows and arrows, but it was the only weapon he had left. When the two Comanche warriors saw Corporal Decker had only a knife for a weapon, they both halted their horses. They both nocked arrows to their bowstrings and grinned confidently as they pulled back their bowstrings and aimed their arrows at Corporal Decker. Both Comanches' grins faded suddenly, however, when they heard gunfire and felt hot burning bullets penetrate deep into their bodies.

Corporal Decker smiled from ear to ear after he heard the gunfire and watched both Comanche warriors fall off their horses. He then turned around and saw Cooper and Sergeant Black riding their horses toward him at a fast gallop. He stood up and waved joyfully at his two comrades as they rode their horses toward him. He was thankful to be alive and was eager to thank the two men who just saved his life.

*****

"Are you okay?" Sergeant Black asked Corporal Decker after he and Cooper both halted their horses next to him.

"I am thanks to you two," Corporal Decker replied wearing a smile on his face. "You two just saved my life."

"You're welcome," Sergeant Black responded. He then pointed at Cooper and said, "I would be dead but for our friend Cooper here. He saved my life."

"Do you still think he's a coward?" Corporal Decker asked.

"Not anymore," Sergeant Black replied.

Cooper smiled at the two soldiers and then said to both soldiers, "Let's find Corporal Decker's revolver and pull his rifle out from underneath his dead horse."

"Yes, sir," a happy-looking Corporal Decker and Sergeant Black replied concurrently.

Cooper dismounted his horse and walked slowly up to a horse belonging to one of the Comanches they had just shot and killed. He grabbed the horse's leather reins then petted it gently on its forehead and then looked back at the two soldiers and said, "Take the saddle off Corporal Decker's dead horse and bring it over here. This horse once belonged to a ranch located not too far from here. I recognized the ranch's brand on this horse's right thigh."

"It looks like Cooper found you a horse you can ride," Sergeant Black said.

"Good because I wasn't looking forward to riding double with you," Corporal Decker said as he and the sergeant approached his dead horse.

"Why?" a curious Sergeant Black asked.

"Because you fart too much."

"No, I don't!" Sergeant Black exclaimed before saying, "It's my horse that farts a lot."

"You both fart too much," Corporal Decker stated.

"No, we—"

"Hurry up you two!" Cooper interrupted. "We have a long way to ride before we reach Blanco Canyon, and we're wasting time here."

"Yes, sir!" both soldiers replied.

7

Captain Josh Stephens and his company of Texas Rangers rode out of Lubbock, Texas, and headed for Blanco Canyon. Their orders were to locate and then rescue three white women whom the Comanches had kidnapped and taken back to their village located somewhere inside Blanco Canyon. Josh and his men stayed alert as they rode their horses down Tomahawk Trail knowing at any moment; they could be attacked by Comanche warriors or Comancheros. They traveled for eight hours before setting up camp alongside a stream.

Josh and his men were exhausted from their ride and enjoyed the bacon and beans they cooked for themselves. They groomed, fed, and watered their horses before gathering around the several campfires they made for themselves. They chatted with each other for a while before lying out their bedrolls. Josh ordered several of his men to take turns guarding their campsite while he and the others slept. Before he closed his eyes, Josh said a short prayer thanking God for protecting him and his men so far.

*****

"Wake up!" Anton Rollins said with a stern voice when he saw Isaac Canterbury sleeping on his stomach. "You're on sentry duty!"

When Isaac didn't respond, Anton knelt down beside him and shook his shoulders. Anton became furious when Isaac didn't respond and yelled, "Wake up!" He then rolled Isaac over onto his back.

Anton's lower jaw dropped opened when he saw Isaac had been killed. Blood covered Isaac's upper body. A knife had sliced opened his body from his throat down to his belly button. It was a horrific sight.

I need to warn Captain Stephens and the other rangers, Anton thought to himself. He stood up, turned around, and then froze when he saw four Comanche warriors standing in front of him with their bowstrings pulled back and nocked with arrows. Before he could sound the alarm, four arrows penetrated his chest. He fell backward and landed on his back gasping for air. Just before he passed away, he saw four hostile Comanche warriors looking down at him.

*****

The sounds of gunfire woke Captain Josh Stephens up. He drew his revolver from his gun belt that was lying on the ground next to him and looked toward the sounds of gunfire. He saw several of his men lying on the ground with arrow shafts sticking out of their bodies.

Josh stood up and yelled, "We're under attack!" He then aimed his revolver at a Comanche warrior that was charging toward him and pulled its trigger. His bullet slammed into the Comanche, knocking him onto his back. He ran up to the Comanche and shot him in the chest, making sure he was dead.

A ranger named Jonah Buchanan came running up to Josh and asked, "All you all right, Captain?"

"Yes," Josh replied. He then looked around the campsite and saw his men defending their lives against the attacking Comanche warriors. He quickly turned his attention back to Jonah and said, "We need to get ourselves and the rest of the rangers back to those trees before the Comanches slaughter us all. Tell the rangers over there to retreat to those trees, and I'll go tell the others."

"Yes, sir!" Jonah said and then took off running.

Josh saw a small group of his men pinned down by the hostile Comanche warriors. He slid his revolver back into its leather holster and picked up his Henry lever-action repeating rifle. He targeted the first Comanche warrior he saw, cocked his rifle's lever, and then pulled its trigger. His rifle's bullet slammed into the warrior's chest. He quickly cocked the lever on his rifle, aimed it at another Comanche warrior, and then pulled its trigger. His bullet hit and killed the warrior he was aiming at.

After killing the two Comanche warriors, Josh ran over to his men and ordered them to withdraw to the group of trees at the north side of their campsite. As his men retreated, Josh gave them cover fire until they all safely reached the trees. He started retreating back toward the trees when his men began giving him cover fire. He shot one and killed one more Comanche warrior as he retreated.

When Josh reached the group of trees safely, he ordered his men to give Jonah and the rangers he was ordered to bring back to the trees cover fire. Comanche arrows ripped into several of the Texas Rangers retreating to the trees with Jonah. Josh and the rangers with him concentrated their fire on the Comanches chasing after Jonah and the other rangers with him. There bullets smashed into several Comanche warriors killing or mortally wounding them. The intense cover fire from Josh and his men forced the Comanches to retreat allowing Jonah and the few rangers with him to reach the group of trees safely.

Josh and his Texas Rangers waited for another Comanche attack. They kept themselves hidden as best they could behind the trees they chose for their defensive position. They didn't have to wait long before the Comanches attacked them again. The Comanches rushed the group of trees the Texas Rangers were defending.

Arrows slammed into the trees the Texas Rangers were standing behind. The Comanches charged toward the trees shooting their arrows as they ran toward the Texas Rangers. As the Comanches drew nearer to the rangers, they started throwing tomahawks and lances.

The Texas Rangers kept their rifles and revolvers aimed at the Comanches as they waited for Captain Josh Stephens to issue the order to fire.

"Pick out your targets!" Josh shouted and then aimed his revolver at a Comanche warrior. He waited a few seconds more and then yelled, "Fire!"

Comanche warriors screamed as bullets ripped into their bodies. Many of them fell to their deaths while others were badly wounded.

The intense fire from the Texas Rangers' weapons drove the remaining Comanches back.

"Hold your fire!" Josh shouted to his men when he saw the Comanche warriors retreating.

"They're running away!" a jubilant-sounding Jonah yelled out.

"Should we chase after them?" a Texas Ranger named JT asked.

"No!" Josh quickly responded. "They are too many, and we are too few."

A Texas Ranger named Chester came running up to Josh and exclaimed, "Our horses are all gone!"

Josh looked over to the area where he and his men had secured their horses and frowned when he saw they were all gone. He then looked at Chester and said, "The Comanches must have stolen them while they were attacking us."

"Without our horses, we will have to quit our rescue mission and return to Lubbock," Chester suggested.

"We're not abandoning our rescue mission," Josh said. "Those three women that we were sent to rescue need our help, and we're not going to quit on them."

"So we're going to walk down Tomahawk Trail to Blanco Canyon?" Chester asked.

"We sure are, and if we're lucky, we might run into those Comanches that stole our horses along the way," Josh replied. Josh looked around the campsite at all the death that surrounded it. Bodies of dead Texas Rangers and Comanche warriors littered the campsite. He then looked at Jonah and asked, "How many casualties did we suffer?"

"It looks like we lost half the company, sir."

"How about the injured?"

"A few suffered flesh wounds but nothing serious."

"Order the men to dig shallow graves for our men who died during the Comanche ambush," Josh said. He holstered his revolver and then picked up his lever-action repeating rifle. He then looked at Jonah and said, "I'm going to see where those Comanches are heading, and if they stop and set up camp somewhere near, we can ambush them and get our horses back."

"I hope we can ambush them," Jonah said. "They killed a lot of our friends tonight."

"They sure did," Josh concurred, wearing a frown on his face. He then walked away from Jonah wondering how the Comanche warriors had gotten by his sentries without being seen. *I wonder if they dozed off while they were on sentry duty,* he thought to himself as he followed the tracks of his and the other rangers' horses the Comanches had stolen.

8

"My whole body aches," Katherine White said while lying down on her blanket inside a small tepee that her and Jennie Farmer had been sharing inside Chief Black Hawk's village.

"My body is sore too," Jennie said as she, too, lay down on her blanket.

Both women picked up buffalo hides, lying on the ground next to them, and covered their sore and badly bruised bodies. They both lay still trying to forget another day they had both spent in captivity living in the Comanche village. They talked a bit but soon were sound asleep.

*****

Two young Comanche warriors, Jumping Wolf and Little Hawk, had fallen hard for Katherine and Jennie and decided to pay them a visit. There intentions, however, were not friendly as they approached the tepee that the two whites female captives occupied.

"Which one do you want?" Jumping Wolf asked.

"The taller one that calls herself Jennie," Little Hawk replied.

"Good because I like the other one," Jumping Wolf said as they arrived at the captives' tepee.

Jumping Wolf pulled back the deerskin covering the tepee. He and Little Hawk grinned at each other before walking into the tepee. As they entered the tepee, they saw the two white female captives lying on the ground sound asleep. The two Comanche warriors stood still for a moment admiring the two beautiful women sleeping on the ground in front of them. They heard footsteps outside the tepee as they stared down at the two beautiful white women but chose to ignore the sounds of someone walking near the tepee.

Both Comanche warriors wore evil smiles on their faces as they slowly walked toward Katherine and Jennie. Their evil smiles were quickly replaced with expressions of anger when they heard a familiar voice behind them.

"What are you two doing inside this tepee?" the Comanche squaw named Sun Flower asked.

"Get out of here before we hurt you," Jumping Wolf warned.

"You wouldn't dare touch me," Sun Flower responded. "I'm White Buffalo's squaw, and he'll kill the two of you if you hurt me."

Both Katherine and Jennie woke up but kept quiet while watching the two Comanche warriors argue with Sun Flower. They both knew why Jumping Wolf and Little Hawk came to visit them and hoped Sun Flower could chase them away. They both felt their bodies trembling with fear as they watched the three Comanches arguing.

"We're not scared of White Buffalo!" Jumping Wolf exclaimed. "He's not even a Comanche!"

"Yes, he is!" Sun Flower shouted back.

"He's too white to be a Comanche warrior!" Little Hawk said sternly.

"Little Hawk is right," Jumping Wolf stated. "He has no Comanche blood inside him. He was born white and will always be white."

"He's a Comanche warrior just like you two are!"

When Jumping Wolf heard Sun Flower's response, he slapped her across her face. Sun Flower felt a burning sensation on the side of her face after she was struck. She tried to fight back, but Little Hawk grabbed her and then threw her body down on the ground. She heard both Little Hawk and Jumping Wolf laughing out loud as she pushed herself up off the ground. She became furious and charged toward both Comanche warriors. She stopped suddenly when she saw a familiar face standing behind Jumping Wolf and Little Hawk.

"Now you both will pay for what you just did to me!" Sun Flower warned and then pointed her right finger toward the tepee's entrance.

Jumping Wolf and Little Hawk spun around and saw an angry-looking Comanche warrior named White Buffalo facing them. They both drew their hunting knives from their leather sheaths and glared at White Buffalo. Jumping Wolf lunged forward as White Buffalo drew his tomahawk from his leather belt. White Buffalo threw his tomahawk at Jumping Wolf and watched it slashed into Jumping Wolf's forehead. Jumping Wolf fell backward and landed on his back. He died a few moments later.

Little Hawk looked back and saw his friend lying on his back with a tomahawk blade embedded in his skull. He quickly returned his attention to White Buffalo and charged toward him. As Little Hawk ran toward White Buffalo, he saw a knife flying toward him. Before he had a chance to dodge it, the knife sliced into the middle of his chest. Little Hawk stumbled forward and fell on his knees. He looked down and saw White Buffalo's knife's handle sticking out of his chest.

Little Hawk heard footsteps quickly approaching him and looked up and saw an angry-looking White Buffalo standing over him. He watched White Buffalo reach for the knife that was embedded in his chest and then felt the knife's blade twisting inside his body. He felt the knife's blade cutting his vital organs as his life slipped away. Little Hawk watched White Buffalo pull the knife out of his body just before his spirit left his lifeless body.

White Buffalo pulled his knife out of Little Hawk's carcass and slid it back into its colorful decorated leather sheath. He then walked over to Jumping Wolf and pulled his tomahawks' blade out of the dead Comanche warrior's skull. As he slipped his tomahawk underneath his leather belt, he heard footsteps quickly approaching him. He looked up and then smiled when he saw Sun Flower standing in front of him.

"Are you all right?" White Buffalo asked as Sun Flower fell into his arms.

"I am now," Sun Flower replied.

"What happened here?" he asked as he held on to his wife tightly.

"I caught Jumping Wolf and Little Hawk inside this tepee, and they were getting ready to have their way with our two captives," she replied.

White Buffalo looked at the two frightened captives, Katherine and Jennie, and then said, "Gather up your buffalo robes and follow us."

Katherine and Jennie nodded their heads and then picked up their buffalo robes. They both followed Sun Flower and White Buffalo out of the tepee. They saw many squaws, children, and a few warriors surrounding the bodies of Jumping Wolf and Little Hawk and began worrying about their own safety as they followed White Buffalo and Sun Flower.

Sun Flower and White Buffalo stopped in front of a large tepee. Sun Flower turned around and faced the two whites female captives while White Buffalo entered the tepee. Jennie and Katherine heard sounds of women and children mourning behind them as they waited for Sun Flower to speak to them.

"This will be your new home for a while," Sun Flower said and then pointed at the large tepee that White Buffalo had just entered. "You two will now live with White Buffalo and I."

*****

When Katherine and Jennie first saw White Buffalo sitting near a small campfire inside his and Sun Flower's tepee, they noticed his skin color was white. He also had long brown hair with blue eyes. His jaw was chiseled. His shoulders were very broad, and his arms were muscular and strong. He wore a buckskin shirt with no sleeves, a breechcloth with leather leggings and moccasins on his feet.

Katherine looked at Sun Flower after she and Jennie sat down inside the tepee and asked, "Was your husband born a Comanche?"

"No," Sun Flower quickly responded. "He was kidnapped a long time ago by Chief Black Hawk and his warriors during an attack on one of your peoples' wagon trains. Chief Black Hawk then took a liking to White Buffalo, took him into his family, and raised him."

"So he could be chief of this village one day?" Jennie asked.

"He could be, but Chief Black Hawk has another son that doesn't like White Buffalo much and will do all he can to prevent White Buffalo from becoming chief when Chief Black Hawk dies."

"Enough talk," White Buffalo said. He then handed Katherine and Jennie some food and said, "Eat."

Both Jennie and Katherine ate the food White Buffalo had handed them. They didn't know what they were eating, but it tasted good. They both wondered if White Buffalo had thoughts of leaving this Comanche village and living again with his own people. Neither one of them realized that the Comanches were White Buffalo's people, and he had no plans of ever leaving them.

9

Cooper McCaw, Sergeant Otto Black, and Corporal Luther Decker rode their horses up to a Swing Station. A Swing Station was a small stagecoach station where a stagecoach's team of horses was exchanged for a new team. This Swing Station consisted of a small cabin, a barn, and a corral. Cooper, Black, and Decker noticed right away that this Swing Station looked deserted. There were no horses in the corral, and no one had come out to greet them after they dismounted their horses.

Cooper yelled out, "Hello!" He then waited a few moments before shouting, "Is anyone here?"

When he and his two companions heard no response, they walked into the small cabin. They stopped dead in their tracks when they saw three male corpses lying on the cabin's floor.

It was a ghastly sight. The three male carcasses were stripped naked and were covered with blood, maggots, and blowflies. As they approached the three bodies, they saw internal organs exposed where the carcasses had been sliced opened. Blood also covered their heads where their scalps had been sliced off their heads.

"Who could have done this awful act of cruelty?" Corporal Luther Decker asked.

"The Comanches!" Cooper exclaimed.

"They're savages!" Decker said as he turned away from the gruesome sight.

"They sure are," Cooper concurred as he, Decker, and Black started walking toward the cabin's door. Once they exited the cabin, Cooper said, "Let's check out the barn."

When they reached the barn, they walked inside and found eight empty stalls. They did, however, find plenty of hay for their horses to eat. They also inspected the well and found plenty of water in it.

"It's going to be dark soon. Let's spend the night in this barn tonight," Cooper suggested. He then said, "Let's feed, water, and groom our horses then bury those three dead men we found in the cabin and then we can eat some food before turning in for the night."

Sergeant Black and Corporal Decker nodded their heads in agreement and followed Cooper to their horses.

*****

Cooper and his two companions were exhausted and slept soundly through the night. They all woke up refreshed when the sun rose the following the day. They fed, watered, and saddled their horses and then ate a little breakfast themselves. While eating their breakfast, Sergeant Black and Corporal Decker became curious why Cooper McCaw was branded a coward, stripped of his rank, and then dishonorably discharged from the United States Cavalry.

"I heard why you were branded a coward, but after what Corporal Decker and I have witnessed over the past few days, we both know you're not a coward," Sergeant Black said. He then asked, "Will you tell us why you were really branded a coward, stripped of your rank, and then kicked out of the cavalry?"

"Sure," Cooper replied.

"You don't have to," Corporal Decker said. "We both know that you're not a coward."

"I don't mind telling you two what really happened, but let me ask you both first what you heard happened."

"We were told you were the only survivor at the Battle of White River. Corporal Decker and I lost a lot of goods friends at that battle, and we both blamed you for their deaths after you were found alive with no serious injuries," Sergeant Black replied.

"Yes, we did blame you, but after what we've seen these past few days, we no longer blame you but still are curious why you survived and the rest of your men didn't," Corporal Decker asked.

"I honestly don't know why the Comanches didn't kill me," Cooper replied. "All I remember is fighting for my life with the rest of my men against an overwhelming force of Comanche warriors. We were outnumbered ten to one but still stood our ground and fought bravely. We knew if we surrendered, the Comanches would kill us all, so we decided to fight to the death while still hoping reinforcements would arrive before we were all slaughtered."

"No one would brand you a coward for choosing to fight to the death with your men," Corporal Decker stated.

"You're right, no one would, but when the reinforcements finally arrived, I was found two hundred yards away from where my command was massacred by the Comanches."

"So that's why they thought you deserted your command," Sergeant Black said.

"Yes, that's why," Cooper admitted. "When they found me waking up from being unconscious two hundred yards away from where all the men under my command lay dead, they came to the conclusion that I had deserted my command before I was knocked unconscious."

"So how did you get two hundred yards away from your men?" a curious Corporal Decker asked.

"I honestly don't know," Cooper answered.

"Was that the answer you gave to the Military Court that convicted you at Fort Concho?" Sergeant Black asked.

"Yes, it was," Cooper replied.

"There must be an explanation how you got so far away from your men when you got knocked out," Corporal Decker said.

"I wish I had one, but I don't," Cooper said while wearing a frown on his face. "There's not a single witness living that can tell me how I ended up two hundred yards away from the rest of my men."

"What was the last thing you remember from that battle?" Sergeant Black asked.

"I remember looking at dozens of my men lying dead or badly hurt all around me. It was a horrific sight," Cooper said. "I called out to my men to retreat to a deep gully that was nearby and then I remember my men and I running toward it."

"What else do you remember?" Sergeant Black asked.

"That's it," Cooper replied.

"How far was that gully that you ordered your men to run to?" Corporal Decker asked.

"Twenty to thirty yards," Cooper replied. "I can't really remember."

"How were you knocked out?" Sergeant Black asked.

"I'm not sure, but there was a large bump on the back of my head when the reinforcements found me," Cooper responded.

"One of the Comanches must have hit the back of your head with his war club while you were running toward that gully," Sergeant Black suggested.

"One must have, but why didn't that Comanche then kill me?" Cooper asked.

"He probably thought he had and then rode his horse off to kill another one of your soldiers," Corporal Decker said.

"Unfortunately, we'll never know," Cooper said as he mounted his horse.

"Decker and I will do all we can to help you deliver the Comanche warrior called White Buffalo to his father so you can be reinstated into the Cavalry with your old rank and no longer be branded a coward. Won't we, Corporal?"

"We sure will," Corporal Decker replied.

"Wow, I never thought you two would help me try to get my reputation back," Cooper said. He then smiled and said, "Thank you."

"We rather be your friends now than your enemy since we both now know you can kick our butts in a fight," Corporal Decker said, wearing a smile on his face.

"The corporal is right about that," Sergeant Black concurred. "We have a lot less bruises, cuts, and scrapes fighting with you than against you."

"Mount your horses," Cooper ordered while chuckling. "We still have a long way to go down Tomahawk Trail till we get to Blanco Canyon."

As Sergeant Black and Corporal Decker were mounting their horses, Cooper saw smoke rising from an area north of their position. He wondered if a prairie fire was starting as he reached for his binoculars. He raised his binoculars and then looked through them.

After mounting his horse, Sergeant Black saw Cooper looking through his binoculars and asked, "Have you spotted some Comanches?"

"I'm not sure," Cooper said as he continued looking through his binoculars. He then said, "I see smoke, but I'm not sure if it's from a prairie fire or something else."

"Could it be Comanches sending up smoke signals," Corporal Decker asked.

"The smoke I see are not smoke signals," Cooper replied as he lowered his binoculars and then slipped them back into his saddlebag.

"Then where's that smoke coming from?" Corporal Decker asked.

"I'm not sure, but we're going to find out," Cooper said and then kicked his horse into a fast gallop and rode it toward the smoke.

Sergeant Black and Corporal Decker yelled simultaneously, "Wait for us!" And then they kicked their horses into a fast gallop and chased after Cooper.

*****

Cooper, Sergeant Black, and Corporal Decker halted their horses when they reached the top of a small hill. All three drew their rifles from their saddle scabbards when they saw two covered wagons being attacked by a small band of Comanche warriors. They cocked the levers on their rifles then aimed them down at the hostile Comanches. They each picked a target and then squeezed their rifles' triggers. Their bullets ripped into three Comanche warriors knocking them off their horses.

"There's a few settlers still alive defending those wagons," Cooper said. "Let's go help them."

"There's a lot of Comanches between us and them," Corporal Decker warned.

"If we don't help those settlers, they'll be wiped out!" Cooper exclaimed. He then slid his rifle back into its saddle scabbard and then drew his revolver from its gun belt.

"We'll be right behind you," Sergeant Black said as he too slid his rifle back into is scabbard and then drew his revolver. The sergeant then looked over at a nervous-looking Corporal Decker and asked, "Won't we, Decker?"

Decker put his rifle back into its scabbard and then answered with a jittery voice, "Yes, we will." He then drew his revolver from its holster while feeling his body shake with fear.

Cooper kicked his horse into a fast gallop and then rode it toward the two covered wagons. He then looked back over his left shoulder and saw his two new friends riding their horses closely behind his. He understood why Corporal Decker was a little reluctant to help the settlers out. The odds of them making it past the Comanches and reaching the two covered wagons alive were slim. But Cooper was willing to risk his and his two companions' lives to try to save a few settlers' lives he didn't even know. He had seen enough settlers and soldiers massacred by Comanche warriors and would do anything he could to prevent more from being killed.

*****

A few Comanche warriors saw Cooper, Sergeant Black, and Corporal Decker charging toward them and broke off from the rest of their small war party. The warriors kicked their horses into a gallop and charged them toward the three white men. As they rode their horses, they nocked their arrows and then pulled back their bowstrings. Just as they were aiming their arrows at Cooper, Sergeant Black, and Corporal Decker, bullets ripped into them. The Comanche warriors fell off their horses, watched the three white men ride their horses past them, and then died moments later.

The settlers defending the two covered wagons saw Cooper and his two companions riding their horses toward them. The settlers gave the three riders cover fire and killed several Comanche warriors. More Comanche warriors spun their horses around when they noticed Cooper and his two comrades. They charged their horses toward the three white men intending to kill and then take their scalps.

Cooper saw a Comanche warrior charging toward him. He raised his revolver and aimed it at the Comanche. An arrow whizzed by Cooper's left shoulder as he pulled his revolver's trigger. He watched his bullet rip through the Comanche's throat. The Comanche warrior fell off his horse gasping for air and died a few moments later after landing on his back.

Sergeant Black saw a bare-chested Comanche bearing down on him. He quickly aimed his revolver at the warrior and then pulled its trigger. His bullet smashed into the warrior's chest. As he watched the bare-chested warrior falling off his horse, an arrow flew by the right side of his face.

Sergeant Black spun his horse around and saw a Comanche warrior nocking an arrow while sitting tall on his horse. He targeted the Comanche with his revolver and then pulled its trigger. His bullet slammed into the Comanche's right shoulder causing the Comanche to drop his bow. The Comanche drew his tomahawk from his leather belt with his left hand, kicked his horse into a gallop, and charged toward Sergeant Black.

Sergeant Black aimed his revolver at the charging Comanche and then pulled its trigger. When no bullet discharged from his revolver's barrel, he quickly realized his revolver was out of bullets. He slid his revolver back into its holster and then drew his hunting knife out of its leather sheath. He threw his knife at the Comanche warrior bearing down on him. Just as the Comanche warrior was getting ready to throw his tomahawk at Sergeant Black, he saw a knife flying toward him. He tried to dodge out of the way but was too slow. Sergeant Black's knife's blade imbedded deep into the Comanche warrior's heart. The Comanche dropped his tomahawk and then slumped over his horse's neck. A few moments later, he slid off his horse, landed on his chest, and died.

Corporal Decker shot and killed two Comanche warriors as he rode his horse toward the two covered wagons. He made it to the wagons unscathed and dismounted his horse. He saw two male settlers standing behind one of the wagons. He drew his Henry lever-action repeating rifle from its saddle scabbard and ran over to them.

"My name is Decker, and we need to give my two friends cover fire."

Both settlers nodded their heads and aimed their rifles at two Comanche warriors near Cooper and Sergeant Black. They squeezed their rifles' triggers and watched their bullets kill the two Comanche warriors they were aiming at.

"Good shooting," Corporal Decker said after he watched the two settlers shoot and kill the two Comanche warriors.

"Thanks," a settler named Cory said. He then aimed his rifle at another Comanche and said, "We'll need to kill more of them if your two friends want to make it here alive."

"You two take the four on the left, and I'll concentrate on killing the two Comanches on the right," Corporal Decker said.

"We can handle that," the other settler named Ben said as he targeted a Comanche warrior with his rifle.

Ben pulled his rifle's trigger and watched his bullet slammed into a Comanche warrior's right knee. The Comanche warrior pulled back his bowstring while feeling Ben's bullet burning inside his knee. Before the wounded Comanche warrior could release his bowstring, another bullet slammed into the middle of his forehead killing him instantly. Before Ben could target another Comanche warrior with his rifle, an arrow hit his right shoulder. As he was looking at the arrow shaft sticking out of his right shoulder, another arrow penetrated the middle of his chest. Ben dropped his rifle, stumbled forward, and then died before his body hit the ground.

"The Comanches got Ben," Cory said as he looked down at his deceased friend.

"They'll kill us too unless you concentrate on killing them," Corporal Decker warned as he targeted another Comanche warrior with his lever-action repeating rifle.

Cooper and Sergeant Black reached the two covered wagons safely and dismounted their horses. They drew their rifles out of their saddle scabbards and ran over to the wagon that Corporal Decker and Cory were defending.

"Thanks for the cover fire," Cooper said as he greeted Corporal Decker. "We wouldn't have made it here alive without you and the settlers killing the Comanches that were bearing down on us." Cooper then look at the settler named Cory and asked, "How many in your group are still alive?"

"Just my wife, two daughters, and I," Cory replied.

"Where are your wife and two daughters at?" Cooper asked.

"Hiding in the bed of the other wagon," Cory replied. "My two sons were defending that wagon but were killed by the Comanches just before you and your friends arrived."

Cooper looked at Corporal Decker and Cory and said, "Go over and defend that wagon while Sergeant Black and I defend this one."

"Yes, sir," Corporal Decker replied before he and Cory ran over to the wagon where Ben's wife and daughters were.

"The Comanches are regrouping, sir," Sergeant Black said as he pointed toward the Comanche war party.

Cooper looked toward the war party as he cocked the lever on his Henry lever-action repeating rifle. He then shouted, "Get ready. They're going to hit us hard!"

10

"Hold your fire!" Cooper shouted while watching the small Comanche war party approach him and the other three defenders of the two covered wagons. "The closer we let those Comanches get to us, the more damage our lever-action repeating rifles can do to them!"

Cooper, Sergeant Black, Corporal Decker, and the settler named Cory all waited patiently as the Comanches drew nearer to them. As the gap between them and the Comanches became smaller, Cooper told the men to each pick out a Comanche to shoot at and great ready to pull their rifles triggers. When Cooper felt the Comanches were close enough so he and the other defenders' bullets wouldn't miss, he yelled, "Fire!"

Bullets ripped into the attacking hostiles, knocking them off their horses. Cooper cocked his rifle's lever quickly and then aimed his rifle at a Comanche. He dropped the Comanche with one shot, cocked his rifle's lever again, and quickly targeted another Indian. He pulled his rifle's trigger and saw the Comanche fall off his horse after a bullet smashed into his chest.

Cooper glanced over to the other covered wagon while he cocked his rifle's lever. He saw Corporal Decker and Cory bravely defending it, but something caught his attention that he didn't like. He saw one of Corey's daughters sticking her head out of the wagon's bed.

She's going to get herself killed doing that, Cooper thought.

Before Cooper could warn Cory about her daughter, an arrow slashed through her neck. She fell out of the wagon and landed on her back gasping for air. As she choked on her own blood, she felt her life quickly fading away and then she died a few moments later.

"Keep your wife and other daughter down in the bed of that wagon or the Comanches will kill them too!" Cooper shouted to Cory who was staring down at his blood-covered deceased daughter.

Cory ran back over to the wagon that he and Corporal Decker had been defending and told his wife and other daughter to keep down inside the bed of the wagon. Both his wife and daughter were crying, and their bodies shook with fear. An arrow slammed Cory's forearm. Cory spun his body around and then shot and killed the Comanche before the Comanche could nock another arrow.

Cory looked down at his left forearm while feeling a burning sensation and saw an arrow shaft sticking out of it. He tried to ignore the pain as he cocked the lever of his rifle. He targeted a Comanche warrior and pulled the trigger. His bullet hit the Comanche's right hip. Cory cocked his rifle's lever again, squeezed its trigger, and watched his bullet hit and kill the Comanche warrior.

"Is your forearm okay?" Corporal Decker asked when he saw the arrow shaft sticking out of Cory's left forearm.

"It stings a lot, but I can still use it," Cory replied.

"Good," Corporal Decker said as he targeted a Comanche with his rifle and then pulled its trigger.

"We're killing a lot of Comanches, but they're not giving up," Cory said.

"They're like deerflies. They keep attacking you until you kill them," Corporal Decker replied. He then looked over at Cooper and Sergeant Black and saw both of them shooting their rifles as fast as they could at the hostile Comanches. He then returned his attention to the Comanches attacking the covered wagon he and Cory were defending.

*****

"Do you see that Comanche wearing the war bonnet with the red, black, and white feathers," Cooper asked after he had shot and killed a Comanche warrior.

Sergeant Black saw a Comanche sitting tall on his horse wearing a colorful war bonnet and then answered, "Yes, I do."

"That's the chief of this war party," Cooper said. "If we kill him, the Comanches just might break off the attack."

"Let's kill the chief then!" Sergeant Black exclaimed.

Cooper and Sergeant Black cocked their rifles' levers and took careful aim at the Comanche war chief. They both squeezed their rifles' triggers and watched their bullets ripped into the Comanche war chief's chest. The chief wore a shocked facial expression as he looked down at his bare chest and saw blood seeping out of his two bullet wounds. He then lost control of his body and slid off his horse. When he landed on his back, he saw some of his warriors gathering around him. Before he could order them to fight on, he died.

"We got him!" a happy-sounding Sergeant Black shouted out.

"We sure did!" Cooper responded.

"They're breaking off the attack!" Sergeant Black exclaimed as he and Cooper lowered their rifles.

Cory and Corporal Decker lowered their rifles as well when they saw the Comanche war party spin their horses around and ride away. Even though Cory was happy to watch the Comanche war party retreat, he was saddened when he looked over at his deceased daughter's body lying on the ground.

"We'll help you bury her and the others in your group that were killed," Corporal Decker said when he noticed Cory looking at his deceased daughter.

"Thank you," Cory said. "And thank you for saving our lives too. If you and your two friends hadn't show up when you did, my wife, other daughter, and I would have been killed too."

11

"When can we stop and rest?" a tired-looking Texas Ranger named Chester asked.

"Soon," Captain Josh Stephens replied.

"The bottom of my feet are raw," Chester said.

"If you and the rest of the rangers want your horses back, we need to keep moving," Josh said. "The Comanches who stole our horses are close by. The tracks we've been following are now fresh."

"We can keep going, Captain," a Texas Ranger named Jonah Buchanan said. "If Chester would have gotten himself a new pair of boots back in Lubbock when I told him too and thrown away his old rotting boots he's wearing now, he wouldn't be complaining about his sore feet."

"Shut up, Jonah!" an angry-looking Chester said. "I don't have money to buy things I need."

"That's because you gamble all your money away playing cards," Jonah quickly stated. "As soon as we get our pay, you go to the nearest saloon and look for a—"

"Quiet!" Josh interrupted after he had squatted down in front of his small company of Texas Rangers and then looked back over his left shoulder at them. He then motioned to all his rangers to get down and stay quiet. He then looked through his binoculars and saw the remnants of the Comanche war party that had stolen his and his rangers' horses. He then smiled when he saw the horses that the Comanches had stolen from them.

Josh lowered his binoculars and then motioned for his men to join him on top of the small hill he was squatting down on. The

Ranges obeyed and quickly joined their captain. Josh laid down on his chest and quietly ordered his men to do the same. He then pointed down the hill at the small Comanche war party.

"There's no more than twenty of them down there," Jonah whispered.

"We must have killed more of them then we realized," Josh whispered back.

"Or more of them could have been killed by settlers or a cavalry troop they might have attacked since they ambushed us," Jonah quietly suggested.

Chester looked at Josh and quietly asked, "Can we go kill those Comanches so we can get our horses back?"

"Not yet," Josh replied. "We'll wait till it gets dark so we can sneak up on them. In the meantime, stay down, eat some jerky, drink some water from your canteens, and get some rest."

"Yes, sir," Chester replied, wearing a frown on his face. He then mumbled to himself, "My feet are killing me!"

*****

Under the cover of darkness, Josh and his men crawled toward the Comanche campsite. They left their lever-action repeating rifles behind and only took their revolvers and hunting knives with them. They crawled unnoticed through the prairie tall grass. When they reached the Comanche campsite, they noticed the Comanches were sleeping. Josh waited for all his men to catch up. He then quietly ordered them to attack the Comanches with their hunting knives first and only use their revolvers if a Comanche warrior calls out and warns the rest of the camp of the attack.

Josh crawled up to the first Comanche warrior he saw. The Comanche warrior was lying on his back on top of a buffalo hide sound asleep. Josh quickly covered the warrior's mouth with his left hand and then used his knife and sliced the warrior's neck. He kept his left hand covering the warrior's mouth while the warrior took his final breaths.

Josh saw another Comanche warrior sleeping nearby and started crawling toward him. As he crawled toward the warrior, he witnessed some of his men quietly killing Comanche warriors. So far his plan of attack was working with no Comanche warrior sounding the alarm. But that all changed when the Comanche warrior he was sneaking up on pushed himself up off the ground and alerted the rest of the Comanches that they were being attacked.

Josh threw his knife at the Comanche warrior who was sounding the alarm. His knife penetrated deeply into the Comanche's stomach, but it didn't prevent the Comanche from alerting the rest of the camp. Josh ran up to the Comanche, tackled him, grabbed his knife's handle, and then twisted his knife's blade several times before pulling his knife out of the Comanche's belly. Josh slid his knife back into its leather sheath, drew his revolver, and then shot and killed the Comanche.

Gunfire erupted throughout the Comanche camp after the rest of the Comanche warriors were awakened. Some Comanches grabbed their old rifles while others picked up their bows and arrows. Bullets and arrows whizzed by the Texas Rangers as they fired their revolvers at the Comanche warriors.

A Texas Ranger named Glenn Fowler aimed his revolver at a Comanche warrior charging toward him. He felt his anxiety kick in after he pulled his revolver's trigger and no bullet discharged from its barrel. He slid his revolver back into its holster and drew his hunting knife out of its leather sheath. But before Glenn could use his knife to defend himself, a tomahawk sliced deep into his chest. He staggered backward a few feet before falling onto his back. He died moments later while watching the Comanche warrior pull the tomahawk out of his chest.

Two bullets whistled by Jonah as he drew his revolver from its gun belt. He looked toward the direction where the bullets had come from and saw two Comanche warriors reloading their muzzle-loading rifles. He aimed his revolver at one of the Comanche warriors then pulled its trigger. His bullet slammed into the Comanche's left shoulder. While the injured Comanche struggled to hold on to his rifle, Jonah pulled his revolver's trigger again. Jonah's second bullet smashed into the warrior's chest knocking him backward.

Jonah turned his attention toward the second Comanche warrior who was reloading his muzzleloader and targeted him with his revolver. He pulled his revolver's trigger and watched his bullet hit and kill the Comanche warrior. He saw another Comanche running toward a group of Cottonwoods and chased after him. As he closed the gap between him and the Comanche he was chasing, a bullet ripped through his left forearm. He ignored the burning sensation from the bullet wound as best he could and continued chasing after the Comanche warrior.

When Jonah reached the cottonwoods, he lost sight of the Comanche he was chasing. He ducked behind a tree and reloaded his revolver hoping the Comanche wouldn't see him. When he came out from behind the Cottonwood, he saw the Comanche warrior standing in front of him holding a tomahawk in his right hand. The Comanche swung the tomahawk violently at Jonah.

The Comanche's tomahawk knocked Jonah's revolver out of his right hand. A stunned Jonah saw his life flash in front of him as he watched his revolver fall to the ground. He tried to reach for his hunting knife, but the Comanche's tomahawk slashed open his skull before he had the chance to draw his knife from its leather sheath. The Comanche warrior knelt down next to Jonah's lifeless body. The warrior wanted to take Jonah's scalp so he could hang it outside his lodge, but a bullet penetrated the middle of the warrior's back, killing him before he could take Jonah's scalp.

Chester felt tears running down his cheeks as he stood over his friend's lifeless body. Jonah befriended Chester when other rangers wouldn't, and now his friend was dead. When Chester saw Jonah's boots, he pulled them off his dead friend's feet. He quickly took his boots off and slipped Jonah's boots on. He then looked down at his deceased friend and said, "You always told me I could take your boots if you no longer needed them, my friend. And thanks to your generosity, my feet will no longer be sore."

After Chester stood up, he heard someone running toward him. He drew his revolver from its holster, spun around, and looked for a

Comanche warrior to shoot at. He was relieved when he saw Captain Josh Stephens running toward him.

"Are you alright?" Josh asked after he stopped in front of Chester.

"I am, but Jonah's dead," Chester replied.

Josh looked down at their fallen comrade and saw the tomahawk's blade embedded in Jonah's skull. He then said, "Poor guy. He probably never saw it coming toward him."

Josh then returned his attention to Chester and said, "Glenn got it too."

"That's too bad," Chester said, wearing a sad expression on his face. He then asked, "Do we have time to bury Jonah and Glenn?"

"We'll make time," Josh replied.

"Did we get our horses back?"

"We sure did!"

"Good," Chester responded. "At least Jonah and Glenn didn't die in vain."

After the Texas Rangers had buried their two fallen comrades, they gathered up the horses that the Comanche warriors had stolen from the previous night. They mounted their horses and rode away from the Comanche campsite and headed toward Blanco Canyon. Captain Josh Stephens and his surviving rangers were determined to rescue the three young women who had been kidnapped. They didn't know that the hostile Comanche warriors had killed one of the women, Lillie Spencer.

12

A group of Comanche squaws that were scraping hides and drying meat paused when they saw a band of Comanche warriors riding their horses into the village. As the band of Comanche warriors rode their horses by several tepees, the crowd of spectators grew. The small band of Comanches halted their horses in front of Chief Black Hawk's lodge. One of the warriors named Rising Sun dismounted his horse and then walked into Chief Black Hawk's lodge. Moments later, he walked back out followed by a weeping squaw named, White Sun.

"Why is White Sun crying?" a curious Sun Flower asked.

"I'm not sure, but we'll find out soon," White Buffalo replied.

The Comanche village gathered around Rising Sun and then waited patiently for him to tell them where Chief Black Hawk was. As White Sun continued crying, Rising Sun told the village that Chief Black Hawk had been killed in a battle with the bluecoats. He then asked several warriors in the camp to ride back with him to the battle site to retrieve their deceased chief's body so he could be buried in a shallow trench nearby the village.

White Buffalo turned to Sun Flower and said, "I'm going with Rising Sun to retrieve my father's body and bring it back here to be buried."

"Be careful," Sun Flower said.

"I will," White Buffalo said before mounting his horse. He then left the village with Rising Sun and a dozen other warriors to retrieve Chief Black Hawk's body.

*****

White Buffalo, Rising Sun, and the other Comanche warriors halted their horses when they saw a dozen US Cavalrymen gathering around Chief Hawk's carcass. White Buffalo looked at Rising Sun and asked, "Are those the same bluecoats that killed Chief Black Hawk?"

"Yes," Rising Sun replied. "I recognized their leader. He's the large one with the red hair and beard."

"There's only one thing to do then," White Buffalo said. "We're going to kill every one of those bluecoats, take their scalps, and then bury their scalps with our chief."

"I was hoping you would say that," Rising Sun said.

"They still haven't seen us, so let's go surprise them," White Buffalo said to the Comanche warriors with him. He then kicked his horse into a fast gallop and charged toward the bluecoats with his fellow Comanche warriors chasing after him.

When the cavalrymen heard gunfire erupting behind them, they spun around and saw White Buffalo leading a small band of Comanche warriors toward them. The cavalrymen grabbed their single-shot Springfield rifles and started firing at the attacking hostiles. Bullets fired from the Comanches' rifles killed several cavalrymen as White Buffalo and his warriors charged their horses toward the dozen soldiers.

The Comanches' battle cries sent chills down the cavalrymen's spines. Their leader named Lieutenant James Vogel ordered his men to mount their horses. As the cavalrymen were mounting their horses, Comanche bullets and arrows cut them down. Lieutenant Vogel was the only one that was able to mount his horse without getting shot or mortally wounded. He spun his horse around and rode it as fast as he could away from the attacking Comanches.

White Buffalo kicked his horse into a fast gallop and pursued Lieutenant Vogel. His horse quickly closed the gap between him and the lieutenant. The lieutenant shot his revolver several times at White Buffalo. His bullets whistled by White Buffalo while the warrior was pulling back his bowstring and aiming his arrow at the lieutenant's back. The lieutenant felt an arrowhead penetrate deep into the middle of his back moments later.

As his life was fading away, the lieutenant let go of his horse's reins and fell off his horse. When his body hit the ground, he fell unconscious and died moments later.

White Buffalo pulled back on his horse's reins, jumped off, and ran over to the lieutenant's lifeless body. He then knelt down next to the lieutenant, drew his knife from its decorated leather sheath, and then used it to take off the deceased lieutenant's scalp. He then wiped off the blood covering his knife's blade onto the lieutenant's uniform before sliding it back into its sheath. He then mounted his horse and rode it back to the area where his warriors were celebrating their victory.

*****

"They're coming back!" a Comanche squaw named Smiling Star exclaimed.

Sun Flower smiled when she saw White Buffalo leading his small band of Comanche warriors into their village. Her smile quickly faded away, however, when she saw her husband and the warriors accompanying him draw closer to her. The heart-wrenching wailing of squaws and children could be heard all around the Comanche village as White Buffalo led the horse carrying Chief Black Hawk's lifeless body through the village. The men of the village wept silently as the body of their chief passed by them. White Sun pushed her way through the crowd so she could walk next to the horse carrying the body of her deceased husband.

"Where will they bury Chief Black Hawk?" Katherine White asked while standing next to Sun Flower.

"Somewhere near the river," Sun Flower replied.

"Will White Buffalo become the chief of this village now since his father is dead?" Jennie Farmer asked.

"I'm not sure," Sun Flower answered. "Chief Black Hawk has another son who could become chief."

"What's his name?" Jennie asked.

"Raven," Sun Flower responded. She paused for a moment before saying, "He hates White Buffalo. If he becomes chief, he will banish White Buffalo from this village."

"I've heard some warriors talking about Raven," Katherine said. "They fear him!"

"Who will choose the next chief?" Katherine asked.

"A council will decide who replaces him," Sun Flower replied.

"Who picks the members of the council?" Jennie asked.

"A group of elders that were handpicked by Chief Black Hawk in case he got killed or died," Sun Flower responded.

"When will the council meet and pick the new chief?" Katherine asked.

"Soon!" Sun Flower replied. She paused for a moment and then said, "But not before Raven arrives."

*****

White Buffalo and several other warriors finished digging the grave for Chief Black Hawk. They laid the chief's carcass down into the grave and then covered it up with the freshly dug-up dirt. The entire Comanche village encircled their deceased chief's grave and mourned his loss. Their mourning was interrupted moments later by thundering sounds of horses approaching the village. White Buffalo, Sun Flower, and the rest of the village turned toward the thundering sounds of the fast approaching horses and saw the fierce Comanche warrior called Raven leading a band of fifty warriors toward their village. Ravens and his warriors rode their horses through the village and then halted them near the area where everyone was mourning their fallen chief.

Raven jumped off his horse and walked up to White Buffalo who was standing next to Chief Black Hawk's freshly dug gravesite. He glared at his adopted brother and then asked, "Whose grave is that?"

"Our father's," White Buffalo replied.

"How did he die?" a hostile-sounding Raven asked.

"The bluecoats killed him," White Buffalo replied.

"We need to catch the bluecoats who killed our father, torture them, and then burn them all alive!" Raven exclaimed.

"They've already been killed, and their scalps are all buried with our father," White Buffalo said.

"Did you avenge our father's death without me?"

"Yes, because no one knew where you were," White Buffalo said.

"My warriors and I were out raiding many white-eyes homes," Raven said. "We brought back many scalps to hang outside our lodges."

"We need to mourn our father's death and allow the council to name a new chief of our village," White Buffalo said.

"The council doesn't have to meet," Raven said with a stern look on his face. He then turned toward everyone in the village and said defiantly, "I am the only true son of Chief Black Hawk and deserve to be your chief." Raven then pointed at White Buffalo and said, "White Buffalo has no Comanche blood inside him. He is and will always be a full-blooded white-eye."

Rising Sun stepped in front of Raven and said, "Chief Black Hawk adopted White Buffalo as his son." He then pointed at his friend, White Buffalo, and said, "He is and will always be a Comanche. It doesn't matter if he wasn't born a Comanche like we were. He was adopted by our chief and therefore he is a Comanche and has the right to lead us if the council chooses him to be our new chief."

"Fine!" Raven said with anger in his voice. "We'll let the council decide who the new chief will be."

"The council will meet tonight and decide whether you or White Buffalo will become our new chief. Until then, you two can mourn the loss of your father," Rising Sun said.

Rising Sun and the rest of the Comanche village left the two brothers alone to grieve the loss of their father. Neither brother spoke to one another as they stood over their deceased father's gravesite. Raven never liked White Buffalo and had never accepted him as a brother. If he became chief of their village, one of his first acts would be to banish his adopted brother from the village and never allow him to come back. White Buffalo, on the other hand, had no hard feelings toward his brother and would make sure no harm came to Raven if the council chose him as the new chief instead of Raven.

13

Cooper McCaw, Sergeant Black and Corporal Decker bade farewell to the settler named Cory and his family and then rode their horses toward Blanco Canyon. They felt terrible for Cory and his family. They lost a family member plus the rest of their small wagon train. Cooper tried to talk them into going to Lubbock so they could hook up with a larger wagon train traveling west, but Cory and his family were determined to keep traveling to California and didn't want to wait around for another wagon train.

The farther Cory and his family traveled on the clear sunny day, the safer they felt. They had gone ten miles without seeing any signs of Comanches or Kiowas. Cory's wife, Martha, never wanted to leave their small farm they had in Bath, Ohio. Her husband, however, had heard stories about California his whole life and wanted to move his family there. When Cory approached her about moving their family to California, she tried to talk him out of it at first but then caved in and supported his desire to move there.

When Cory pulled back on the reins of the team of horses pulling their covered wagon, Martha asked, "Why are we stopping?"

"I thought I saw an Indian on top of that hill over there," Cory replied while pointing toward a small hill.

Martha looked at the hill her husband was pointing at and then said, "I don't see any Injuns."

"I know I saw one!" Cory said confidently.

"Why did we stop?" Cory and Martha's daughter named Holly asked.

"Your father thought he saw something up on that hill over there," Martha replied as she pointed at the hill.

"What did you see, Pa?" a curious Holly asked.

"It doesn't matter now," Cory replied. "Whatever I saw is gone now."

Cory didn't want to scare his daughter and tell her that he thought he saw an Indian sitting tall on his horse on top of the hill they all were looking at. A Comanche arrow killed her sister, and the last thing Cory wanted to do was worry his daughter that Indians might be attacking them again.

"The sun will be going down soon," Martha said. "Maybe we should stay here for the night."

"I guess this place is as good as any to set up camp," Cory said.

"Good," Martha said. "I'll start—" Martha paused when she saw a dozen Indians riding their horses at a fast gallop. She then yelled, "Injuns!"

"They're going to kill us jus' like they killed my sister!" a terrified Holly screamed.

Cory reached for his Winchester and then jumped off the wagon's driver's seat. He looked back at Martha and told her to hide in the bed of the wagon with Holly. A nervous-looking Martha nodded her head and then jumped back into the bed of the wagon and tried to comfort her terrified daughter. She then hid herself and Holly as best as she could knowing if the Indians killed Cory, their hiding place would quickly be discovered.

Cory knelt down next to his wagon and aimed his rifle at one of the Indians. He didn't know whether the Indians were Comanches or Kiowas, but it really didn't matter since both tribes were at war with the bluecoats and settlers that invaded their lands. He pulled his rifle's trigger and watched his bullet strike and kill the Indian he was aiming at. He quickly cocked the lever on his rifle and then targeted another Indian.

Bullets whistled by Cory as he pulled his rifle's trigger. His bullet struck the Indian he was aiming at. As he was cocking the lever on his rifle, a bullet struck his left forearm. He felt a burning sensation while he targeted another Indian. He pulled his rifle's trigger and watch his bullet smash into Indian's forehead killing him instantly.

Just as Cory was cocking the lever on his rifle, he felt another burning sensation inside his right knee. He looked down at his right knee and saw blood seeping through his trousers. He returned his attention to the small band of Indians attacking him and targeted one of them. As he was pulling his rifle's trigger, he felt a sharp pain slice through his chest. He began to panic when he saw an arrow shaft sticking out the middle of his chest. He knew an arrowhead was imbedded deep in his heart as he felt his life quickly fading away. He lost control of his rifle just before he fell over.

As Cory lay on the ground fighting for his life, he heard his wife and daughter screaming. He tried to push himself up off the ground but lacked the strength to do so. He then felt several pairs of hands grabbing him just before he lost consciousness.

*****

"Draw your revolvers and get ready to use them!" Captain Josh Stephens ordered his company of Texas Rangers as he lowered his binoculars.

Josh slid his binoculars back into his saddlebag, drew his own revolver, and then ordered his men to follow him just before he used the heels of his boots to kick his horse into a fast gallop. He then led his company of rangers toward a covered wagon that was being attacked by a small band of Indians. As he and his men drew closer to the Indians, he recognized what tribe the Indians were from. They were Kiowas.

Josh aimed his revolver at the one of the Kiowas and then squeezed his revolver's trigger. His bullet struck the Kiowa warrior's chest knocking him onto his back. Several Kiowas spun around when they heard gunfire. Before the Kiowa warriors could defend themselves, their bodies were riddled by bullets. Josh and his rangers pulled back on their horses' reins when they reached the covered wagon. They dismounted their horses and then killed any injured Kiowa they saw. After checking to make sure all the Kiowa warriors were killed, they looked for the owners of the covered wagon hoping they still were alive.

Josh and two of his rangers ran to the back of the covered wagon and looked inside it. They all frowned when they saw the mutilated bodies of a woman and a little girl. Both corpses were covered with blood, and their scalps had been taken off their heads. As they turned away from the covered wagon, they saw several Texas Rangers waving at them. They ran over to where the rangers were and saw them kneeling next to a middle-aged man who was lying on his back.

"Is he still alive?" Josh asked as he knelt down next to his men.

"Barely," Chester replied as he tried to comfort the mortally wounded settler.

"What is your name?" Josh asked the settler.

"My name is Cory." He then looked over at his covered wagon and asked, "Is my wife and daughter still alive?"

"No," Josh replied. "They were dead when we found them."

"I should never have left my farm in Ohio," Cory said before he coughed up some blood. He then said, "If I would have stayed in Ohio, my family would still be alive." He coughed up some more blood while gasping for air. "I wish I would have listened to—" Death interrupted Cory as his badly mutilated body gave up and died.

"He's dead," Chester said as he and the other rangers looked down at Cory's lifeless body.

"We'll give Cory, his wife, and daughter a proper Christian burial before we continue our journey to Blanco Canyon," Josh said.

"I saw some shovels inside the wagon," a Texas Ranger named Elmer said.

Josh looked at several of his men and said, "Go get the shovels and dig three graves."

"Yes, sir," they all replied.

Josh said a short prayer over Cory's body and then walked over to his horse. He reached into one of his saddlebags and pulled out his dusty old Bible. He read it while his men dug three shallow graves. Once the graves were dug, the rangers lay the three corpses down into the graves. After the rangers threw the fresh dug-up dirt back into the graves, they all stood around the graves with their hats off and waited for Josh. After clearing his voice, Josh read a few passages from the Bible and then said a short prayer. He and his men then put their hats back on their heads and walked toward their horses.

As they were mounting their horses, the Texas Rangers noticed vultures circling the sky above them. A few of the vultures began swooping down at the dozen dead Kiowa warriors' bodies that scattered the ground around the covered wagon.

"Those vultures look hungry," Chester said as he watched two vultures attack one of the carcasses.

"They are hungry, and they will be well fed today," Josh said.

"Why was that family traveling through Injun country all by themselves?" Chester asked.

"We'll never know," Josh said as he and his men rode their horses away from the covered wagon, twelve dead Kiowas lying around it, and three gravesites belonging to a family that should have stayed at their farm in Ohio.

14

White Buffalo pulled back the deerskin flap covering his tepee's entrance and then walked inside it. He saw his wife, Sun Flower, adding some wood to a small fire she had built. He heard some giggling coming from behind Sun Flower and saw the two white female captives, Katherine and Jennie, doing some chores. All three women stopped what they were doing when the saw a concerned-looking White Buffalo standing near the tepee's entrance.

"What's wrong?" Sun Flower asked after seeing a worried expression on her husband's face.

"The council has picked a new leader for our village," White Buffalo replied.

"Who?" Sun Flower asked.

"Raven," White Buffalo replied after he knelt down next to the small fire located in the middle of the tepee.

"That's terrible news," Sun Flower said. "He'll make your life a living hell!"

"He might. He's hated me ever since Chief Black Hawk adopted me. He never wanted a brother, and he told me so over a hundred times since I became part of his family."

"What did you say to Raven and the council after they selected Raven as our new leader?"

"I told them that my warriors and I would support Chief Raven."

"How did Raven react to you when you said that?"

"He just glared at me for a while then nodded his head at me before he turned his attention to the council and thanked them for choosing him to be the new chief."

"How many of your warriors will still be loyal to you?" Sun Flower asked.

"I'm not sure," White Buffalo replied. "I know my friend Rising Sun will always be loyal to me, but I'm not too sure about the others. Most of them are scared of Raven."

"Should we flee and move to another village?"

"If we leave this village, Raven will make sure that no other Comanche village takes us in."

"What should we do then?"

"Stay here for now and hope Raven believes that I will be loyal to him and let us live here in peace." White Buffalo stayed quiet for a while and thought about what his and Sun Flower's future would be like with Raven as their leader. He then looked at Sun Flower, rubbed his belly, and said, "I'm hungry."

Sun Flower smiled at her husband and then said, "I'll get some meat and cook it for you."

*****

Raven gathered some of his warriors together and told them to bring him the two female captives living in White Buffalo's tepee. He handpicked his strongest warriors for this task. The four warriors he selected were Two Wolves, Red Hawk, Yellow Bear, and Howling Wolf. He instructed these warriors to kill White Buffalo if he tried to prevent them from taking the two female captives. None of these warriors liked White Buffalo, so they all hoped he would try to protect the two female captives.

The four Comanche warriors waited till late at night to make their move. They snuck up to White Buffalo's tepee and were relieved when they saw it was dark inside. Two Wolves along with his three companions pulled their knives out from their leather sheaths. The four warriors then nodded their heads at each other before they pulled open the deerskin covering to the tepee's entrance and then rushed inside it.

The four warriors searched for White Buffalo, his squaw, and the two female captives inside the tepee but quickly realized that the tepee was emptied. They spun around when they heard someone whistling at the tepee's entrance and saw White Buffalo standing in front of them holding two tomahawks, one in each hand.

"Were you looking for me?" White Buffalo asked as he stared down the four Comanche warriors facing him.

"No, we weren't," Red Hawk replied.

"Then what are you doing in my lodge?"

"Chief Raven sent us here to find the two white women you are protecting and bring them to him," Red Hawk replied.

"Is that true, Howling Wolf?" White Buffalo asked.

"It's true," Howling Wolf replied.

"Why does Chief Raven want the two white women?" White Buffalo asked as he continued staring down the four Comanche warriors.

"He didn't tell us," Yellow Bear replied.

"What did he tell you to do if I refused to allow you to take the two white women with you?" White Buffalo asked.

"He told us to kill you," Two Wolves replied.

"You four will have to try to kill me then because I'm not letting you take the two white women," White Buffalo said.

White Buffalo backed out of his lodge and moved toward a large campfire so he could see the four Comanche warriors that were planning on killing him. He told several squaws who were sitting around the fire to move, and they quickly obeyed and scattered. The four Comanche warriors stepped out of tepee and slowly walked toward White Buffalo holding their hunting knives in their hands. None of the four warriors liked White Buffalo, but they respected his fighting skills so they all approached him cautiously.

White Buffalo attacked Red Hawk first. He slashed Red Hawk across the chest with a tomahawk. Before Red Hawk could react, White Buffalo slammed his other tomahawk into the Red Hawk's skull. Red Hawk fell backward and died before his body hit the ground.

Yellow Bear lunged his knife at White Buffalo, but White Buffalo's two tomahawks blocked it. As Yellow Bear was pulling back his knife, White Buffalo attacked him. He used both his tomahawks and quickly killed Yellow Bear. He then saw the warrior named Two Wolves charging toward him. He threw a tomahawk and watched it penetrate the middle of Two Wolves's chest. Two Wolves staggered forward a few feet before he fell forward and landed on his chest.

White Buffalo heard a Comanche war cry and then saw Howling Wolf charging toward him. He raised his second tomahawk and threw it at Howling Wolf. His tomahawk slashed into the top of Howling Wolf's skull and stopped him dead in his tracks. He looked at White Buffalo while wearing a stunned expression on his face. He felt woozy, stumbled backward, and then fell onto his back. He saw White Buffalo kneeling down next to him just before he died.

White Buffalo pulled his tomahawk out of Howling Wolf's skull and then walked over to Two Wolves's body. He rolled Two Wolves over onto his back and then pulled his other tomahawk out of the dead warrior's chest. He saw his friend Rising Sun approaching him as he wiped the blood on his two tomahawks' blades off on Two Wolves's buckskin shirt.

"What happened?" Rising Sun asked.

"These four warriors were told to kill me if I refused to give them the two white women who are living with Sun Flower and me," White Buffalo replied.

"Who gave them that order?"

"Chief Raven did."

"You need to gather you stuff and flee before Chief Raven finds out you killed these four warriors," Rising Sun warned.

"I was already planning on leaving," White Buffalo said. "Sun Flower and the two white women are waiting for me in a group of cottonwoods on the other side of the river. I was coming back to my lodge for a couple of buffalo robes we forgot when I caught Howling Wolf and the three other warriors inside my lodge."

"You need to go now! Chief Raven will know what happen here soon!"

"I'm going," White Buffalo said. "I'm going to grab those buffalo robes and then leave."

"I'll stall Chief Raven as long as I can to allow you, Sun Flower, and the two white women to flee."

"I'll miss you, my blood brother."

"I'll miss you too," Rising Sun said as he hugged White Buffalo. He then asked, "Where will you go?"

"I don't know," White Buffalo replied. "This Comanche village will never welcome me back, and I'm sure Chief Raven will make sure no other Comanche villages allow me to live with them."

"You should go back to the white-eyes," Rising Sun said. "They were your people before we kidnapped you."

"Yes, they were, but I doubt they'll welcome me back now. I've killed too many whites who have trespassed on our Comanche lands."

"Yes, you've killed a lot of Whites, but they don't know that," Rising Sun said. "And don't give up on being a Comanche either. This village will be angry once they heard what Chief Raven did."

"They'll be angry but won't be able to stop Chief Raven from making sure I never come back here again."

"Don't give up hope, my blood brother," Rising Sun said and then bade farewell to White Buffalo.

White Buffalo returned to his lodge, grabbed the buffalo robes he had forgotten, and then ran as fast as he could to the cottonwoods on the other side of river where his wife, Sun Flower, and the two white women named Katherine and Jennie were waiting for them. He had no idea where he would go, but he knew he had to flee the lands of the Comanches as soon as he could. He knew Chief Raven would send warriors after him to kill him, Sun Flower, and the two white women. Chief Raven knew that as long as White Buffalo was alive, he would pose a threat to him.

White Buffalo told Sun Flower, Katherine, and Jennie what happened when he reached them. He told them that Rising Sun would stall Chief Raven and his warriors as long as a he could, but he wouldn't be able to stall them for long.

"We need to get out of this area now!" White Buffalo exclaimed as he mounted his horse.

"Where will we go?" Sun Flower asked.

"I don't know yet, but we need to get as far away from this village as we can."

"We'll follow you wherever you take us," Sun Flower said. She then looked at Katherine and Jennie and asked, "Won't we?"

"We sure will," Katherine replied.

White Buffalo spun his horse around and said, "Follow me!" He then used the heels of his moccasins and kicked his horse into a fast gallop.

Sun Flower, Katherine, and Jennie kicked their own horses into a fast gallop and followed White Buffalo. As they rode their horses across the plains, White Buffalo thought of places he could take his wife and the two white women and hide out until Chief Raven and his warriors gave up looking for them. He knew if Raven caught them, he and his warriors would torture them first and then burn them alive. He knew Raven hated him and would love to watch him burn alive.

15

Chief Raven was growing impatient waiting for the two white female hostages to be brought back to him. He had sent four of his best warriors to White Buffalo's lodge over thirty minutes ago, and they still hadn't brought back the two hostages to him. He knew White Buffalo was a great warrior, but he had doubts that White Buffalo could defeat the four warriors he had sent to fetch the women. He pushed opened the deerskin flap on his tepee and went looking for his four warriors as his impatience grew. As he was walking toward White Buffalo's lodge, he saw Rising Sun running toward him.

"What's wrong?" Chief Raven asked after Rising Sun stopped in front of him.

"The bluecoats are near!" Rising Sun exclaimed.

"Did you see them?"

"No, but White Buffalo did."

"Where is White Buffalo?" Chief Raven asked.

"He's waiting for you a little ways up the river," Rising Sun replied. "He asked me to come back here to get you and asked you to bring all the warriors you can with you so we can drive the bluecoats away from our lands."

"Have you seen Howling Wolf, Yellow Bear, Red Hawk, and Two Wolves?"

"Yes, and they're already heading up the river to help White Buffalo."

That explains why they haven't brought the two female captives to me yet, Chief Raven thought and then said, "Gather up our warriors and meet me by the river!"

Rising Sun nodded his head at Chief Raven then spun around and howled a loud Comanche war cry to alert the warriors inside the village. As Chief Raven ran toward his horse, he heard shouting throughout his village. When he reached his horse, he grabbed its reins and jumped on its back. He then heard his warriors approaching and signaled them to mount their horses. He then looked for Rising Sun and saw the warrior mounting his horse. Chief Raven rode his horse over to Rising Sun and then ordered him to lead the war party to the place where White Buffalo was waiting for them. He and his warriors were anxious to engage the bluecoats. As Chief Raven and his warriors rode their horses at a fast gallop away from their village, they all had only one thought on their minds: *Take as many bluecoats scalps as possible and then bring those scalps back to their village to hang outside their lodges.*

Rising Sun, however, had other thoughts on his mind. He had hidden the four warriors' bodies that White Buffalo had slain inside White Buffalo's lodge. He then lied to Chief Raven that White Buffalo had spotted bluecoats nearby the village. He was now leading Chief Raven and a Comanche war party in the opposite direction that his friend White Buffalo along with his wife and the two white female hostages were heading.

Rising Sun knew that Chief Raven would soon find out that he had been lied to, and when he did, Rising Sun faced certain death. *I need to buy my blood brother, White Buffalo, as much time as I can. And if I get killed doing it, then it is worth it,* he thought as he led the Comanche war party far away from the direction that White Buffalo and his companions were heading.

After riding for more than two miles, Chief Raven grew impatient. He signaled his warriors to halt their horses while pulling back on his horse's reins. He then looked over at Rising Sun and asked, "Where is White Buffalo?"

"He's up the river just a little further," Rising Sun replied.

"He better be!" Chief Raven warned before kicking his horse into a gallop.

The war party followed their chief and was eager to engage the bluecoats. Rising Sun gradually pulled back on his horse's reins to allow the warriors to pass by him. He then spun his horse around, kicked it into a fast gallop, and rode his horse away from the war party. One of the Comanche warriors spotted Rising Sun riding his horse away. The warrior called out to Chief Raven. The chief looked back at the warrior and saw him pointing at someone riding his horse away from the war party.

When Chief Raven realized it was Rising Sun who was deserting his war party, he called out to his warriors to chase after him. He and his warriors spun their horses around and chased after Rising Sun. As Chief Raven and his warriors closed the gap, his anger grew.

Why did Rising Sun lie to me? Chief Raven wondered.

Rising Sun rode his horse as fast as he could, but he knew his horse was getting tired fast and couldn't gallop much longer. He looked for a place where he could try to defend himself but saw nothing but tall grass and the river he was riding parallel too. Bullets whistled by him as he continued riding his horse. He looked back over his left shoulder and frowned when he saw Chief Raven and his war party closing on him.

Rising Sun pulled back on his horse's reins when he heard a loud squeal. He felt his horse stumbling underneath him and jumped off it before it fell to the ground. He crawled behind his fallen horse and saw two bullet holes on its right hip. He pulled his rifle from its deerskin scabbard and then cocked its lever. He then aimed his rifle at one of the Comanche warriors charging toward him and pulled its trigger. His bullet ripped into the warrior's chest and knocked him off his horse.

While Rising Sun was cocking his rifle's lever, a bullet slammed into his left shoulder. As he was feeling the bullet burning inside his left shoulder, he aimed his rifle at another warrior and then squeezed its trigger. He watched his bullet hit and kill the warrior he was aiming at. Before he could cock his rifle's lever again, a bullet struck his forehead and killed him instantly.

Chief Raven and his warriors encircled Rising Sun and his horse. It only took a few moments to realize that Rising Sun and his horse were dead. Chief Raven was noticeably frustrated that one of his warriors killed Rising Sun. He wanted to question Rising Sun and find out why he had lied. He then looked at his warriors and yelled out, "We're riding back to our village to look for White Buffalo, Sun Flower, and the two white women who are living with them!" He then kicked his horse into a fast gallop and rode it toward his village with his warriors following closely behind him.

*****

When Chief Raven and his warriors arrived back at their village, they rode their horses through the village and halted in front of White Buffalo's lodge. A warrior named White Owl jumped off his horse and ran into White Buffalo's lodge. Moments later, he exited the lodge, looked up at Chief Raven who was sitting tall on his horse, and said, "White Buffalo, Sun Flower and the two white women along with their possession are gone." White Owl then cleared his voice before saying, "I also found four of our warriors."

"You what?" Chief Raven asked before jumping off his horse.

"I found—"

Before White Owl could finish his answer, Chief Raven pushed him out of the way and entered White Buffalo's lodge. Clearly stunned, Chief Raven's lower jaw dropped open when he saw four of his warriors lying on the ground inside White Buffalo's tepee. He quickly identified the four warriors as the ones he sent to fetch the two white female hostages.

White Buffalo must have killed my warriors and then fled with Sun Flower and the two white women, he thought. *Rising Sun must have known and made up the story of White Buffalo spotting the bluecoats so he could give them a chance to get far away from this village.*

Chief Raven felt his anger reaching a boiling point when he exited White Buffalo's lodge. He was angry that Rising Sun had betrayed him and that White Buffalo fled the village with Sun Flower and the two white women that he wanted for himself. He told his warriors to rest their horses, get some rest, and be ready to ride in a few hours. Chief Raven was determined to find White Buffalo, kill him, and then take his scalp as a trophy. He then would force Sun Flower and the two white women to become his squaws.

As Chief Raven walked toward his lodge, he thought of ways to torture his adopted brother, White Buffalo. Before he reached his lodge, he settled on his favorite method of torture. After he took White Buffalo's scalp, he would tie him to a large wooden pole and then burn him alive.

Watching flames engulf my brother's body will make me smile and then laugh out loud, he thought as he pulled open the deerskin flap to his tepee. He entered his lodge and then settled down to rest for a few hours before he and his warriors pursued and tried to capture White Buffalo and his companions.

*****

"Can we stop and rest?" Sun Flower asked.

"Not yet," White Buffalo replied.

"But our horses are getting tired."

"They can be ridden a little longer."

"When do you think Chief Raven will find out that you killed four of his warriors?"

"He probably already knows."

"Rising Sun won't tell him where we're going, will he?"

"My blood brother will die before he tells Chief Raven where we're going."

"I hope we seen Rising Sun again one day."

"So do I," White Buffalo said as he and his companions rode their horses slowly out of Blanco Canyon.

White Buffalo knew Chief Raven would be coming after him. He looked over at his beautiful wife and then at Katherine and Jennie and then wondered how he could find a safe place that would afford him and his companions protection before Chief Raven and his warriors caught up with them. He had no idea where he would go but knew he would no longer be welcomed in the lands occupied by the Comanches. He was a man with no place to call home, but at least he had the woman he loved with him and the two white women that he and Sun Flower have befriended.

White Buffalo often thought about his real father, Clayton Fitzpatrick. He wondered why his father had never rescued him from the Comanches after he was kidnapped. He remembered his father being an officer in the United States Cavalry but had forgotten what his father looked like. He was closer to his mother since his father was always away fighting Indians.

After Chief Black Hawk adopted him and raised him to be a Comanche warrior, White Buffalo was taught to hate the whites. He killed many white men who had trespassed onto the Comanche lands after he had become a Comanche warrior, but he never killed their women and children. He did, however, watch his fellow warriors torture, kill, and then mutilate many white women and children. He didn't like watching it but knew if he didn't his fellow warriors would bully him.

White Buffalo found a gully with a stream running through it. The gully was deep and would help hide them and their horses. He knew their horses were exhausted and needed to be fed, watered, and rested. He and his companions were exhausted, thirsty, and hungry too. So he led his companions down into the gully. He halted his horse then looked back at Sun Flower, Katherine, and Jennie and said, "We'll rest here for a while before we continue."

"I'm starving," Sun Flower said.

"So are we," Katherine said.

"We can eat a little food and drink some water from the stream," White Buffalo said. "We need to feed our horses and let them drink from the stream too."

"How long can we stay here?" Jennie asked.

"A few hours then we need to start moving again," White Buffalo said.

"Will Chief Raven come looking for us?" Katherine asked.

"He sure will," White Buffalo replied.

"What will he do if he catches us?" Katherine asked.

"He'll torture my husband before he kills him," Sun Flower replied.

"What will he do to us?" Katherine asked.

"Chief Raven will torture us too and then he'll either kill us or take us back to the village."

"If he takes us back to the village, what will happen to us?" Jennie asked.

"We'll become his or some of his warriors' squaws."

"If we keep moving and only rest for a few hours at a time, he and his warriors may not catch us," White Buffalo said. "We need to quit thinking of what might happen if he catches us and instead concentrate on trying to escape from him and his warriors."

"White Buffalo is right," Sun Flower said as she and the others dismounted their horses.

"Let's feed and water our horses first," White Buffalo said. "Then we can eat, have some water and then get some rest. We have a long way to go before we reach safety."

"Where are we going?" Sun Flower asked.

"I'm not sure yet, but we need to get as far away from Blanco Canyon as we can," White Buffalo replied as he led his horse to the stream.

16

Cooper McCaw, Sergeant Black, and Corporal Decker halted their horses when they saw a skeleton staked out spread-eagled on the ground with a lance stuck in the ground next to it. They dismounted their horses and walked cautiously toward the skeleton.

"I wonder who this was?" a curious Corporal Decker asked.

"It was either a soldier or a settler," Cooper replied.

Corporal Decker pulled the lance out of the ground and inspected it. He then handed it to Cooper and asked, "Is this a Comanche warrior's lance?"

"It sure is," Cooper replied after he looked at it. He then stuck the lance back into the ground next to the skeleton before saying, "The Comanches left this skeleton here to scare settlers, buffalo hunters, and soldiers away."

"So we're nearing Blanco Canyon?" Sergeant Black asked.

"Its entrance is two miles straight ahead," Cooper replied. "Straight down this Tomahawk Trial we've been following."

"Why is this trail called Tomahawk Trail?"

"Not sure why, but it's what the soldiers at your fort have always called it," Cooper replied. "The Texas Rangers call it Tomahawk Trail too."

"Where will we find White Buffalo?" Sergeant Black asked.

"Somewhere along the banks of the White River," Cooper responded as he and his two companions walked back to their horses.

"Is that river nearby?" Corporal Decker.

"No," Cooper responded. "It's located deep inside Blanco Canyon."

"Oh crap," Corporal Decker said while looking down Tomahawk Trail toward Blanco Canyon.

Cooper and the two soldiers mounted their horses and then rode slowly toward Blanco Canyon. As they drew nearer to the canyon's entrance, they saw several vultures circling up in the bright sunny sky. All three of them knew that a sighting of vultures circling up in the sky meant either dead animals or humans were up ahead.

*****

When Cooper saw a horrific sight, he pulled back on his horse's reins and signaled Sergeant Black and Corporal Decker to halt their horses. They dismounted their horses and walked slowly up to an Indian lying on his back next to his dead horse. As they drew near to the Indian, they all concluded that he was dead. They saw two bullet wounds. The first one on the Indian's left shoulder. The second one was located in the middle of his forehead.

"Was he a Comanche?" Sergeant Black asked.

"He sure was," Cooper replied.

"I wonder if there's a Comanche village nearby?" Corporal Decker asked.

"I'm not sure, but if we follow all those unshod hoofprints, we'll find a Comanche village eventually," Cooper answered while pointing at the hoofprints. He then examined the unshod hoofprints closer and determined there were between forty to fifty horses that made the prints. He then turned his attention back to Sergeant Black and Corporal Decker and said, "Let's mount up and follow these hoofprints."

After Corporal Decker mounted his horse, he asked Cooper, "Why would the Comanches leave one of their dead warriors here?"

"The only reason I can think of is that they killed this Comanche lying here," Cooper replied.

"Why would they kill one of their own?" Corporal Decker asked.

"He must have done something to upset them," Cooper replied and then kicked his horse into a slow walk. He then looked back at his two companions who were riding their horses behind him and said, "Stay alert and be ready to defend yourselves."

*****

A Comanche warrior named Dancing Bear opened his eyes when he felt someone shaking his left shoulder. He saw Gray Deer kneeling beside him and asked, "What's wrong?"

"I've spotted three white-eyes approaching our canyon," Gray Deer replied. "We need to warn our village."

"We can kill those white-eyes ourselves," Dancing Bear said confidently as he pushed himself up off the ground. He then looked down from the top of the cliff that he and Gray Deer were on and saw the three white-eyes riding their horses. He turned toward Gray Deer and said, "There's only three of them." He paused for a moment before saying, "We're Comanche warriors. We can kill those three white-eyes easily."

"You're right!" Gray Deer concurred. "Those three white-eyes are no match against two Comanche warriors." He then asked, "When do we attack them?"

"Now," Dancing Bear replied. He reached for his rifle and said, "Grab your rifle and follow me!"

*****

Cooper, Sergeant Black, and Corporal Decker pulled back on their horse's reins when they heard gunshots. They looked in the direction they heard the gunfire and saw two Comanche warriors aiming their rifles at them. They heard gunfire and saw muzzle flashes coming from the Comanche's rifles and then heard bullets smash into a boulder behind them.

"Head for those boulders over there!" Cooper ordered and then kick his horse into a fast gallop.

Sergeant Black and Corporal Decker kicked their horses into a gallop and chased after Cooper. As they were approaching the boulders, they heard bullets whistling by them. They reached the boulders unscathed and halted their horses behind them. They drew their lever-action repeating rifles from their leather saddle scabbards and then dismounted their horses. They took cover behind some boulders and then looked for the two Comanche warriors who were shooting their rifles at them.

"Do you see them?" Corporal Decker asked.

"I do now," Cooper replied while cocking his rifle's lever. "They're on top of that cliff over there."

Cooper pointed to a tall cliff and then aimed his rifle toward it. He waited for one of the Comanches to show themselves, and when one finally did, he squeezed his rifle's trigger. His bullet whizzed by the Comanche warrior, causing him to duck behind a small boulder. Sergeant Black and Corporal Decker aimed their rifles at the same area where Cooper spotted the Comanche warrior and opened fire. They saw only two Comanches but knew that there were probably more.

*****

"Our bullets are missing those white-eyes," a disappointed Gray Deer said after he watched his bullet smash into one of the boulders the white-eyes were hiding behind.

"We should move closer to them," Dancing Bear suggested. "If we do, our bullets will not miss."

"Should we take our horses or move closer on foot?"

"We'll leave our horses up here."

"Maybe we should go back and warn Chief Raven and the rest of our village about these three white-eyes approaching," Gray Deer suggested.

"Are you becoming afraid of those three white-eyes?" Dancing Bear asked.

"No. I just think our rifles are too old to use to fight them. Those three white-eyes have those fast-shooting rifles."

"Our rifles are good enough to use to kill those white-eyes, so shut your mouth and follow me!"

Dancing Bear and Gray Deer ran down the back side of the cliff and then followed an narrow trail down to the bottom of the canyon. When they reached the bottom of the canyon, they both ducked down behind a few medium-sized boulders. They both peeked over the boulders and saw the three white-eyes kneeling behind a group of boulders.

"We're close enough," Dancing Bear said. "Our bullets can kill those white-eyes easily now."

Dancing Bear and Gray Deer aimed their rifles at the three white-eyes they wanted to kill. They both were eager to kill the three white men and then use their hunting knives to slice off the white-eyes' scalps. They each had a couple of Kiowa warriors' scalps hanging outside their lodges back at their village. Neither one of them, however, had a bluecoat or settler's scalp as a trophy yet. And they both desperately wanted one.

They both aimed their old rifles at the three white-eyes they wanted to kill and then pulled their rifles triggers. Gray Deer's bullet missed and whizzed by the left ear of the white-eye he was aiming at. Dancing Bear's bullet, however, ripped into the white man he was aiming at. Dancing Bear wasn't sure if his bullet killed the white man, but he was sure it severely wounded him.

*****

"I'm hit!" Corporal Decker called out while falling backward.

Cooper and Sergeant Black both looked down at their fallen comrade and saw blood seeping through Corporal Decker's shirt. Corporal Decker had just been shot through the heart, and he knew his life was fading away fast. He looked up at Cooper and Sergeant Black and tried to speak but couldn't. Cooper and Sergeant Black knelt next to Corporal Decker and watched the corporal struggle to talk.

"Don't try to talk," Cooper said.

"I'm—"

Corporal Decker started coughing up blood, which prevented him from getting his words out that he wanted to say. He struggled to stay alive but soon lost his battle and died.

"He's gone!" a sad-looking Sergeant Black said. "He was my one true friend I had in the cavalry, and now he's gone." He then looked at Cooper and said, "We need to kill the Comanches that killed my friend."

"Let's get to it then!" Cooper said as he leaned his rifle against a boulder. He drew his revolver from his gun belt and said to Sergeant Black, "When I draw them out into the open, shoot them with your rifle."

"Yes, sir!" Sergeant Black responded and then cocked the lever on his lever-action repeating rifle.

*****

"One of the white-eyes is charging toward us," Gray Deer said.

Dancing Bear peeked over the boulder he was hiding behind and saw a white man running in a zigzag pattern toward the boulders that he and Gray Deer were kneeling behind. He then looked over at Gray Deer and said, "His scalp is mine if I kill him before you do."

"His scalp will be mine because I will kill him first," Gray Deer said and then stood up from behind the boulder and aimed his single-shot rifle at the white man charging toward him.

As Gray Deer was pulling his rifle's trigger, he was confident his bullet would strike and kill the white-eyes he was aiming at. His confidence, however, evaporated when his bullet missed hitting the white man. Dancing Bear laughed out loud at Gray Deer knowing his fellow Comanche warrior was now out of ammunition. He then lifted his own rifle and aimed it at the white man charging toward the boulders that he and Grey Deer were defending.

Dancing Bear's laughter ceased when he saw a muzzle flash coming from a boulder behind the white man running toward him. He felt a bullet rip through his neck and dropped his rifle while he fell backward. When he hit the ground, he began coughing up blood and died choking on it moments later.

Gray Deer was stunned momentarily when he saw his fellow warrior lying on his back with a blood-covered neck and blood spilling out of his mouth. He then drew his tomahawk from his leather belt. He looked at the white man running toward him and cried out a Comanche war cry. He then ran out from behind the boulder he was defending and sprinted toward the white man. As he drew closer to the white man, his anger grew, and he was looking forward to killing his enemy with his tomahawk.

Gray Deer saw the white man stop dead in his tracks and aim his revolver toward him. He then attempted to throw his tomahawk at the white man, but a bullet struck him first. He felt a burning sensation in the middle of his chest. He stumbled forward as he lost control of his body. He felt another bullet strike the top of left shoulder as he was falling face forward. He died moments after he landed on his chest.

Cooper spun around when he heard someone running up behind him. He then slid his revolver back into its holster when he saw Sergeant Black approaching him.

"Did we get them all?" Sergeant Black asked.

"I think we did," Cooper replied. "It looks like there were only two of them." He and Sergeant Black inspected both Comanche bodies making sure both were dead. Cooper then returned his attention back to Sergeant Black and said, "Thanks for killing these two Comanches before they could kill me."

"No thanks necessary," Sergeant Black said. "You saved my life a few times since we left Fort Concho."

"Let's go back and bury our friend, Corporal Decker. Then we can hide these two Comanches bodies before the vultures spot them. After that, we can hide out until dark. The Comanche village we're looking for must be nearby, so we'll use the cover of darkness to sneak up on it," Cooper said.

"I hope we find White Buffalo in that village," Sergeant Black said.

"I do too," Cooper said as he and the sergeant walked back to the area where they left Corporal Decker's body lying.

17

Cooper McCaw and Sergeant Black ate some dinner after they buried their friend, Corporal Decker. They kept quiet while they ate and then spoke only a few words to one another while they fed and watered their horses. They mounted their horses when they saw the sun setting in the west and then rode their horses slowly on Tomahawk Trail toward the entrance to Blanco Canyon while mourning the loss of Corporal Decker.

Cooper and Sergeant Black pulled back on their horses' reins when they heard the familiar sounds of horses galloping toward them. They spun their horses around and saw a small dust cloud.

"Are they Comanches?" Sergeant Black asked.

"Most likely," Cooper replied.

"We better find some place to hide quickly so they don't spot us," Sergeant Black said as he and Cooper quickly looked for a place to hide.

"I see a small opening at the base of that cliff over there," Cooper said as he pointed at a cave. He then asked, "Do you see it?"

"Yes, I do."

"Let's ride our horses into it and hide out there," Cooper suggested. He then kicked his horse into a fast gallop and rode his horse toward the cave.

This Tomahawk Trail is like a hornet nest, Sergeant Black thought while following Cooper toward the cave.

After both men rode their horses into the cave, they quickly dismounted. They drew their rifles from their saddle scabbards and then ran toward the entrance to the cave. They saw some tumbleweed at the entrance to the cave and dove behind it so whoever was approaching would have difficulty spotting them.

"I still can't tell if they're Comanches, can you?" Sergeant Black asked.

"Not yet, but as they draw nearer to us, we will be able to see who they are," Cooper replied.

Both men cocked the levers on their rifles so they would be ready to shoot if they were spotted and then attacked by whomever was approaching them. As the dust cloud approached them, they were finally able to identify who the riders were and were both relieved that the horsemen were not Comanches.

"Thank God they're not Comanches," Sergeant Black said as he and Cooper lowered their rifles.

"I recognize the man leading the column," Cooper said. "His name is Captain Josh Stephens and those men following him are Texas Rangers."

"What are the Texas Rangers doing here?" Sergeant Black asked.

"I have no clue, but if they keep stirring up dust by riding their horses at a fast gallop, every Comanche nearby will spot them," a very concerned Cooper replied.

"We better warn them," Sergeant Black said.

"Let's wave at them and hopefully they'll spot us and ride their horses toward us," Cooper suggested.

"Why can't we shoot our guns so they'll see us for sure?"

"Because the Comanches will hear our gunshots," Cooper replied. "We're too close to Blanco Canyon now, and the Comanche village could be nearby."

"You're right," Sergeant Black concurred as he and Cooper both stood up and started waving their hands above their heads hoping the Texas Rangers spotted them before riding past them.

"They're not seeing us!" Cooper exclaimed as he and Sergeant Black kept waving their hands at the Texas Rangers.

"If we don't stop them, they might ride into an ambush," Sergeant Black warned.

"Mount your horse!" Cooper ordered. "We got to catch up to those Texas Rangers and stop them before they ride into Blanco Canyon."

*****

Captain Josh Stephens and his column of Texas Rangers rode their horses toward Blanco Canyon without fear of being ambushed by Comanche warriors. Their confidence evaporated when they heard gunfire and saw muzzle flashes coming from behind boulders on both sides of their column. The Texas Rangers drew their revolvers from their gun belts and looked for Comanches to shoot at. Bullets ripped into several rangers, killing some and wounding others. It didn't take long for Captain Josh Stephens to realize that if he didn't order his men to retreat, he and his men would be massacred.

"Retreat!" Josh called out as bullets continued ripping into his men.

A few of the Texas Rangers heard Josh's order but most did not. The majority of the rangers continued battling the Comanches while Josh and the few rangers who heard his order retreated. It only took a few moments for Josh to realize that the loud gunfire prevented most of his men from hearing his retreat order. He spun his horse around and then kicked it into a full gallop. He rode it toward the rest of his men who were still engaging the Comanches.

As Josh rode his horse toward his men, he kept yelling, "Retreat!" More of his men heard his order but were shot and killed when they tried to retreat. Josh managed to reach the few rangers who hadn't been shot yet and signaled them to retreat. They spun their horses around and followed their captain. Bullets whistled by the Texas Rangers as they rode their horses as fast as they could away from the Comanches.

Josh saw two white men sitting tall on their horses signaling his men to ride their horses into a nearby cave. As he drew nearer to the two men, he saw that one of them was a soldier. The other man wore a buckskin shirt, trousers, and a wide-brimmed hat on his head. He didn't recognize the men but was grateful they were helping him and his men.

Josh and the rest of the Texas Rangers followed the two horsemen into the cave They all dismounted their horses then drew their lever-action repeating rifles and ran to the cave's entrance.

"Thanks for helping us out," Josh said as he knelt next to the strangers. He then introduced himself.

"You're welcome," Cooper said and then introduced himself and Sergeant Black to Josh and his men.

"I've heard of you," Josh said as he looked at Cooper. "You were—"

"If we don't start killing the Comanches attacking us, we'll all be killed and scalped!" Sergeant Black warned while glaring at Josh.

"You're right," Josh concurred and then cocked the lever on his rifle.

*****

A Comanche warrior named Yellow Jacket looked at the Comanche warriors surrounding him and ordered them to make sure all the Texas Rangers lying on the ground near them were dead before they started taking their scalps. He also ordered his warriors to gather any weapons and ammunition the fallen rangers had in their possession. A warrior named Soaring Eagle approached Yellow Jacket while the other warriors obeyed Yellow Jacket's command.

"Shouldn't we send one of our warriors to warn Chief Raven that we caught Texas Rangers entering our canyon?" Soaring Eagle asked.

"No," Yellow Jacket replied. He then glared at Soaring Eagle for a few moments before saying, "Don't you think we can kill these white-eyes ourselves?"

"Yes, but Raven is our new chief, and he should be told that the rangers are near our village," Soaring Eagle said with a stern look on his face.

"He'll be told but after we kill them all and take their scalps," Yellow Jacket replied. He then paused for a few seconds before saying, "Chief Raven put me in charge of our village until he returns knowing that I would make sure that any white-eyes entering our canyon would be killed. I'm not sending one of our warriors to tell him what happened here until we kill all the rangers that attacked us. He's going to know that he can trust me to defend our village in the future when he wants to take a war party to attack the white-eyes."

Soaring Eagle nodded his head in agreement even though he disagreed with Yellow Jacket. He walked away from Yellow Jacket looking for a dead Texas Ranger that hadn't been scalped yet. When he found one, he knelt down next to the carcass then drew his hunting knife from its decorated leather sheath. He used his knife to slice off the dead ranger's scalp. He then put the scalp inside his leather pouch and would keep it there until he returned to his village where he would hang it outside his lodge.

After the Comanche warriors were finished taking scalps and collecting the deceased rangers' weapons and ammunition, Yellow Jacket ordered his warriors to mount their horses. He put his war bonnet on top of his head and drew his rifle out of its deerskin scabbard. He raised his rifle above his head to get his warriors attention. He then shouted out a Comanche war cry and used his rifle to signal his warriors to attack the cave where the surviving Texas Rangers were.

18

"Here they come!" Captain Josh Stephens called out.

"Don't fire until I say so!" Cooper McCaw commanded.

"We only take orders from our captain," Chester said while staring at Cooper.

"You can take orders from him too," Josh said while pointing at Cooper. "He has more experience fighting Indians than all of us. He's fought Comanches, Kiowas, and Apaches. He's become the best Indian fighter in Texas, so if he tells you to do something, you better do it!"

"Yes, sir!" Chester replied even though he didn't like taking orders from a man who was branded a coward and kicked of the cavalry. Chester hated cowards and therefore despised Cooper. He would, however, obey any orders issued by Cooper since he was just ordered to by his captain. He then looked over at Cooper and warned, "Those Comanches are almost on top of us!"

"Hold your fire!" Cooper ordered once again as he and the others aimed their lever-action repeating rifles at the fast-approaching Comanche warriors.

I hope he orders us to fire our rifles before they're close enough to scalp us, Chester thought to himself as he felt chills running up his spine.

*****

Yellow Jacket and his warriors' confidence grew as they drew nearer to the white men they were attacking.

The white-eyes must be getting ready to surrender to us since they're not firing their guns at us, Yellow Jacket thought as he and his warriors rode their horses at a fast gallop toward the white men.

Yellow Jacket and his warriors shouted out their war cries as they quickly closed the gap between them and the cave that the white men were defending. The Comanche warriors were eager to kill the white men and then take their scalps. They knew if they massacred these white men they were attacking, it would scare off any other settlers, buffalo hunters, Texas Rangers, and bluecoats from entering Blanco Canyon.

Yellow Jacket signaled his warriors to open fire as they neared the cave. His warriors obeyed. They pulled their rifles' triggers and released their bowstrings. As they watched their bullets ricochet off the boulders in front of the cave and their arrows slam into them, they all wondered why the white men still hadn't fired their weapons. It didn't take long for them to find out why.

*****

"Fire!" Cooper called out to Sergeant Black and the Texas Rangers defending the cave with him.

Cooper, Sergeant Black, and the Texas Rangers pulled their rifles' triggers and watched their bullets rip into the attacking Comanches. They continued cocking and squeezing their rifles' triggers as fast as they could as their bullets continued slamming into the Comanche warriors. They watched over a dozen Comanche warriors fall off their horses as they continued firing their rifles. The Comanches broke off the attack after suffering severe casualties and retreated farther back into Blanco Canyon.

"They're breaking off their attack!" a jubilant Chester exclaimed.

"They're running away!" a Texas Ranger named Elmer called out.

"We whipped them!" a Texas Ranger named Willie yelled.

"We didn't beat them yet!" Cooper shouted. "They're regrouping and getting ready to attack us again!"

Cooper pointed to a dust cloud forming where the Comanches had retreated. The men defending the cave with Cooper were all shocked when they saw the surviving Comanche warriors charging their horses toward them again.

"Make sure your rifles are fully loaded and get ready to use them!" Captain Josh Stephens called out as he started loading cartridges into his lever-action repeating rifle.

Cooper, Sergeant Black, and the Texas Rangers loaded their rifles as fast as they could. When they were all finished, they aimed their rifles at the fast-approaching Comanche warriors. Most of the men defending the cave had fought Indians in the past, but none except Cooper had fought Indians as fierce as the Comanche warriors they were facing now. Josh along with his men and Sergeant Black all looked toward Cooper and waited for his instructions.

Cooper saw the men all looking at him before he called out, "Don't fire until I say so!"

Cooper then heard Sergeant Black and the Texas Rangers reply, "Yes, sir!"

Sergeant Black and the rangers waited for Cooper to order them to fire their rifles as they watched the Comanche warriors galloping their horses toward them. They heard bullets whistling pass them and then ricocheting off the cave wall behind them. This time their nerves were calm knowing that Cooper would order them to fire their rifles before the Comanches were on top of them.

*****

"Steady your aim, men!" Cooper called out as he watched the Comanche warriors draw nearer. He quickly cocked the lever on his own rifle, targeted a Comanche warrior, and then shouted, "Fire!"

Cooper, Sergeant Black, and the Texas Rangers fired their lever-action repeating rifles as fast as they could. They saw their bullets cut down the Comanche warriors attacking them. The Comanche warriors killed two more Texas Rangers before breaking off their attack. As the Comanches retreated, the Texas Rangers, Sergeant

Black, and Cooper continued firing their rifles at them. Their bullets killed and injured several more Comanches.

Yellow Jacket felt a burning sensation in his lower back as he was rallying his warriors for another attack. He spun his horse around and felt another bullet penetrate his chest. Within moments of the second bullet striking him, he lost full control of his body. As he was falling off his horse, he wondered what death would be like.

The surviving Comanche warriors encircled their fallen leader and watched him die moments later. They now realized they were too few to continue attacking the white-eyes. They looked down at their fallen leader for a few more moments before riding their horses away from Yellow Jacket's lifeless body and heading back into Blanco Canyon toward their village.

"They won't be attacking us again today," Cooper assured the men defending the cave with him. "We've killed most of them along with their leader."

"Hallelujah!" a jubilant Chester exclaimed. He then looked over at Cooper and said, "I'm sorry for refusing to take orders from you. It will never happen again."

"Don't worry about it," Cooper said as he and Chester shocked hands. "I don't blame you and the others for not wanting to take orders from a man who has been branded a coward and kicked out of the cavalry."

"You're no coward!" Chester quickly responded. "None of us here believe you are and all of us hope that you will fight with us again in the future."

Thank you," Cooper said, wearing a smile on his face. He then looked at Captain Josh Stephens and asked, "What are you and your men doing here?"

"We were ordered to rescue three young women who were kidnapped by Comanches who live somewhere inside this canyon," Josh replied. He then paused for a moment before asking Cooper, "What are you and Sergeant Black doing here?"

"We came here to kidnap a Comanche warrior called White Buffalo and bring him back to Fort Concho with us," Cooper replied.

"I've heard of White Buffalo," Josh said. "He's known as one of the fiercest warriors of the Comanche Nation. Why do you and Sergeant Black want to risk your scalps to kidnap White Buffalo?"

"If we bring White Buffalo safely back to Fort Concho, then Cooper here will be reinstated back into the cavalry at his old rank and will no longer be branded a coward," Sergeant Black replied as he joined the conversation.

"It looks like we're heading to the same Comanche village but for different reasons," Josh said.

"It sure does," Cooper concurred.

"Should we join forces so we can help each other in our quests?" Sergeant Black asked.

"I think we should," Cooper replied.

"So do I," Josh said.

"Good. It's settled then," Sergeant Black said.

"It won't be easy," Josh warned. "The Comanches know we're here now."

"They sure do, but as long as I'm alive, I'm not going back to Fort Concho without White Buffalo," Cooper said.

"Neither am I," Sergeant Black said.

"My men and I feel the same way about those three white women the Comanches kidnapped," Josh said.

"How are we going to rescue those three women and kidnap White Buffalo if the Comanches know we're here now?" a curious Chester asked.

"We're going to bury our dead first," Cooper said. "Then we're going to mount our horses and ride away from this canyon so the Comanches believe they've beaten us. Then in a few days, we'll sneak back into this canyon and find the Comanche village where those three white women and White Buffalo are residing. Then if we're very lucky, we'll take the four of them out of that village and make it back to Fort Concho before the Comanches can catch up with us."

"That sounds risky," Josh said.

"It is so I won't be upset if you and the other rangers change your minds and decide not to go with the sergeant and me."

"We're definitely going with you two even if your plan is risky," Josh responded.

"Good. I was hoping you all would join us," Cooper said.

19

White Buffalo pulled back on his horse's reins. He then raised his right hand and signaled his three companions to halt their horses as well.

"What's wrong?" Sun Flower asked as she halted her horse next to her husband.

"I'm tired of running," White Buffalo said. "I did nothing wrong. My brother, Raven, sent those four warriors to take Katherine and Jennie away from us. I was told Raven ordered his warriors to kill me if I refused to allow them to take Lillie and Katherine."

"You refused and then killed all four of them," Sun Flower said.

"I had no choice," White Buffalo replied. "They attacked me."

"And I believe you," Sun Flower said. "But that won't matter to Raven. He will use those four warriors deaths to turn the entire village against you. We cannot go back. If we do, they will kill us all."

"I need to go back and face Raven."

"You cannot go back!" Sun Flower said while wearing a stern look on her face. "Raven hates you. He and his warriors will kill you as soon as they see you."

"A lot of warriors in our village are my friends and have fought and hunted with me for many years. I don't believe they would fight me even if Raven ordered them to."

"Those warriors might not try to kill you if Raven tells them to, but will they protect you against Raven and all the warriors loyal to him?"

"I don't know," White Buffalo replied. "I think they would."

"You think, but you're not sure, are you?"

"No, I'm not," White Buffalo answered.

"That's why we can't go back," Sun Flower said.

"You, Katherine, and Jennie are not going back with me."

"If you go, then we go with you."

"No, you won't!" White Buffalo stated. "You must—"

"No!" Sun Flower interrupted. "If you go back to the village, then Katherine, Jennie, and me will go with you." Sun Flower then looked over to Jennie and Katherine and asked, "Won't we?"

"Yes," both women answered concurrently even though neither one of them wanted to go back to the Comanche village where they were tortured, raped, and bullied until White Buffalo and Sun Flower took them in.

"If we don't go back to the village, where will we go?" White Buffalo asked.

"We can go live with the Kiowas," Sun Flower suggested.

"The Kiowas would never welcome us," White Buffalo said. "I've killed too many of them. They would kill us as soon as we step foot in their territory."

"What about the Apaches?" Sun Flower asked.

"They hate and fear all Comanches, so they would never let us live with them."

"We could travel north to the lands of the Sioux, Cheyenne, Crow, and Arapaho," Sun Flower suggested.

"I thought about that, but the journey would be long, and the winter months are almost upon us."

"We could go to the white man's fort called Fort Concho and see if they would take us in. You are white just like the bluecoats are, and when they see us bringing back Katherine and Jennie, they should let us live among them."

"I thought about that too, but I've killed a lot of bluecoats and some other whites too so they would probably take you and me hostage and then kill us."

"No, they wouldn't!" Katherine exclaimed. "Our parents would be very grateful for you and Sun Flower rescuing us and would make sure the bluecoats wouldn't harm either one of you."

"She's right!" Jennie concurred. "Our parents would make sure that no harm came to you and Sun Flower. They probably would insist you two live with one of our families."

"I have a father who might take me back if he's still alive," White Buffalo said. "He was a bluecoat when the Comanches kidnapped me so long ago."

"So it looks like going to Fort Concho is our best option," Sun Flower said wearing a smile on her face.

"Fort Concho is our best option," Katherine concurred. She then looked at Jennie and asked, "Isn't it?"

"It sure is," Jennie agreed.

Sun Flower, Jennie, and Katherine turned their attention toward White Buffalo and waited for his response. White Buffalo pondered whether they should go to Fort Concho and whether the bluecoats would kill him as soon as they saw him or allow him and Sun Flower to live among them. He then returned his attention to the three women staring at him and said, "I guess Fort Concho is our only option right now."

"It is!" a jubilant Sun Flower exclaimed.

"You won't regret it," Katherine said, wearing a huge smile on her face.

"No, you won't," a happy Jennie concurred.

"Which way is Fort Concho?" Sun Flower asked.

"That way," White Buffalo answered while pointing to the west.

*****

"How long will it take us to ride to Fort Concho?" Sun Flower asked as she, White Buffalo, Katherine, and Jennie slowly rode their horses toward the Fort.

"Several days," White Buffalo replied.

"That's not too—"

A loud thundering noise interrupted Sun Flower. She and the others looked back over their shoulders and saw a dust cloud fast approaching them.

"What's causing that dust storm?" a curious Jennie asked.

"You don't want to know," White Buffalo replied. He then paused for a moment before saying, "Kick your horses into a fast gallop and follow me."

White Buffalo used the heels of his moccasins and kicked his horse into a fast gallop. He looked back over his left shoulder and saw his three companions chasing after him. He knew what was causing the dust cloud and hoped they wouldn't catch up with him, Sun Flower, and the two white women accompanying them.

White Buffalo knew he and his companions couldn't keep riding their horses at a fast gallop much longer. He looked for a place where they might be able to hide but saw none. They were surrounded by tall grass with nowhere to hide. He looked back over his shoulder and frowned when he saw a Comanche war party chasing them.

White Buffalo felt his horse getting tired and knew it would collapse due to exhaustion if he didn't slow it down soon. He looked back Sun Flower, Katherine, and Jennie who were still behind him and signaled them to slow down their horses as he pulled back on his horse's reins. A nervous-looking Sun Flower rode her horse up alongside White Buffalo and asked, "Why are we slowing down? That's Raven behind us!"

"Our horses are exhausted and can't go much further at the pace we were riding them."

"If we stop now, Raven will surely catch up with us," Katherine warned as she and Jennie rode their horses up alongside White Buffalo and Sun Flower.

"We have no choice but to stop our horses now," White Buffalo said as he halted his horse. "They can't go on."

Sun Flower, Katherine, and Jennie halted their horses next to White Buffalo. Sun Flower then looked at her husband and asked, "So what do we do now?"

"Wait until Raven and his warriors catch up with us."

"What happens after they catch up with us?" Sun Flower asked.

"They'll probably kill me and then take you, Katherine, and Jennie back to the village with them."

"I can't go on living without you!" Sun Flower cried out as tears started flowing down her cheeks.

"You'll have to," White Buffalo said as he and the others watched Raven and his warriors encircle them.

20

The Comanche warriors sat tall on their horses while encircling White Buffalo and his three female companions. Raven rode his horse slowly forward and then halted it in front of White Buffalo. He then glared down at his adopted brother and asked, "Why did you kill four of my warriors?"

"They attacked me first," White Buffalo replied.

"I told them to kill you only if you refused to give me those two white women you're riding with," Raven replied. "I guess you refused and killed my warriors before they could kill you."

"I did refuse, and that's when they attacked me."

"Since you killed four of my warriors, I'm going to have to kill one of you right now!"

"Kill me then!" White Buffalo said.

"I can't kill you, you're my adopted brother." Raven then looked over at Katherine and Jennie and said, "I'm not going to kill those two white women with you because I want them both as my wives." Raven paused for a moment before looking at Sun Flower. He wore an evil-looking smile on his face before saying, "That leaves only your wife, Sun Flower."

"If you kill her, I'll—"

"You'll do what?" Raven interrupted.

"I'll kill you!" White Buffalo exclaimed.

"You can try!" Raven then looked at his warriors and ordered them to grab White Buffalo. Over a dozen warriors dismounted their horses and cautiously approached the white Comanche warrior. Raven glared toward his warriors and hollered, "I said take him!" He then jumped off his horse and walked behind his warriors toward White Buffalo.

White Buffalo drew his to two tomahawks from his leather belt before jumping off his horse. He took a few steps toward the warriors approaching him and then stopped dead in his tracks and waited to attack. He quickly looked back over his left shoulder at Sun Flower, Katherine, and Jennie and shouted, "Ride out of here now!"

Sun Flower, Katherine, and Jennie spun their horses around and tried to break through the Comanche warriors who were in front of them. The warriors quickly used their horses to block Sun Flower and the two white women from escaping. Sun Flower continued trying to break free while several Comanche warriors pulled Katherine and Jennie off their horses. Sun Flower felt something penetrate her stomach. She looked down and saw an arrow shaft sticking out of her stomach.

Sun Flower saw her life flash in front of her when she saw a Comanche warrior pulling back his bowstring back. She saw his arrow pointing toward her right before the warrior let go of his bowstring. She then felt the warrior's arrow penetrate her chest. She then felt her body slipping off her horse just before she died.

White Buffalo felt his heart torn in two when he saw Sun Flower falling off her horse. He ran to her lifeless body and saw two arrow shafts sticking out of her body. He felt his anger boiling as he turned away from his deceased wife and returned his attention to the warriors approaching him. He cried out a short Comanche war cry before he attacked his enemies.

*****

Katherine and Jennie tried breaking free from their captors while watching White Buffalo kill and injure several Comanche warriors with his tomahawks. They both cried out when they saw Sun Flower killed and lost all hope of ever escaping the lands belonging to the Comanches when they saw White Buffalo fall down onto his knees. As they were being dragged away, they saw Raven and his warriors encircle White Buffalo.

"We'll never escape these savages!" Katherine cried out as Comanche warriors were tying strips of leather around their wrists and ankles.

"There has to be someone coming to rescue us!" Jennie shouted back.

"If there was, we would have been rescued by now!"

"We need to keep praying to God to send soldiers to rescue us!"

"It's too late," Katherine called out after her body was thrown across a horse's back. She then cried out, "God has deserted us!"

"I can't believe that!" Jennie yelled back as two Comanche warriors lifted her body up off the ground.

"I do! We're in hell, and there's no way out!" Katherine cried out just before a Comanche warrior used his war club to knock her out.

*****

Several Comanche warriors forced White Buffalo down onto his chest and held him down while his wrists and ankles were being bound. White Buffalo fought hard to break free from his enemies, but the wounds he suffered made his body too weak. After two Comanche warriors rolled White Buffalo onto his back, he saw Raven staring down at him.

Before Raven could speak, White Buffalo shouted, "You told your warriors to kill my wife!"

"I sure did!" Raven admitted while wearing an evil smile on his face.

"You know how much I loved her. She was everything to me! I'm going to kill you for killing her!"

"You'll never have the chance to," Raven responded. "We're taking you back to our village so everyone can watch us torture you before we roast you alive."

"You wouldn't dare!" White Buffalo said while glaring at Raven.

"Oh yes, I would!" Raven replied while wearing an evil smile on his face.

21

Major Kevin Cooney stood up from his chair when he saw General Clayton Fitzpatrick walk into his office. The major quickly stood at attention, saluted, and patiently waited for the general to return the salute.

"As you were!" General Fitzpatrick said in a commanding voice after as he returned the major's salute.

"We weren't expecting you for three more weeks, sir!" Major Cooney said before shaking the general's hand.

"I wanted to arrive here at Fort Concho early so I could help you all locate my son," General Fitzpatrick responded after he quickly shook the major's hand.

"We still haven't found him, General, but we're looking for him now."

"Who's looking for him?"

"The man you chose plus two of my best soldiers," Major Cooney replied.

"So Cooper McCaw agreed to find my son in return for being reinstated in this army at his old rank?"

"Yes, sir, he did."

"Good. I was hoping he would." He then asked, "Have you heard from him?"

"No, I haven't, sir."

"Do you know where Cooper and those two soldiers are searching for my son?"

"Yes, sir. They're searching for your son inside Blanco Canyon."

"Do they think my son is somewhere inside that canyon?"

"Yes, they do, sir! The Comanche tribe he's rumored to be living with has its village somewhere inside that canyon."

"Is there a scout inside this fort that can take me to Blanco Canyon?" General Fitzpatrick asked.

"We have several scouts that know the way to Blanco Canyon and one who knows that canyon inside and out," Major Cooney replied.

"What's the name of the scout who knows Blanco Canyon inside and out?"

"His name is Siringo. He's a half-breed. He's half-Choctaw and half-white. His mother was a Choctaw squaw, and his father was a rancher before he was killed by the Comanches during one of their raids."

"Was Siringo at his father's ranch when the Comanches attacked it?"

"No. He was with is mother visiting his mother's village," Major Cooney replied. "He hates the Comanches and seeks vengeance for his father's death every chance he gets."

"I'll choose him as my scout," General Fitzpatrick said.

"How many soldiers will you be taking with you?" a curious Major Cooney asked.

"Zero."

"You can't go to Blanco Canyon with only one scout accompanying you, General. If the Comanches catch you near Blanco Canyon, they'll torture you first and then roast you alive," Major Cooney warned. "Our army cannot afford to lose you!"

"I'll be leaving this fort tomorrow with Siringo and no one else," General Fitzpatrick said in a stern voice.

"If the Comanches or Kiowas see you outside this fort wearing your uniform with no troop of soldiers accompanying you, they will surely attack you," Major Cooney cautioned.

"I won't be wearing my uniform," General Fitzpatrick said. "I'll be dressed like a cowboy tomorrow morning when I leave."

"Why did you send Cooper to look for your son if you were planning on searching for him by yourself?"

"I still believe Cooper is the only man that can find my son, but he might need some help once he does. And if he does, I want to be there to help Cooper bring my son safely back here," General Fitzpatrick replied. He then paused for a moment before saying, "My son has been living with the Comanches for a very long time and has now become a fierce Comanche warrior. As you know, the Comanches call him White Buffalo and the Comanches enemies fear his name. Rumor has it that he has killed many Kiowas, Utes, and Apaches. I haven't heard if he's killed any soldiers or settlers yet, but if he has, it's not his fault. The fault is mine for not rescuing him earlier."

"Your son might not want to go back to his former civilized life once Cooper finds him. He might even try to kill you when he sees you," Major Cooney warned. "He's a Comanche now, and they hate anyone who is not Comanche."

"I know and that's why I need to help Cooper bring my son back here. I sent Cooper on a suicide mission for find my son because everyone else who tried to rescue my son in the past had failed. I was always too busy to help find my son, but now I'm in a position where no one out here in Texas can stop me."

"You should take a detachment of cavalry with you," Major Cooney suggested.

"No. I don't want to risk any soldiers' lives trying to rescue my son who might not even want to be rescued anymore. I'm choosing Siringo to go with me since he knows the Blanco Canyon and hates Comanches. He'll want to go with me because he'll have a chance to kill Comanches who he hates. I won't have to force him to go with me. He'll be willing and ready to go with me as soon as you tell him I need a scout to take me to Blanco Canyon."

"That's true, he will," Major Cooney concurred. He then asked, "When are you planning on leaving for Blanco Canyon?"

"Early tomorrow morning," General Fitzpatrick replied.

*****

After General Fitzpatrick finished putting on his new clothes, he walked over to a long wall mirror, stood in front of it, and stared at it. He hadn't worn civilian clothes in over twenty-five years and didn't recognize the man in the mirror even though it was him. He then grinned after seeing himself in cowboy clothes.

I definitely look like a rancher now, he thought and then fastened his new gun belt around his waist.

No one recognized General Fitzpatrick as he exited his private officer's courters and walked across the parade grounds of Fort Concho. He saw a rough-looking half-breed standing near the front gate of the Fort holding the reins of two horses.

That must be Siringo, he thought as he approach the scout.

"Are You General Fitzpatrick?"

"Yes, I am." The general then asked, "Are you Siringo?"

"Yes, sir!"

"Thanks for meeting me here at six sharp."

"You're welcome, sir," Siringo said as he handed General Fitzpatrick the reins of a horse. He then said, "I picked out the best horse I could find in the stables and bought a new tack for it."

"I love the saddle you picked," the general said after he mounted his horse.

"I was hoping you would," Siringo said before mounting his own horse.

"I hear you hate Comanches."

"I sure do!" Siringo exclaimed.

"Good because we're going to have to kill a lot of them to get my son out of Blanco Canyon and back to this fort alive."

"Can we take the scalps of the Comanches we kill?"

"You can," General Fitzpatrick replied. "I just want my son."

"I'll help you find your son, but I can't guarantee that we'll make it out of Blanco Canyon alive," Siringo warned.

"I know our chances are slim, but I owe it my son to try."

"What's your son's name?"

"His name is David, but all the Comanches call him White Buffalo."

"White Buffalo is your son?"

"Yes, he is," General Fitzpatrick replied.

"I've heard of him," Siringo said. "He's a great Comanche warrior!" Siringo paused a moment before saying, "I heard Cooper McCaw along with two soldiers set out to bring White Buffalo back to this fort?"

"They did, but no one has heard from them since they left to bring my son back here. I have a feeling we'll run into their dead bodies on the way to Blanco Canyon."

"I hope not," Siringo said. "I used to scout for Cooper before he was kicked out of the cavalry and branded a coward. He's a good man, and he's no coward!"

"Let's get moving," General Fitzpatrick said. "We have a long ride to Blanco Canyon."

22

Cooper McCaw, Sergeant Black, and Captain Josh Stephens lay on their chests on top of a small hill and hid themselves as best as they could in the tall grass. They were watching a large Comanche war party riding their horses toward Blanco Canyon. Cooper and Josh looked through their binoculars so they could get a closer look at the hostile war party. Sergeant Black pulled out a small spyglass so he too could zoom in on the Comanches.

"Do you all see that white man with long hair with his hands tied?" Cooper asked.

"Not yet. Where is he?" Josh asked.

"He's the only one walking down there," Cooper replied. "He's being pulled by a rope behind a Comanche's horse."

"Now I see him," Josh said.

"So do I," Sergeant Black said. He then asked, "I wonder who he is."

"That's White Buffalo," Cooper replied.

"So that's the fierce Comanche warrior you were sent to kidnap," Josh said. He then paused for a moment before saying, "He doesn't look that fierce right now."

"No, he doesn't," Cooper concurred. "He looks like a captive now."

"Looks like we won't have to kidnap him any longer," Sergeant Black said. "We're going to have to rescue him instead."

"He's not the only captive we can rescue," Cooper said. "I just spotted two white women."

"Where?" Josh asked.

"Over there," Cooper said as he pointed toward the two white women.

Within moments, Josh and Sergeant Black zoomed in on two young white women riding their horses slowly with the Comanche war party. As Josh zoomed his binoculars as much as he could on the two white women, he wondered if they could be two of the three white women he and his detachment of Texas Rangers were sent to find and rescue.

"Are those the women you were sent to rescue?" Cooper asked.

"It could be two of them," Josh replied. "My men and I were detached to rescue three young white women who were kidnapped. Those could be two of them. If they are, then I wonder what happened to the other one."

"They could have killed her after they got tired of torturing and raping her, or they could have sold her to the Comancheros or Mexican bandits," Cooper replied.

"Those two women fit the description of two of the three captives my men and me were sent to rescue, so it must be them," Josh said. "Rescuing two is a lot better than none."

"It sure is," Sergeant Black concurred.

"Should we follow that war party back to Blanco Canyon?" Josh asked.

"No," Cooper replied. "We'll wait in the gully where the rest of our men are waiting for us for a couple of days so we can figure a plan to rescue White Buffalo and the two young white women you and your men were sent to rescue. The Comanches will be on the alert for us now since our battle with them. The longer we wait, the more chance the Comanches might let their guard down so we can sneak into that canyon and try to rescue White Buffalo and those two white women."

"The odds are stacked against us, but when haven't they been since leaving Fort Concho," Sergeant Black said. "I think waiting a couple days is a good idea."

Cooper and Sergeant Black then turned their attention to Josh and waited patiently to see if Josh and his men were willing to wait for a couple of days before they tried to rescue the two white women.

"I think we should wait for a couple of days too," Josh said. "We stand a better chance of sneaking into Blanco Canyon if the Comanches aren't expecting us. Plus, if we wait a couple of days, we should come up with a good plan to free the three captives in the Comanche village inside Blanco Canyon."

"I'm glad we're all in agreement," Josh said as he and his two companions continued watching the large Comanche war party traveling toward Blanco Canyon with their three hostages.

*****

Raven rode his horse up alongside White Buffalo. He looked down at the once fierce warrior who was now a captive and laughed out loud. He then started harassing White Buffalo.

"You were once a great warrior, but now you're a broken man on his way to his execution," Raven said, wearing an evil smile on his face.

"So you're going to kill me?" White Buffalo asked as he looked up at Chief Raven.

"Not right away," the Comanche chief responded. "We're going to torture you first."

"Why don't you fight me instead?" White Buffalo asked in a calm voice.

"Because you would be too easy to kill," Raven snapped back.

"You're too scared to fight me!" White Buffalo exclaimed.

"You think I'm scared of you?"

"I know you are," White Buffalo replied.

Raven didn't like White Buffalo's response. He jumped off his horse and drew his wooden war club from his leather belt. He walked up to White Buffalo and swung his war club at the defenseless hostage. He continued swinging his war club at White Buffalo whose wrists were bound. White Buffalo knees buckled after his body weakened from the brutal beating he was taking from Raven's war club. He fell forward and landed on his chest.

White Buffalo felt his body aching as he was forcibly rolled over onto his back. He opened his eyes and saw Raven standing over him holding a war club in his right hand. Raven glared down at White Buffalo for a few moments before walking back to his horse. He slid his war club through his leather belt before remounting his horse. His warriors kept silent as he rode past them but wondered why their chief refused to accept White Buffalo's challenge.

*****

Two warriors named Grey Owl and Talking Bird walked up to White Buffalo. They picked him up off the ground and made sure the leather straps were still tied tightly around White Buffalo's wrists. Both warriors decided to walk with White Buffalo instead of riding their horses. They felt bad for White Buffalo and knew that Raven was planning on killing him. They wanted to help White Buffalo but knew they would be killed if they were caught trying.

"Chief Raven is planning on killing you when we get back to our village," Grey Owl warned.

"I know he is," White Buffalo replied.

"He won't kill those two white women though," Grey Owl said. "He plans on making squaws out of both of them."

"They'll have a rough life, but at least he's letting them live," White Buffalo said.

"Death might be better than living with Raven," Talking Bird said. "I feel bad for those two white women."

"If you feel bad for them, why don't you try to free the two of them from Raven?" White Buffalo asked.

"Raven would kill us if we tried," Grey Owl replied.

"Only if he catches you!"

"He'll catch us if we try," Grey Owl said.

"Will you two do me a favor?" White Buffalo asked.

"Sure, if we can," Talking Bird replied.

"Please bury what's left of Sun Flower's body when you two come back this way."

"I promise you that we will," White Owl said. "I always liked her."

"So did I," Talking Bird concurred.

"He had no reason to kill her," White Buffalo said. "The only reason Raven had her killed was to get at me! I hope I get a chance to kill him."

"You'll never get the chance to kill Raven," Talking Bird said. "Once we get back to our village, he's going to torture you first. Once he gets tired of torturing you, he'll burn you alive."

"His heart is evil," Grey Wolf said. "He'll never give you a chance to kill him because he's always been afraid of you. He knows he could never beat you in a fair fight."

"Thanks for being honest with me and for agreeing to bury my wife's remains. It means a lot to me," White Buffalo said.

"We both were honored to fight by your side in many battles with the Kiowas and white-eyes," Talking Bird said. "We'll never forget you!"

"He's right, we won't," Grey Wolf said before he and Talking Bird walked away from White Buffalo and remounted their horses.

As White Buffalo watched his two friends ride their horses away from him, he thought about all the battles he had fought in against bluecoats, settlers, and Kiowas. He risked his life several times for the Comanche village that was now shunning him. He knew many Comanches still liked him but were too afraid to help him escape. As he was being pulled back to his Comanche village, he thought about the torture and death awaiting him.

23

"Chief Raven is coming!" an excited young Comanche squaw named Dancing Star exclaimed. She dropped the dirty clothes she was carrying toward the river to wash, spun around, and ran toward the village. As she ran, she cried out several times, "Chief Raven is coming!"

The Comanches inside the village stopped what they were doing when they heard their chief and his war party were returning. They all ran toward the front of the village eager to see if Raven had captured White Buffalo, Sun Flower, and the two white female captives. As Raven and his war party entered the village, they were welcome by loud cheering from the villagers. When the Comanches inside the village saw White Buffalo and the two white female captives, they started harassing them.

While White Buffalo was being pulled through the village, he heard two women screaming. He looked over his left shoulder and then frowned when he saw Katherine White and Jennie Farmer pulled off their horses. He saw the two white women pushed to the ground in the middle of the village. Both women were then dragged on their backs behind him while being spit on by squaws in the village.

White Sun felt tears running down her cheeks when she saw her adopted son, White Buffalo, being forcibly pulled through the village. When news reached her that Sun Flower had been killed, White Sun broke down and cried.

Why would anyone kill Sun Flower? White Sun wondered as she continued crying. *She was nice to all who crossed her path.*

When White Sun saw her son, Raven, riding his horse in front of the war party he was leading, she quickly ran as fast as she could toward him. When she drew near, she called out to her son.

"Why was Sun Flower killed?"

Raven pulled back on his horse's reins when he heard his mother shout out the question. After his horse halted, he saw his mother, White Sun, standing nearby. He then glared at her before replying, "I had her killed."

"Why?" White Sun cried out while trying to control her emotions.

Raven slowly looked at the crowd gathering around him and his warriors before answering, "Because she and White Buffalo were helping the two white women escape."

"You could have punished her another way!" White Sun exclaimed.

Raven didn't like being lectured by his mother in front of the warriors, squaws, children, and the elderly living in his village. He was their chief and deserved respect from everyone living in it including his mother. He jumped off his horse and approached his mother. The whole village gasped when they saw their chief slap his mother. White Sun stood still—stunned by what just happened to her.

White Sun felt a burning sensation on her right cheek from Raven's slap. She then felt tears flowing down her face as she lost control of her emotions. She started crying, spun around, and ran toward her tepee.

"Why did you slap our mother?" White Buffalo demanded to know.

"She's not your mother," Raven snapped back. He then turned around and glared at White Buffalo before exclaiming, "She's my mother!"

"Why did you slap her?" White Buffalo asked again.

"She asked too many questions," Raven answered as he continued staring at White Buffalo.

"She's your mother. She's allowed to ask you all the questions she wants," White Buffalo stated.

"Not anymore! I'm her chief, and she needs to respect me just like everyone else has to in this village."

"You've change since our father was killed. You have become evil!"

Raven turned his attention toward a few of his warriors and said, "Take White Buffalo down to the large willow tree at the river and tie him to it." He then returned his attention to White Buffalo and said, "You'll find out how evil I am before there is another full moon. I'm not going to kill you right away. I'm going to torture you over a period of time. When I'm done torturing you, you'll be begging me to kill you. And when you do, you will realize how evil I've become!"

*****

Several warriors dragged White Buffalo down to the willow tree that Raven had ordered them to. They tied him to the tree with leather straps and then harassed him for a while before leaving him and returning to the village. White Buffalo was tied to a tree, alone, and he knew his future looked grim. He didn't want to give up hope of escaping but knew the odds of him doing so were stacked against him.

White Buffalo watched children play near him and thought back to his youth when he was with his father and mother back in Ohio before they came west. He had many friends near his family's farm in Ohio and was sad when his father told him they were moving west to Texas. He loved his family's farm and never wanted to leave it. He now wished he were back in Ohio instead of facing certain death. He knew his adopted brother, Raven, never liked him; but he never thought Raven hated him and always wanted to kill him.

White Buffalo turned his attention toward several squaws who were washing clothes. As he watched them, he thought of his deceased wife, Sun Flower. He missed her and yearned for her company but knew he would never see her again. His heart was full of anger, and he wanted revenge, but he couldn't break free of the leather straps that bound him to the willow tree.

White Buffalo closed his eyes and started praying to God. He gave up on God a long time ago after the Comanches took him from his family, and no one came to rescue him. He never believed in in Manitou, the Comanche Great Spirit. Even though White Buffalo gave up on God, he still believed in him and hoped that God would help him now even though he hadn't in the past.

But wait! God did help me! He realized after thinking about it.

Most male captives were killed by the Comanches after they were tortured and scalped alive. But the Comanches had spared White Buffalo's life and adopted him into their village. He was the first white male captive that Chief Black Hawk and his warriors hadn't killed. He never knew why he was the only male captive the Comanches hadn't killed, but now he realized that God must have had something to do with it.

White Buffalo knew he wouldn't be able to escape death this time but knew he could have eternal life if he could get himself into heaven. He then remembered the one verse his parents had him memorize when he was a child. John 3:16 which said, "For God so loved the world, that he gave his only begotten Son, that whosoever believeth in him should not perish, but have everlasting life." He quoted that verse and then accepted Jesus as his Lord and Savior again just like he did when he was a little child. He continued praying to God while he waited for the Comanches to torture him before they took his life.

White Buffalo knew they would take his scalp before they burned him alive. Even though the Comanches sometimes used other vicious methods of torture like staking out naked male captives spread-eagled over huge ant beds, he knew Raven would instead have his body burned over a campfire after he was scalped alive. Raven always bragged to his warriors how he loved watching captives being burned alive. White Buffalo remembered Raven laughing out loud while he watched white male captives being burned alive. Raven was evil and wanted everyone around him to know it so they would fear him.

Most male captives would have been killed by now, but Raven wanted to make an example out of his adoptive brother, White

Buffalo. He was looking forward to torturing his adoptive brother and White Buffalo knew it. But now White Buffalo would not be scared of death since he knew he was going to heaven after he died. He had just accepted Jesus as his Lord and Savior, and it brought a calm over him that he never thought he would feel knowing he was going to die soon.

24

General Clayton Fitzpatrick and his scout, Siringo, both pulled back on their horses' reins when they saw a horrific sight. Lying in front of them were six skeletons spread-eagle and staked to the ground. They both dismounted their horses and approached the six skeletons cautiously. They both looked around for fresh Indians signs and were relieved when they saw none.

"Who did this?" General Fitzpatrick asked while looking at the six skeletons that were staked spread-eagled to the ground.

"The Comanches did," Siringo answered.

"They were soldiers," General Fitzpatrick said, wearing a frown on his face. "Their uniforms are lying next to their bodies."

"The Comanches must have stripped the clothing off the soldiers before they staked them to the ground," Siringo said.

"What did the Comanches do to these six soldiers after they tore their uniforms off and staked them to the ground?"

"They mounted their horses and rode away."

"They didn't kill them before they rode off?"

"Nope," Siringo replied. "The red ants killed these six soldiers."

"Red ants?" General Fitzpatrick asked. He then looked underneath one of the skeletons and saw a huge red ant mound. He then looked back at Siringo and said, "You're right! Fire ants killed these soldiers." He then paused for a moment before asking, "Why did the Comanches do this to these soldiers?"

"Because they're evil," Siringo responded before he remounted his horse. He then added, "They also do it to warn others not to enter their lands."

"We're going to ignore their warning," General Fitzpatrick said while mounting his horse.

"I knew you were going to say that," Siringo said and then kicked his horse into a slow walk.

General Fitzpatrick used the heels of his boots to kick his horse into a slow walk and then rode it behind Siringo. They both rode their horses on Tomahawk Trail toward Blanco Canyon ignoring the warnings left by the Comanches.

*****

"Two riders are heading toward us," an outlaw named Swalwell said as he looked through his binoculars.

"Are they Comanches or Kiowas?" an outlaw named Schiff asked.

"Neither," Swalwell replied before putting his binoculars back into his saddlebag.

"Then who are they?"

"Looks like two cowboys to me."

"What are they doing in Comanche land?" Schiff asked.

"Maybe they're coming here to hide out like we did," Swalwell replied.

"So they must be outlaws like us."

"They have to be. Why else would they risk their lives riding into Comanche lands?"

"Should we join up with them?" Schiff asked.

"Hell no!" Swalwell answered.

"Are we going to hide from them?"

"Nope."

"Then what are we going to do?"

"We're going to ambush them, and after we kill them, we'll take any valuables we find on their dead bodies."

"I like your suggestion," Schiff said.

"I thought you would," Swalwell said.

*****

General Fitzpatrick and Siringo halted their horses when they both heard bullets whistle by their heads. They both looked toward the direction where the gunfire came from and saw two men aiming their rifles at them.

"We're getting ambushed," Siringo warned.

"We need to find cover, and we need to find it fast!" General Fitzpatrick shouted as more bullets whizzed by him and Siringo.

"I'm looking!" Siringo exclaimed. "We're surrounded by tall grass and nothing else."

"I see a gully! Follow me!" General Fitzpatrick shouted and then kicked his horse into a fast gallop.

Siringo kicked his horse into a gallop and chased after the general. They rode their horses into the gully the general had spotted. Both drew their rifles from their saddle scabbards and then jumped off their horses. They ran to the edge of the gully and dove onto the ground. They cocked the levers on their rifles as bullets whistled over their heads.

*****

"I wish we would have killed them before they reached that gully," Schiff said. "Now it's going to be harder to kill them."

"You should have aimed better," Swalwell said.

"What about your aim?" Schiff asked.

"My rifle's sights are a little off," Swalwell replied.

"It's your eyes," Schiff said. "You're not seeing good anymore."

"Says who?"

"Says I."

"Shut up!" Swalwell said.

"You shut up!" Schiff stated as his anger grew.

"Make me!"

"Okay, you asked for—"

A bullet slammed into Schiff's forehead before he could finish his response. Swalwell saw Schiff's lifeless body fall face-first to the ground. He dove behind the outlaw's body so he could use it for cover. He cocked the lever on his rifle and then aimed it toward the gully where the two men that he and Schiff ambushed were hold up.

As Swalwell was pulling his rifle's trigger, he felt a bullet rip through the top of his right shoulder. As he was cocking his rifle's lever, he felt another bullet penetrate his left shoulder. He dropped his rifle and ran toward his horse. Two bullets slammed into his back before he reached his horse. He fell down on his knees and then onto his chest and died moments later.

*****

"We got two of them!" General Fitzpatrick exclaimed. "I wonder if there are anymore."

"I only saw two men shooting at us," Siringo responded.

"I wonder who they were."

"Just two losers trying to ambush us so they could steal our horses and the little money we have on us."

"Should we bury them?"

"Hell no! They tried to kill us!"

"Good point," General Fitzpatrick said. "We'll let the vultures feast on them."

"I like that idea," Siringo said as he and the general walked back to their horses.

25

Siringo halted his horse and signaled General Fitzpatrick to do the same.

"What's wrong?" General Fitzpatrick asked.

"There's a band of Comanche warriors following us," Siringo replied.

"They must have heard the gunfire from those two outlaws ambushing us."

"They probably did."

"Should we try to escape them?"

"That's the only choice we have because there's too many of them for the two of us fight."

"Just tell me when, and I'll be right behind you."

Siringo drew his revolver from its leather holster and checked to make sure it was fully loaded. He then looked at General Fitzpatrick and yelled, "Now!" He then kicked his horse into a fast gallop.

General Fitzpatrick used the heels of his boots to kick his horse into a fast gallop. He chased after Siringo fearing for his life. He heard Comanche war cries behind him as he and Siringo rode their horses through the tall grass of the Texas panhandle. Bullets whizzed by them as they rode their horses. Both men knew if they fought the Comanche warriors chasing them, they would both lose their lives and scalps. They also knew their horses couldn't run at a full-out fast gallop forever.

Siringo and General Fitzpatrick saw a small, abandoned trading post up ahead and rode their horses toward it. If they were going to die, they both wanted to kill as many Comanche warriors as they could before they were both killed. Neither one of them wanted to be captured knowing they would be tortured before being burned alive or stripped naked and then staked out over fire ants mounds. If they were going to die, both men wanted to die quickly while killing as many Comanche warriors as they could.

*****

Siringo and General Fitzpatrick halted their horses in front of the abandoned trading post. They drew their lever-action repeating rifles out of their saddle scabbards and then dismounted their horses. They took their saddlebags off their horses and then ran into the one-story adobe building. Siringo leaned his rifle against the wall next to the door and walked back outside.

"Where are you going?" General Fitzpatrick asked.

"I'm going to get our canteens off our horses just in case we're lucky enough to survive a while," Siringo replied.

"What about our horses?"

"The Comanches will either try to steal them when it gets dark or kill them right away, so we can't attempt to escape."

"We won't be able to escape," General Fitzpatrick said. "There's too many of them."

"You and I know that, but they still might think we'll try even though we won't," Siringo said as he grabbed his and then the general's canteen off their horses.

Bullets smashed into the one-story building as Siringo was walking through the doorway. He shut the door behind him and picked up his rifle that was leaning against the wall. He knelt down next to one of the two buildings' front windows and signaled the general to kneel next to the other one. He and the general cocked the levers on their rifles and then waited for the band of Comanche warriors to draw closer.

Siringo and the general targeted two Comanche warriors with the sights of their rifles and then pulled their rifles' triggers. Their bullets hit the two Comanches they were aiming at. The two warriors fell off their horses and died moments later. They targeted two more Comanches and shot and killed them. As they were cocking the levers on their rifles, they saw two more Comanches get shot and wondered who shot them.

"Who just killed those two Comanches?" General Fitzpatrick asked.

"I don't know, but it wasn't us," Siringo replied.

"Maybe it's an army patrol or the Texas Rangers."

"It's neither," Siringo said. He then pointed through the window and said, "It's two buffalo hunters, and they're riding their horses toward us."

"I see them now," General Fitzpatrick said after he spotted the two buffalo hunters galloping their horses toward the trading post.

"We just might get out this trading post alive," Siringo said.

Siringo raised his rifle and aimed it at a Comanche warrior. As he was pulling his rifle's trigger, he asked the general to help him give the two buffalo hunters cover fire so they stood a chance of making it to the trading post alive. The general nodded his head before pulling his rifle's trigger. The general's bullet smashed into the Comanche's forehead killing the warrior instantly.

Siringo killed a Comanche that was bearing down on the two buffalo hunters. He quickly cocked his rifle's lever and then shot and killed another Comanche that was aiming his rifle at one of the buffalo hunters. The two buffalo hunters drew their revolvers and shot several Comanches that were closing in on them. When they reached the one-story adobe building unscathed, they rode their horses behind it, dismounted, drew their Sharps .50 caliber rifles from their scabbards, and grabbed their saddlebags before entering trading post through the back door.

"My name is Quill, and this here is Brody. We thought you two could use some help fighting off these Comanches."

"We sure could!" General Fitzpatrick exclaimed, wearing a wide smile on his face. "My name is General Clayton Fitzpatrick, and the man kneeling by the window over there is Siringo."

"You don't look like a general," Quill said. "Where's your uniform?"

"I left it back at Fort Concho," General Fitzpatrick replied.

"Why did you do that?"

"Because I'm out here on unofficial business."

"It must be important business to be here in Comanche country without a troop of your soldiers accompanying you."

"It is, and I tell the two of you about it if we all survive this Comanche attack."

"We'll try our best to fight off the Comanches because I'm interested in hearing your story now." He checked to make sure his Sharps .50 caliber rifle was loaded and then said, "Brody and I will cover the back while you two keep covering the front."

"Okay," General Fitzpatrick said. "Let's get back to killing some Comanches."

"Some you say," Siringo stated. "We better kill them all, or we'll lose our scalps!"

*****

Quill and Brody aimed their Sharps rifles at two Comanches warriors. The two warriors sat tall on their horses believing they were too far away from being targeted by the white-eyes defending the trading post. Quill and Brody were confident the two Comanches were within their rifle's range when they both pulled their rifles' triggers. Both Comanche warriors were shocked when the buffalo hunters' bullets slammed into their chests. The impact from the two bullets knocked both Comanche warriors off their horses. They both died moments later lying on their backs.

"We taught those two Comanches a lesson, didn't we?" Quill asked Brody as he reloaded his rifle.

Brody nodded his head in response and then reloaded his own rifle. When they were finished reloading their rifles, both buffalo hunters targeted two more Comanche warriors and then shot and killed them. Siringo aimed his rifle at a Comanche warrior riding his horse toward the trading post at a fast gallop. He pulled his rifle's trigger and then watched his bullet hit and kill the Comanche he aimed at. He then looked back at Brody curious how he and Quill were doing.

"Hey, Brody, have you and Quill killed any Comanches yet?" Siringo asked loudly.

Brody looked back at Siringo and nodded his head and then loaded another cartridge in his rifle.

"How many have you two killed?" Siringo asked.

Brody showed four fingers on his right hand before aiming his rifle at another Comanche warrior.

"How many Comanches are attacking the rear of this building?" Siringo asked after he shot and killed another Comanche.

Brody pulled his rifle's trigger and watched his bullet rip through a Comanche warrior's neck. The Comanche warrior dropped his rifle as he fell off his horse. The warrior landed on his back, coughing up blood, and died moments later. Brody then looked back at Siringo without answering Siringo's question.

Siringo repeated his question again, but Brody didn't answer him. Instead, Brody reloaded his rifle. Siringo wondered why Brody refused to answer his question. He cocked his lever on his rifle, spun around, and aimed his rifle at a Comanche. He pulled his rifle's trigger and watched his bullet slam into the Comanche's left shoulder. He cocked the lever on his rifle again and then aimed it at the same Comanche warrior. He pulled his rifle's trigger and watched it strike the warrior's chest. The warrior fell off his horse and was dead before he landed on the ground.

"They're breaking off the attack!" a happy-sounding General Fitzpatrick exclaimed. He then turned around and asked the two buffalo hunters defending the rear of the trading post if they saw the Comanches breaking off the attack.

"Yes, they are!" Quill said before leaning his rifle against the wall next to the window he was defending.

"Will they attack us again?" General Fitzpatrick asked.

"You can count on it," Siringo said. He paused for a moment before saying, "They're just regrouping before they attack us again."

"How's everyone's ammunition holding up?" General Fitzpatrick asked.

"Good," Quill and Siringo said simultaneously.

"How's your ammunition holding up, Brody?" General Fitzpatrick asked.

Brody just nodded his head in response.

"Why don't you talk to us?" Siringo asked while glaring at Brody. "You just nod your head or show us your fingers when we ask you questions. You haven't said a word since you walked into this trading post."

"Open your mouth Brody and show them why you can't speak," Quill said.

Brody walked up to Siringo and General Fitzpatrick and then opened up his mouth. The general's and Siringo's lower jaws both dropped opened when they realized that Brody had no tongue in his mouth.

"What happened to his tongue?" General Fitzpatrick asked slowly while still wearing a shock facial expression.

"The Comanches cut his tongue off while they were torturing him," Quill replied. "The only reason he's still alive is because a troop of cavalry rescued him just before the Comanches could kill and scalp him."

"We're so sorry," General Fitzpatrick said while looking at Brody. "We didn't know."

Brody grinned at both Siringo and General Fitzpatrick before he turned around and walked back to the window he had was defending. Siringo and General Fitzpatrick both felt terrible after finding out the reason Brody hadn't spoken to them. They both returned to the windows they had been defending and started reloading their lever-action repeating rifles while waiting for the Comanches to attack them again.

26

"Here they come!" Siringo warned.

"Make your shots count!" General Fitzpatrick called out as he and the others watched a band of Comanche warriors encircle the trading post they were defending.

The four defenders aimed their rifles out the windows they were kneeling behind. They each targeted a Comanche warrior and then pulled their rifles' triggers. They all grinned with satisfaction when their bullets hit and killed the Comanche warriors they were aiming at.

Siringo saw two Comanche warriors spin their horses around and charge toward the window he was defending. He aimed his rifle at one of the Comanches and then pulled his rifle's trigger. He watched his bullet slam into the Comanche knocking him off his horse. He quickly cocked the lever on his rifle and then aimed it at the other Comanche warrior. He pulled the trigger on his rifle and then smiled when his bullet penetrated the Comanche's stomach. As he watched the Comanche slump over his horse's neck, he thought, *I betcha that Comanche's belly's on fire.*

Brody loaded a cartridge in his Sharps .50 caliber rifle and then looked for a Comanche to shoot at. He spotted one right away and aimed his rifle at him. He squeezed his rifle's trigger and watched his bullet tear the top of the warrior's head off. He then loaded another cartridge in his rifle and then took careful aim at a Comanche warrior wearing red war paint on his face who was nocking his arrow. Before the warrior had a chance to pull back his bowstring, Brody shot and killed him.

Quill saw two Comanche reloading their rifles. He quickly shot and killed one of them. As Quill was reloading his rifle, he heard a bullet whistled by his right ear. He spotted the Comanche warrior that just shot at him and targeted that warrior with the sights on his rifle. He then squeezed his rifle's trigger and watched his bullet rip into the warrior's left knee. The Comanche stumbled and fell to the ground. As Quill watched the warrior crawl toward a shrub, he reloaded his rifle. Once it was reloaded, he aimed it at that warrior and pulled its trigger. His bullet hit the warrior's right rib cage. The warrior continued crawling for a few more feet before he collapsed and died.

General Fitzpatrick cocked the lever on his lever-action repeating rifle and then aimed it at a Comanche warrior who just shot at him but missed. He pulled his rifle's trigger just as a bullet whizzed by his head. His bullet hit and killed he Comanche warrior he was aiming at. He quickly cocked the lever on his rifle and targeted another warrior to shoot at. When he knew he couldn't miss hitting the warrior he was aiming at, he pulled his rifle's trigger. His bullet struck and killed the warrior he aimed at.

"How's everyone holding up on ammunition?" General Fitzpatrick shouted.

Brody turned around and gave a thumbs-up with his right thumb while Siringo and Quill both shouted they still had plenty of ammunition.

"Good!" General Fitzpatrick exclaimed. "Conserve your ammunition. If we run out, we're dead!"

*****

Cooper McCaw, Sergeant Black, Captain Josh Stephens, and his small company of Texas Rangers all pulled back on their horses' reins and halted their horses. They all looked toward the old, abandoned trading post that was under attack by a band of Comanche warriors.

"I thought that trading post was abandoned years ago," Sergeant Black said.

"It was," Cooper concurred.

"It's not now!" Josh exclaimed.

"Should we help who's ever being attacked by those savages?" Sergeant Black asked.

"Hell, yes, we should," Cooper said. He then looked back at all the men accompanying him and said, "Make sure your weapons are fully loaded. We're going to help out whoever's inside that old trading post." Cooper checked his revolver and lever-action repeating rifle to make sure they were fully loaded while the rest of the men with him check theirs. After Cooper was sure that his and the men accompanying him weapons were loaded, he raised his right hand to get everyone's attention and then shouted, "Charge!" He then kicked his horse into a fast gallop and charged toward the Comanches that were attacking the old trading post.

Cooper led Sergeant Black and the Texas Rangers toward the band of Comanche warriors. He and his men killed several Comanches before the Comanches realized they were being attacked. The Comanches broke off their attack on the trading post and charged their horses toward Cooper and the men accompanying him.

*****

"They're breaking off their attack again!" an elated Quill exclaimed.

"Yes, they are, but it's not because of us," Siringo said.

"Then why are they?" a curious Quill asked as he and Brody approached Siringo.

"Look and see for yourselves," Siringo said as he moved away from the window he had been defending.

Both Quill and Brody smiled after they saw the reason the Comanches broke off their attack. General Fitzpatrick reloaded his rifle while looking out the window. He didn't know who was attacking the Comanches but was anxious to help them out if he could. He then looked toward Quill, Brody, and Siringo and said, "Don't stand still gazing out the window. Grab your rifles and help those men attacking the Comanches!"

Quill and Brody ran back to the rear of the trading post to fetch their Sharps .50 caliber rifles while Siringo and General Fitzpatrick aimed their lever-action repeating rifle at the retreating Comanches and opened fire. Quill and Brody soon joined Siringo and the general and fired their rifles at the Comanche warriors. Siringo and General Fitzpatrick lowered their rifles after the Comanche warriors were out of range. Quill and Brody, however, kept firing their large-caliber Buffalo Rifles that had greater range.

*****

Captain Josh Stephens saw a Comanche warrior bearing down on him. As bullet whizzed by him, Josh took careful aim and then fired his revolver. His bullet struck the Comanche he was aiming at and killed him instantly. He saw another warrior galloping a horse toward him. He aimed his revolver at the warrior and then pulled its trigger. His bullet tore a chunk of flesh off the warrior's left shoulder but didn't kill him. Josh aimed his revolver at the warrior again and then squeezed the trigger. This time his bullet slammed into the right side of the warrior's face killing him instantly.

Sergeant Black saw a Comanche warrior charging toward Cooper who was busy shooting at another warrior. The sergeant aimed his revolver at the warrior and then pulled its trigger. His bullet penetrated the warrior's right shoulder and knocked the warrior off his horse. The injured warrior landed on his chest then rolled over onto his back. He tried to get up off the ground but was stopped by a bullet that smashed into his forehead and killed him.

Cooper saw a Comanche warrior jump off his horse and run toward a fallen Texas Ranger. Cooper knew what the warrior's intentions were and rode his horse toward him. Just as the warrior was trying to scalp the fallen Texas Ranger, a bullet fired from Cooper's revolver killed him. Cooper saw another Texas Ranger lying on the ground and rode his horse over to where the ranger's body lay.

Cooper dismounted his horse and then knelt down next to the injured Texas Ranger. As he was inspecting the ranger's body, he asked, "What's your name?"

"Bobby," he answered.

"Where did the Comache's bullet hit you, Bobby?"

"In the middle of my lower back," Bobby replied.

"How bad is it?"

"I can't move my legs, feet, arms, or hands. I can't feel them either."

Cooper heard a loud war cry behind him. He drew his revolver and spun around. He saw a Comanche warrior running toward him holding a tomahawk in his right hand. He aimed his revolver at the Comanche and pulled its trigger. His bullet hit the Comanche in the middle of his chest. The Comanche fell backward and died before his body hit the ground.

That Comanche won't be taking Bobby's scalp, Cooper thought as he turned back around.

Cooper frowned after he looked down and saw that Bobby had died. He stood up and grabbed his horse's reins. As he was mounting his horse, an arrow flew by him. He spotted a Comanche that was nocking an arrow and rode his horse toward the warrior at a fast gallop. While his horse was quickly closing the gap between him and the warrior, Cooper aimed his revolver at the warrior. He pulled his revolver's trigger while the warrior was pulling back his bowstring. His bullet hit and killed the warrior before the warrior could release his bowstring.

*****

Quill and Brody lowered their rifles when it became difficult to determine whom they were shooting at. The sun had set, and daylight was quickly disappearing. The two buffalo hunters, Siringo and General Fitzpatrick, heard gunfire and saw muzzle flashes as the battle outside the trading post continued. They still didn't know who the Comanches were fighting but hoped whoever it was would prevail.

When the gunfire finally stopped, they wondered who won. They heard the sounds of horses galloping away. They all wondered out loud whether the Comanches had won or lost the battle. If the Comanches lost, then their lives would be spared; but if the

Comanches had won the battle, then the four of them faced certain death whether it be a quick death or a slow death by torture if they were captured alive.

"Hello, trading post! Is anyone alive inside?"

Siringo, General Fitzpatrick, Quill, and Brody all smiled when they heard the loud voice. Now they knew the Comanches had lost the battle and had retreated into Blanco Canyon.

"Yes, we're still alive!" General Fitzpatrick exclaimed.

"My name is Captain Josh Stephens of the Texas Rangers. I have some men with me who are badly injured and need help and shelter. May we come inside?"

"You sure may," General Fitzpatrick replied. He then turned toward Siringo and said, "Light the lanterns and find some cloths for bandaging."

"Yes, sir!" Siringo replied.

He then asked Brody, "Can you go out the back to the well and fetch some water?"

Brody nodded his head and then walked toward the back door.

The general then looked at Quill and said, "Let's go outside and help the rangers bring in their wounded."

27

The horrific sight they saw when they exited the trading post shocked General Fitzpatrick and Quill. Even though it was dark, they could see dozens of corpses lying on the ground in front of them. They saw a man walking toward them and waited to see who it was.

"Hello," the man said. "My name is Captain Josh Stephens."

"My name is General Fitzpatrick, and this here is Quill." After the three men shook hands, General Fitzpatrick said, "Thank you for saving our lives. If you and your men didn't show up when you did, I doubt the four of us could have lasted much longer."

"So there are four of you?" Josh asked.

"Yes," General Fitzpatrick said. "Brody is out back getting water from the well and Siringo is inside."

"Some of my men are injured pretty bad," Josh said. "Can I bring them inside the trading post?" he asked.

"You sure may," General Fitzpatrick said.

"Thank you," Josh responded. "I'll have some of my men bring them right away."

General Fitzpatrick saw a man wearing a buckskin shirt helping a wounded Texas Ranger into the trading post and said, "Let's lay him down on that bed over there." The general then helped the man carry the injured Texas Ranger over to the bed. After they lay the injured Texas Ranger on his back, the man wearing the buckskin shirt thanked the general for helping him.

"You're welcome," General Fitzpatrick said. He then said, "I haven't met you yet. What is your name?"

"My name is Cooper McCaw."

"Have you found my son whom the Comanches call White Buffalo?"

"You must be General Fitzpatrick," Cooper said.

"Yes, I am, and you haven't answered my question."

"We spotted your son two days ago, but we couldn't rescue him."

"Why not?"

"A large war party of Comanche warriors was taking him and two white female captives back to their camp inside Blanco Canyon. We would have been wiped out if we attacked them, and your son would probably have been killed."

"If you weren't a coward, you would have attacked those Comanches and rescued my son," General Fitzpatrick said while glaring at Cooper.

"He's not a coward," Sergeant Black said as he joined the conversation.

"Who are you?" General Fitzpatrick asked.

"My name is Sergeant Otto Black, and I can guarantee you if we had attacked that war party of Comanches dragging your son back to Blanco Canyon, we would have been massacred."

"Alright, I believe you," General Fitzpatrick said. He then looked at Cooper and said, "I'm sorry for calling you a coward."

"Don't worry about it. I've been called that over a hundred times since I was branded a coward, stripped of my rank, and dishonorably discharged from the cavalry."

"I gave you a chance to clear your name and be reinstated by into the cavalry at your old rank if you rescued my son," General Fitzpatrick reminded Cooper.

"Yes, you did," Cooper concurred. He paused for a moment before saying, "I still plan on rescuing your son or die trying."

"You're going to need more men if you're going to try to rescue my son. The Comanches know we're here and will be watching the trail leading into Blanco Canyon," General Fitzpatrick said.

"There's more than one trail that leads into that canyon, and a few men can sneak into that canyon during the night and try to rescue your son and the two white female captives that were spotted with him," Cooper said.

"How many men would you take with you?"

"Just three."

"So you think you and three men can use one of those other trails your spoke of to sneak into Blanco Canyon and rescue my son and the two female captives you saw with him?"

"Yes, sir!"

General Fitzpatrick kept quiet for a few moments and then asked, "Who would you take with you?"

"Sergeant Black and—"

"I'll go," Siringo interrupted as he approached the general, Cooper, and Sergeant Black. He then looked at Cooper and said, "It's good to see you, old friend."

"It's good to see you too," Cooper said as he and Siringo shook hands.

"You two know each other?" General Fitzpatrick asked.

"We sure do," Cooper said. "Siringo was my chief of scouts before my command was stripped from me."

"Was he with you at the Battle of White River?"

"No," Cooper replied.

"I wish I was, but I was fighting the flu back at Fort Concho during that battle," Siringo said.

"I wish you were there too," Cooper said. "If you were one of my men, I would not have been ambushed by that large Comanche war party. You would have spotted them waiting for us."

"I probably would have," Siringo said confidently. He then asked, "Who was scouting for you that day?"

"Two scouts named One Eye Willliams and Scar Face Armstrong," Cooper replied.

"They're terrible scouts," Siringo said. "How did you get stuck with them that day?"

"Because you had the flu and all the other scouts were out scouting for our patrols that day."

"I felt terrible when I heard what happened to your troop and that you were the sole survivor. I wanted to testify in your defense at your court-martial, but by the time I recovered from the flu, you had already been stripped of your command, dishonorably discharged, and branded a coward. I feel responsible for all of it. If I hadn't caught the flu, that massacre at the Battle of White River probably would never have happened. I'm so sorry," Siringo said, wearing a frown on his face.

"It's not your fault," Cooper said.

"I heard back at Fort Concho that you were given a chance to restore your reputation and get your command back if you can rescue General Fitzpatrick's son," Siringo said.

"You heard right," Cooper responded. He then looked at General Fitzpatrick and asked, "That offer is still on the table, right?"

"It sure is," General Fitzpatrick said.

"Good because that's why I'm going with you to Blanco Canyon so I can help you get back what was wrongfully taken from you. I know you're not a coward, and I know you weren't during the Battle of White River even though I wasn't there," Siringo said.

"I'm glad you're going with me and Sergeant Black."

"You said you wanted three men to go with you," General Fitzpatrick reminded Cooper.

"Yes, I did," Cooper concurred.

"I volunteer to go with you," General Fitzpatrick said. "White Buffalo is my son, and I want to help the three of you rescue him."

"If you go with us, you'll have to obey all my orders. Are you willing to do that, General?"

"Yes, I am."

"I need to talk to Captain Josh Stephens and tell him that I've picked my three men to go with me into Blanco Canyon," Cooper said.

"Is he and his men going back to Lubbock?" Sergeant Black asked.

"He'll have his wounded men who can survive the trip return to Lubbock, but a few of his men won't last till morning and a couple of others won't be able to travel for a while. He and some of his men will have to stay at this old trading post for a while," Josh replied. He then turned away from the three men and walked outside.

Sergeant Black followed Cooper outside. He wasn't happy that General Fitzpatrick was going along. He never liked officers, and now a big shot general was going with him, Cooper, and Siringo to Blanco Canyon. The sergeant heard the general agree to take orders from Cooper, but he doubted the general actually would.

General Fitzpatrick looked at Siringo and said, "I bet you those two buffalo hunters that helped us will want to go with us to Blanco Canyon," General Fitzpatrick said.

"Cooper only wants four of us to go," Siringo reminded the general. He paused for a moment and then said, "If more than four of us go, we'll be spotted for sure."

"Where is Quill and Brody?" General Fitzpatrick asked. "I haven't seen those two buffalo hunters for a while."

"Quill and Brody already left, and they were riding their horses west in the opposite direction of Blanco Canyon," Siringo said.

"I never got to thank them for helping us out," General Fitzpatrick said, wearing a sad expression on his face as he followed Siringo out the front entrance to the trading post.

I wonder why they couldn't wait till morning to leave, General Fitzpatrick wondered to himself as he walked toward a small group of Texas Rangers who were digging graves for their fellow deceased comrades.

*****

"Why are you taking the general with you?" Josh asked.

"Because he asked to go," Cooper replied.

"I think you're making a huge mistake taking him with you," Josh said. "The two other men going with you are good men, but the general will only slow you down and try to boss you around as well."

"He promised me that he would take orders from me," Cooper said.

"Even if he does, he'll still slow you down," Josh said, still stunned that Cooper was allowing the general to go with him.

"He's still in good shape," Cooper said. "Plus, it's his son we're trying to rescue, so how could I say no?"

"Since you put it that way, I guess you couldn't say no to him."

"No, I couldn't."

"Will you try and rescue those two white female captives we saw the Comanches taking back with them to Blanco Canyon?"

"Of course we will," Cooper responded.

"Thank you. Could you also check and see if the Comanches are holding another white woman captive too? I was sent out here to find and rescue three white women, and we only saw two of them."

"The other one might be dead, but we'll do our best to find out whether she's still alive or not. And if she's alive, we'll do our best to rescue her too."

"Thanks."

"Now I need a favor from you," Cooper said.

"Just name it," Josh responded.

"Can you send one of your Texas Rangers to Fort Concho and ask the commanding officer there to bring a troop of cavalry here to this trading post?"

"I sure can."

"Good because if my men and I are lucky enough to find White Buffalo and the two or three white woman who were kidnapped and somehow make it out of Blanco Canyon alive, we're going to need all the help we can get to kill the Comanche warriors who will be chasing after us."

"My men and I will be waiting for you near the entrance to Blanco Canyon and help you fight any Comanches chasing after you."

"Thank you," Cooper replied. "We're going to need all the help we can get if we're lucky enough to find and rescue White Buffalo and those female captives."

"When are you planning on leaving?" a curious Josh asked.

"Tomorrow night," Cooper said. "Until then, we have a lot of graves to dig,"

"We sure do," Josh concurred as he and Cooper looked around the trading post and saw corpses lying on the ground everywhere.

28

White Buffalo saw Katherine White and Jennie Farmer walking toward the river. He felt anger boiling inside him after the two white women turned their heads for a brief moment and looked at him. Both their faces were badly bruised and covered with cuts and lacerations

He knew Raven was responsible for the beatings that Katherine and Jennie had suffered. He knew their bodies were probably covered with bruises, cuts, and lacerations too.

White Buffalo watched Katherine and Jennie wash some clothes in the river. He saw several squaws bully and harass the two white women. He felt bad for Katherine and Jennie and was upset that he couldn't help them. He called out to the squaws to stop bullying the two white women, but his shouts fell on deaf ears.

White Buffalo struggled to break free from the leather straps that bound his wrists behind his back. If he could break free of them, he could use his hands to untie the leather straps tied around his ankles and then chase the squaws away from Jennie and Katherine. After a few minutes, he realized it was useless and gave up struggling to break free. He continued watching the squaws bully and harass Katherine and Jennie and felt terrible he couldn't help stop it.

Several warriors White Buffalo knew stopped by and visited him throughout the day. They warned him that Raven would soon be torturing him and was going to force everyone in the village to watch. Raven wanted to send a loud and clear message to his village to never disobey or betray him and show everyone what the consequences would be if they did.

White Buffalo asked the warriors why Raven hadn't tortured him and killed him already. The warriors told White Buffalo that a group of white men were caught entering Blanco Canyon, and Raven took most of the warriors from the village to battle them. The warriors told him that Raven caught a few more white men at the old, abandoned trading post and fought them until a group of Texas Rangers showed up and forced Raven to break off the attack. White Buffalo was informed that dozens of warriors were killed and wounded yesterday and last night and that Raven was in a sour mood and was looking forward to seeking vengeance.

White Buffalo begged a few warriors that were friends of his to cut the leather straps that bound his wrists and ankles and then turn their backs so he could break free, but none of them would do it. They knew what the consequences would be if they were caught, and none of them were willing to risk it in fear of being caught. White Buffalo knew that Raven was looking forward to inflicting pain on him and was not looking forward to it.

White Buffalo couldn't stop thinking about his deceased wife, Sun Flower, whom Raven was responsible for killing. He loved her and his heart would be forever broken now that she was gone and he would never see her again. He wanted vengeance for her murder but knew his chances of ever getting it were very slim as he waited to be tortured and then most likely burned alive in the middle of the Comanche village he had been living in since being captured so many years ago.

29

Willie Doyle was happy that Captain Josh Stephens picked him to ride to Fort Concho. Willie always wanted to prove to the other Texas Rangers that he was worthy of being a ranger too. So when Captain Stephens asked him if he would ride to Fort Concho for help, he quickly accepted the captain's offer.

Willie had been riding his horse for hours, and both him and his horse were getting exhausted. His horse needed watered and fed, so when he came across a small stream, he halted his horse. He dismounted his horse and led his horse to the stream so it could drink. While the horse was drinking water, he reached into one of his saddlebags and pulled out some large carrots to feed his horse. After his horse quenched its thirst, Willie fed it several carrots.

After his horse was finished eating, Willie wrapped his horse's reins around a small tree so he could eat some food himself and drink some water from his canteen. After his hunger subsided and he was no longer thirsty, he filled his canteens up. He then mounted his horse and then rode it toward Fort Concho.

After riding his horse for twenty minutes, he halted his horse when he saw four Indians sitting tall on their horses on top of a small hill. *Are those Indians Comanche or Kiowa?* he wondered. After a brief moment staring at them, he concluded they were Kiowas. Captain Stephens warned him that he had to cross through a small area of land the Kiowas claimed as their hunting grounds. *I must be in Kiowa Territory*, he thought.

When he saw the four Kiowas ride their horses toward him, he used the heels of his boots and kicked his horse into a fast gallop. He hoped his horse could outrun the four Kiowas chasing after him as he rode it toward Fort Concho. He looked back over his left shoulder and frowned when he saw the Kiowas closing on him. Other Texas Rangers had told him that Kiowa warriors were great horsemen. He never believed them, but now he realized they had been telling him the truth.

*****

"Hold up!" Quill called out to Brody. After he and Brody halted their horses, Quill said, "It looks like someone is about to lose his scalp." He then looked at Brody and asked, "Should we help?"

Brody nodded his head and then drew his .50 caliber Sharps rifle from its leather saddle scabbard. Quill drew his Sharps out of its scabbard and then the two buffalo hunters dismounted their horses. They both loaded a cartridge in their Sharps rifles and then knelt down. They each picked a Kiowa warrior to shoot at, took careful aim, and then pulled their rifles' triggers.

*****

Willie heard gunshots behind him, but no bullets hit or whistled by him. He looked back over his left shoulder and saw only two Kiowas still chasing him.

What happened to the two other Kiowas that were chasing me? he wondered as he continued riding his horse at a fast gallop.

Willie heard two more gunshots but again no bullets hit or whizzed by him. He halted his horse, spun it around, and was stunned by what he saw. The two remaining Kiowa warriors were on the ground lying on their backs while their horses were still galloping.

Who killed the four Kiowas that were chasing after me? he wondered as he looked around the hilly landscape covered by tall grass.

Willie drew his rifle from its saddle scabbard and then cocked its lever after he saw two men riding their horses toward him. He lowered his rifle after he recognized the two buffalo hunters. As the two buffalo hunters drew closer, Willie slid his rifle back into its saddle scabbard and then waved toward the two men who just saved his life.

Willie thanked Quill and Brody after the two buffalo hunters halted their horses next to his. He knew he would have been killed if the two buffalo hunters hadn't killed the four Kiowas chasing him.

"What are you doing out here all alone?" Quill inquired. "You almost lost your scalp!"

"Captain Stephens dispatched me to ride to Fort Concho for help," Willie replied.

"Are the Comanches attacking that old trading post again?"

"No."

"Then why do the Texas Rangers need help?"

"Because Cooper McCaw, General Fitzpatrick, and two other men are going into Blanco Canyon to rescue three to four captives. And if they succeed, they're going to have all the Comanche warriors in the area looking for them. Captain Stephens, and what's left of his company of rangers, will be waiting just outside of Blanco Canyon to help fight the Comanches if the rescue mission is successful. But his company of rangers won't be able to hold off the Comanches for long. And unless I get through to Fort Concho for help, I'm afraid everyone I left back at the trading post will be killed trying to rescue those hostages the Comanches are holding inside Blanco Canyon."

"You're in Kiowa land right now, and you might run into more Kiowas along the way to the fort," Quill warmed.

"I know, but I have to try to make it."

"We'll help you get through to the fort," Quill promised. He then looked over at Brody and asked, "Won't we?"

Brody nodded his head in agreement even though he knew their chances of making it to the fort alive were slim. The Kiowas were on the warpath too and would be looking for the three of them once the four warriors they had just killed were discovered.

Quill looked back at Willie and said, "Let's get going! We have a long way to ride and some hostile land to ride through before we get to Fort Concho."

"Thanks for offering to help me. I really appreciate it," Willie said before he kicked his horse into a fast trot.

Quill looked back at Brody and said, "Let's ride!" He and Brody then used the heels of their boots and kicked their horses into a fast trot and followed Willie hoping they would make it to Fort Concho alive.

30

White Buffalo felt a sharp pain in left side. He opened his eyes and saw his adoptive brother, Raven, staring down at him.

"What do you want?" White Buffalo asked as he tried to ignore the pain in his left side.

"Half my warriors want me to kill you today, but the other half don't," Raven said as he continued glaring down at the White Buffalo.

"So what warriors are you going to make happy?"

"The warriors that don't want me to kill you today. But the warriors who want you killed will still be happy when I allow them to start torturing you later today."

"Why don't you show the entire village how great a warrior you are by challenging me to a fight to the death today?

"I rather watch you being tortured," Raven replied.

"You're a coward!"

"No, I'm not!"

"Then fight me and prove to this village that you deserve to be their chief."

"I am the chief, and I don't have to prove anything to anyone!" Raven looked away from White Buffalo for a moment and signaled four of his warriors to come over. He then looked back down at White Buffalo and said, "My warriors are going to strip you naked and then stake you out on the ground so the sun can bake your body today."

"I don't see any red ant mounds around here," White Buffalo said.

"Don't worry," Raven said. "I'm not going to let red ants bite you to death. That's a slow death."

"I thought you would enjoy watching red ants bite me to death," White Buffalo stated.

"That takes too long, and it's no fun watching it."

After the four warriors stripped White Buffalo's clothes off and staked him spread-eagle on his back, White Buffalo asked Raven, "So how are you going to kill me tomorrow?"

"I'm going to burn you alive tomorrow night in the center of our village with everyone watching the flames burn the flesh off your body. And right before I have you burned alive, I will use my knife and slice the flesh and hair off the top of your head."

"You're going to scalp me?"

"You bet I am and then I'm going to hang it outside my lodge."

"It's easy to scalp your enemy when your enemy is staked to the ground and cannot defend himself. No one who walks by your lodge and sees my scalp hanging on it will consider it a trophy. Instead, my scalp will remind everyone in this village how scared you were to fight me."

"No, they won't!"

"Yes, they will," White Buffalo warned.

"I'm getting tired talking to you," Raven said. "I need some excitement. I'm going back to my lodge and have some fun with those two white women you and Sun Flower cared for while you lay here naked and feeling the sun burning your body."

"You're a coward!" White Buffalo called out after Raven turned away from him and started walking toward his lodge.

Raven stopped dead in his tracks, spun around, and shouted back, "I forgot to tell you that I told my warriors to urinate on your body throughout the day to help cool your body from the sun's rays burning it!" Raven then laughed out loud for a few moments before he turned around and continued walking toward his lodge.

White Buffalo tried to break free from the leather straps tied around his wrists and ankles. His efforts failed. He wanted to die a warrior's death, but Raven wouldn't allow him to. All he could do now was lay on his naked body's back with his arms and legs spread-eagled and wait to be tortured and then burned alive tomorrow night in the center of the village where he had lived since being kidnapped as a child so many years ago.

*****

"Did you find it?" Katherine White asked.
"I'm still looking," Jennie Farmer replied.
"Hurry up before he gets back!"
"Are you still watching for him?"
"Yes," a nervous-sounding Katherine replied.
"I found it!" Jennie exclaimed and then held up a hunting knife.
"Great. Now hide it underneath your buffalo hide so he won't find it."
"Won't he miss it?"
"He shouldn't because he has a few of them, and he always keeps his favorite in a leather sheath attached to his belt," Katherine replied.

Jennie took Katherine's advice and hid the hunting knife she found underneath her buffalo hide that she uses as her blanket at night. She then turned around and called out to Katherine, "I hid it!"

"Good because he's walking this way," Katherine warned.
"I hope he doesn't beat us!"
"He usually does."
"Why?" Jennie asked. "We submit to him anytime he wants us too."
"He loves being violent and beating women."
"He must because he beats us all the time," Jennie said. "Our bodies are covered with scrapes and bruises. I'm afraid to look in a mirror because I know I won't even recognize myself anymore."
"Glad we don't have a mirror in this village to look at," Katherine said.
"So am I," Jennie concurred.
"Try to look happy when he enters this lodge."
"I'll try but my body is already trembling with fear."

"So is mine," Katherine said. She then turned around, walked over to where Jennie was sitting, and sat down next to her. She looked at Jennie and reminded her to smile and then forced a smile on her face as Raven walked into the lodge.

*****

White Buffalo tried to break free from the leather straps that bound his wrists and ankles to the stakes that were buried deep in the ground. He was a strong but still couldn't break free. As he lay on his back with his arms and legs outstretched, he thought about his upcoming death. In the past, he would have been a nervous wreck knowing he would be burned alive in the very near future. But instead, he was very calm knowing that he would cross over the bridge and walk through the gates of heaven. He hadn't given up all hope of escaping, but if he couldn't, he was prepared to meet his Lord and Savior.

A few warriors had already urinated on White Buffalo's body while several others tried but were stopped by warriors who were still loyal to him. White Buffalo felt the sun's rays burning his body throughout the day and knew his body looked like a red tomato by now. He thought some of his friends would have tried to break him free, but when none did, he concluded they were all afraid of Raven.

White Buffalo prayed to God and thanked him for allowing him to live as long as he had. He had given up all hope of escaping death and now was asking God to allow him to pass through the gates of heaven. He didn't know whether God was listening to him but hoped that he was. He asked God again to forgive him for all his sins. He also thanked God for allowing his son to die on the cross so his sins could be forgiven. He then pleaded with God to help ease his pain and suffering if possible.

After White Buffalo finished praying, he heard sounds of thunder in the distance. He no longer felt the hot sunrays on his body and face. He opened his eyes and saw the skies above him full of darkness. He then felt raindrops hitting his sunburnt body and realized a storm was approaching. He smiled and thanked God for hearing his prayer.

31

"Change of plans!" Cooper McCaw called out. "We're leaving now!"

General Fitzpatrick, Sergeant Black, and Siringo looked up at the dark skies and smiled knowing that Cooper wanted to take advantage of the bad weather that was fast approaching. They saw lightning bolts in the sky followed by sounds of thunder as they mounted their horses. As they used the heels of their boots and kicked their horses into a trot, they felt raindrops hitting their bodies.

The thunderstorm produced gusty winds and heavy rain, giving the four men great cover as they rode toward Blanco Canyon. Earth-shattering roars followed lightning bolts that filled the skies above them. Amazingly their horses were not spooked as the thunderstorm raged all around them.

As the four men rode their horses near Blanco Canyon, they were ready to draw their revolvers and defend themselves if Comanche warriors attacked them. Their visibility was very poor as they rode their horses into Blanco Canyon. They needed to find shelter for their horses, and they needed to find it quickly as the storm grew stronger. Siringo rode his horse alongside Cooper and suggested where they could find a nearby cave.

Within ten minutes, they found the cave Siringo told them about and rode their horses into it. They dismounted their horses, secured them, and then walked to the cave's entrance. While looking outside, they saw a lightning bolt split a cottonwood in two. They backed up into the cave, sat down, and then discussed how they were going to rescue White Buffalo and the white female captives.

*****

White Buffalo lay spread-eagled on his back all alone as the thunderstorm raged all around him. His body no longer felt burned from all the raindrops that have been cooling his body. He had given up all hope of being able to escape the torture and death he would face as soon as the storm passed by. But then something happened that brought him hope of living a longer life.

White Buffalo felt the ground softening all around him. He pulled hard on the stakes that his wrists and ankles were tied to and smiled when he felt all of them move. He pulled again with his arms and legs and all four stakes came out of the ground. He then used his hands to untie the leather straps that were tied around his wrists and ankles. He was free for the moment and was determined to stay free.

White Buffalo pushed himself off the ground, stood up, and ran toward a familiar tepee. While he was running, he felt the rain hitting him and wind blowing hard against his body. When he reached the tepee, he pulled back the buffalo hide covering its entrance and then heard a woman's voice call out to him.

"What are you doing here?" his adoptive mother, White Sun, asked. Before White Buffalo could answer her, she said, "Come inside before someone sees you."

White Buffalo walked into the tepee and pulled the buffalo hide back down so it covered the tepee's entrance. He saw White Sun sitting next to a small campfire in the middle of the tepee and sat down next to her. He then looked at her and said, "The rain made the ground really soft so I could pull the stakes out."

"You must be cold," White Sun said. "Dry off with this buffalo robe while I get you some clothes." White Sun handed White Buffalo her buffalo robe before searching for some clothes for her adoptive son to wear. A few moments later, she sat down next to him and handed her son some clothes. She then said, "These belonged to your father, and I know he would want you to wear them."

White Sun handed White Buffalo her deceased husband's buckskin war shirt, breechcloths, leggings, and leather belt. She told him that Chief Black Hawk loved him as much as he loved Raven. While White Buffalo put his adoptive father's clothes on, White Sun continued talking to him.

"Where will you go?" she asked. "You can't stay here."

"I'll try to live with my own people again."

"The white-eyes?"

"Yes," White Buffalo replied. "They were my people before warriors from this village kidnapped me, and hopefully, they'll take me back."

"They will," White Sun said with confidence. "You were forced to live with us, and when you tell them that, they'll let you live with them again."

"I could have escaped many times after you and Black Hawk adopted me, but I stayed and fought and hunted with the warriors of this village."

"You don't have to tell them that," White Sun said. She then paused for a few moments before saying, "Go to the bluecoats' fort and look for your father. If he's still alive, the bluecoats should know where to find him."

"Okay, I will," White Buffalo promised.

"You look good in Black Hawk's clothes. Now try these on," White Sun said and then handed White Buffalo a new pair of moccasins. "I made these for Black Hawk, but he was killed before he had a chance to wear them."

White Buffalo slipped the moccasins on and then said, "They fit perfectly."

"Good!" White Sun said. "I have some more things to give you before you leave." She walked away and returned moments later. She handed White Buffalo a tomahawk, hunting knife, a bow, and a leather quiver full of arrows. She then looked deeply into White Buffalo's eyes and said, "Black Hawk would have wanted me to give you his weapons. He always loved you just as much as I do still. Now get going before this storm stops and Raven finds out that you've escaped."

White Sun and White Buffalo hugged each other tightly while saying their goodbyes to each other. White Buffalo then stepped outside into the raging storm and ran toward the area where the horses were kept. He saw a Comanche warrior standing near the horses and drew his tomahawk from his leather belt. He ran toward the warrior as fast as he could and then stopped dead in his tracks when he was within throwing range. He threw his tomahawk just as the warrior spotted him. Before the warrior could react, the tomahawk's blade penetrated the middle of the warrior's chest. The stun-looking warrior fell down onto his knees as White Buffalo ran toward him.

White Buffalo pulled his knife from its sheath and then used it to slice the mortally injured warrior's neck. He then pushed the warrior onto his back and pulled his tomahawk out of the dying warrior's chest. He slid his knife back into its sheath and shoved his tomahawk underneath his belt. He quickly scanned the area where the horses were corralled and smiled when he located his own horse. He ran over to his horse, grabbed its leather reins, and then jumped onto its back.

White Buffalo used the heels of his moccasins and kicked his horse into a fast gallop and then rode it away from the Comanche village that he had been living for many years. While he was riding away from the village, he thought about the two female captives, Katherine and Jennie, he left behind. He wanted to help them both escape but knew he couldn't right now. The storm would be ending soon, and he had to get as far away from the village as he could before Raven discovered he had escaped.

The rain stopped, and the winds died down after White Buffalo had rode his horse for a little more than a mile. The severe thunderstorm had ended, and the sun was starting to shine again. White Buffalo frowned as he kept riding his horse knowing that Raven and his warriors would be looking for him soon.

*****

Raven exited his lodge when he heard one of his warriors calling out for him. He stood in front of this tepee and waited for the warrior that was running toward him. After the warrior stopped in front of him and was trying to catch his breath, Raven asked, "What's wrong?"

"He's escaped!" the warrior named Grey Owl exclaimed.

"White Buffalo?" Raven asked.

"Yes!"

"We need to find him before he gets out of this canyon! He can't be far!"

"I'll gather up the warriors," Grey Owl said.

"Good," Raven responded. He then said, "Meet over where our horses are kept with our warriors mounted and ready to ride."

Grey Owl nodded his head before spinning around and leaving to gather the warriors. Raven turned around and walked back into his lodge. He roughed up Katherine and Jennie before threatening both of them not to try to escape while he and his warriors were gone looking for White Buffalo. He then gathered up his weapons and left his lodge. Katherine's and Jennie's faces were sore from being slapped by Raven's hands but rejoiced after hearing the news of White Buffalo's escape.

"I hope he makes it out of this canyon and back to civilization," Katherine said.

"So do I," Jennie concurred.

"As soon as Raven and his warriors are gone looking for White Buffalo, we're going to try to escape this village," Katherine said.

"The squaws, elderly, and children of this village will be watching our every move," Jennie warned.

"That's why we'll wait till dark before we try to escape." Katherine then opened up the deerskin flap, looked up into the sky, and then said, "It will be dark soon, so we better start planning our escape."

"Escaping from this village without getting caught won't be easy," Jennie warned.

"True, but we have to try. If we stay here, Raven will eventually beat us both to death."

32

White Buffalo pulled back on his horse's reins and then spun his horse around. He grinned when he saw no Comanches following him.

By now, Raven and his warriors know I've escaped and will be searching for me. If I continue riding my horse, its hoofprints will be easy to track. I better continue my escape on foot, he thought.

White Buffalo jumped off his horse and then hit it on its rear. He frowned while watching his horse gallop back toward the village knowing he would never see it again. He then returned his attention on escaping and began jogging through Blanco Canyon. He knew the canyon better than most of the Comanche warriors that would be looking for him did and would use that knowledge to his advantage.

White Buffalo first heard and then saw several Comanche warriors riding their horses. He dove behind two large boulders and hid himself before the warriors could spot him. He drew an arrow from his quiver, notched it on his bowstring, and then waited patiently for the warriors to ride by him. If they spotted him, he was determined to kill as many of them that he could before they had an opportunity to kill him.

White Buffalo kept hidden behind the boulders as the Comanche warriors approached. He stayed quiet as they rode their horses by him and was relieved when they didn't spot him. After the warriors disappeared, he stood up and then put his arrow back into his quiver. He then thought about Katherine and Jennie who he had left behind and knew his deceased wife, Sun Flower, would be upset with him for deserting the two young white women.

*****

"Raven and his warriors have gone looking for White Buffalo," Katherine said. "We need to sneak out of this camp before they come back.

"How are we going to sneak out of here with all the squaws, children, and elderly walking around the village?" Jennie asked.

"We're going to go outside, pretend to do our chores, and when we see an opportunity to escape, we'll take it," Katherine said.

"That's your plan?" a stunned-looking Jennie asked.

"It sure is," Katherine replied before asking, "Do you have a better plan?"

"No, I do not," Jennie replied. She then asked, "Do you have the knife?"

"Yes. It's hidden underneath my dress."

"I hope we don't have to use it."

"If we do, I won't hesitate to defend ourselves with it."

*****

White Buffalo kept in the shadows as best as he could and used the shrubs scattered throughout Blanco Canyon for cover as he slowly moved back toward the Comanche village that he had called his home since being kidnapped by the Comanches. He felt guilty for leaving Katherine and Jennie behind after he escaped. He couldn't stop thinking about them. He knew Raven would continue beating and raping them if they were not rescued. He was determined to free them both and then help them escape from Raven and his warriors.

When White Buffalo heard voices behind him, he stopped dead in his tracks. He pulled an arrow from his quiver and notched it on his bowstring. He ran into the shadows of the tall canyon wall and then waited to see how many warriors were approaching. His wait was short when he saw two Comanche warriors, who he knew were loyal to Raven, walking toward him.

White Buffalo pulled his bowstring back before the two warriors saw him. When he knew his arrow wouldn't miss, he released his bowstring and watched his arrow pierce the chest of the warrior he was aiming at. As the warrior fell to the ground, White Buffalo quickly pulled another arrow from his quiver and notched it. Before the second warrior could react, White Buffalo released his bowstring and watched his arrow slam into the second warrior's belly.

The second warrior stumbled forward while trying to pull the arrowhead out of his stomach. He then fell to his knees, looked up, and saw White Buffalo staring down at him. Before the warrior could utter a word, White Buffalo pulled his hunting knife out of its sheath and used it to slice open the warrior's throat. The warrior fell onto his back gasping for air and then died moments later.

White Buffalo wiped the blood that covered his knife off on the warrior's tunic then slid it back into its decorated leather sheath. He made sure both warriors were dead before dragging their bodies behind some nearby boulders. He then picked up his bow and ran low to the ground back toward the Comanche village he had escaped from. As he ran toward the village, he knew Raven and his warriors were looking for him all over Blanco Canyon.

*****

Katherine and Jennie walked casually through the village. They acted like they normally would so they wouldn't draw anyone's attention. They stopped a few times and engaged in conversations with squaws that had been friendly with them in the past. They both were relieved when none of the squaws suspected them of wanting to escape. All of the squaws they visited with thought Katherine and Jennie were looking forward to marrying Raven in the near future.

As Katherine and Jennie approached the river, they saw several children playing nearby. They noticed a few squaws washing clothes in the river and a few elderly men fishing. A few squaws that were cleaning fish saw Katherine and Jennie approaching and asked for their help.

"Can you help us clean all these fish that those elders caught?" a squaw named Smiling Star asked as she pointed at a pile of fish laying one the ground in between her and a squaw named Little Feather.

"We sure can," Katherine replied, knowing to refuse the request would draw attention to her and Jennie.

Jennie and Katherine sat down next to the two squaws. Little Feather handed them each a hunting knife so they could use the knives to skin the fish. For the next hour, Katherine and Jennie helped Smiling Star and Little Feather clean the fish. The pile of fish started shrinking as the two piles of bones and filets got taller. As they were helping the two squaws clean the fish, Jennie and Katherine quietly thought of ways of excusing themselves so they could continue trying to escape from the Comanche village. When Katherine realized the sun was beginning to set, she decided to act.

"Oh no!" Katherine exclaimed.

"What's wrong?" Smiling Star asked.

"Raven will be back soon, and Jennie and I haven't prepared dinner for him yet," Katherine replied.

"Take a few of these filets and prepare dinner for him," Little Feather offered. She then handed Katherine some filets before saying, "I hear he loves eating fish."

"Thank you," Katherine said. She then looked at Jennie and said, "We need to gather some wood so we can make a fire and cook these filets."

"We sure do," Jennie concurred. She then pointed toward a group of river birch trees on the other side of the river and said, "We can find a bunch of broken branches laying around those trees over there."

"You're right we can," Katherine said. She then looked at Smiling Star and Little Feather and said, "Thanks for the filets."

Both squaws smiled in response and then continued using their knives to skin the fish. Katherine put the filets into the leather pouch she had with her as she and Jennie walked away from the two squaws. Katherine and Jennie used a shallow area in the river to walk across it.

When they reached the other side, they walked toward the group of river birch trees hoping no one was watching them. They took their time gathering broken branches as the night sky settled in.

Katherine set the broken branches she had gathered down on the ground and then walked up to Jennie and asked, "Are you ready?"

Jennie dropped the branches she was carrying and replied, "Yes!"

33

"Take cover!" Cooper McCaw called out when he saw a small group of Comanche warriors riding their horses nearby.

Sergeant Black, General Fitzpatrick, and Siringo dove into a gully near a group of boulders after hearing Cooper's order. They drew their revolvers from their holsters and were ready to use them. Cooper dove into the gully and drew his revolver too. All four men heard the sounds of horses fast approaching them.

"I wish we had our rifles with us," General Fitzpatrick said. "We should never have left them back in the cave with our horses."

"They would have slowed us down," Cooper said.

Cooper then reminded the general the reason they left their rifles behind. They needed the free use of their hands in case they needed to climb over boulders or scale cliffs while inside Blanco Canyon. Carrying their rifles with them would have slowed them down and could have prevented them from entering certain areas of the canyon they needed to go to prevent the Comanches spotting them.

"You're right! They would have slowed us down."

The four men kept themselves hidden while listening to the sounds of horses growing louder. They held their revolvers' grips tightly and rested their index fingers on their triggers. They were all ready to shoot and kill as many Comanches as they could if their hiding place was found.

They kept silent as the group of Comanche warriors drew near. They were ready to fight but only if they had too. They knew if the Comanches discovered them, their hopes of rescuing White Buffalo and the white female captives would vanish. They had to keep themselves hidden and hope the Comanches would not discover them.

Cooper and his three companions felt their hearts pumping when they heard the band of Comanches stop their horses above the gully they were hiding in. They heard the warriors talking among themselves. Both Siringo and Cooper understood the language spoken by the Comanches and listened closely as the warriors spoke among themselves. When they heard the warriors ride their horses away, they all breathed a sigh of relief.

"Thank God they didn't find us!" a joyous Sergeant Black exclaimed. He then looked at Siringo and Cooper and asked, "Did either of you understand what those Comanches were talking about?"

"Yes," Siringo replied. "Those Comanches are looking for a captive who escaped from their village."

"I wonder if my son is the one who escaped," General Fitzpatrick said.

"They didn't say who it was," Siringo said.

"It could be one of the women were looking for," Sergeant Black suggested.

"Yes, it could be," Cooper concurred.

"We need to decide if we should turn back because every warrior in the village we're looking for is searching all over this canyon for whoever escaped," Siringo said.

"The village is only a few miles away," Cooper said. "If White Buffalo and the female hostages we're looking for are still there, it will be a lot easier to sneak into that village with all the warriors out here searching for someone else."

"True," General Fitzpatrick concurred.

"So what are we sitting around here for?" Cooper asked. Before anyone could answer he said, "Let's get off our butts and get inside that Comanche village and find White Buffalo and those female hostages. We don't have much time. We need to use the cover of night to help hide us as we go into and out of the Comanche village."

*****

Katherine and Jennie ran as fast as they could through the cottonwoods. They heard no one behind them and were confident they had escaped the Comanche village without being seen. When they reached the tall grass within Blanco Canyon, they stopped to catch their breath. They scanned the large area in front of them, but the night sky reduced their visibility so they couldn't see as far as they would have been able to in the daylight.

"Do you see any Comanches?" Jennie asked.

"No, but I can't see that far because it's dark tonight," Katherine replied. "The clouds above are covering the moon and stars tonight."

"Where do we go?" Jennie asked.

"I'm not sure, but we need to keep heading away from the village.

"Let's keep heading in the same direction that we have been then."

"That sounds good to me," Katherine said. She said, "From now on, we need to whisper and stay alert until we get out of this canyon. If we see any movement or hear horses or Comanches approaching us, we need to hide ourselves immediately."

"What happens if we don't see any place to hide?" Jennie asked.

"Throw ourselves on the ground, stay still and quiet, and pray we're not found," Katherine replied before leading Jennie into the tall grass.

*****

Two Comanche warriors named Little Bear and Black Feather stopped dead in their tracks when they saw two people walking toward them. It was too dark to tell who it was, so they both knelt down in the tall grass to hide themselves in case it was an enemy of the Comanches approaching them. They notched their arrows to their bowstrings just in case they needed to use their bows and arrows.

Little Bear and Black Feather stood up when they recognized Jennie and Katherine. Both warriors always wanted to make the two white women their squaws and were upset when Raven claimed both women to be his. Now they were both eager to know why the two women had left the village. It didn't take long for the two warriors to realize why. As soon as Katherine and Jennie saw the two Comanche warriors, they spun around and ran as fast as they could away from the two warriors.

"They must be running away from Raven!" Little Bear exclaimed as he and Black Feather chased after Katherine and Jennie.

"Let's catch them and have some fun with them before we take them back to Raven!" Black Feather hollered.

"Or we can do whatever we want with them and then kill them so Raven will never know we touched them!" Little Bear shouted back.

"Yes. Let's do that instead!" Black Feather yelled, wearing a wide smile on his face.

*****

"Keep running!" Katherine shouted out to Jennie. "If they catch us, they will rape us for sure and then either take us back to Raven or kill us!"

Jennie looked back over her left shoulder and then exclaimed, "They're catching up with us!"

Jennie and Katherine ran as fast as they could, but both knew the two Comanche warriors chasing them would soon catch them. They've been raped many times since being kidnapped by the Comanches and their bodies beaten too. Their bodies were covered with cuts, scrapes, and bruises and both now suffered from depression. They both wanted to go back to civilization, but their hopes of doing so were quickly fading away as the two Comanche warriors chased after them.

"It's hopeless!" Jennie cried out. "We can't outrun them!"

"We can't give up!" Katherine exclaimed.

"Sorry, but I already have," Jennie responded and then stopped running.

"Don't stop!" Katherine shouted after seeing Jennie standing still.

"Keep going!" Jennie shouted. "You've always been the stronger one!"

Little Bear and Black Feather caught up with Jennie and tackled her to the ground. Katherine heard Jennie screaming as she continued running as fast as she could. She felt tears running down her cheeks as she left her friend behind with the two savages. She knew Jennie was buying her some time to get away from those two Comanche warriors. She was now more determined than ever to make it back to civilization so Jennie's sacrifice wasn't wasted.

34

"Hurry up!" Little Bear said exclaimed. "I want her now!"

"You already had her!" Black Feather said as he continued forcing himself upon Jennie. "It's my turn now!"

"Just hurry up so I can have some fun with her again," Little Bear said while watching Black Feather rape Jennie. "I don't enjoy watching you having fun with her!"

"Just turn around then and keep quiet until I'm done!"

"Alright!" Little Bear said before turning himself around.

Jennie struggled with her two attackers even though she knew it was useless to. The two warriors hit Jennie often while sexually abusing her. She called out to God several times while she was being raped begging him to rescue her. She was sick and tired of the life she had been living since being captured by the Comanches. Her body was a sore all over and covered with cuts, scrapes, and bruises. She hated her life and didn't want to be dragged back to the village that she and Katherine had escaped from. She knew that Raven would be furious with her for escaping and would torture her upon her return and maybe even kill her.

"You can have her now," Black Feather said.

"Good! Now get out of the way!" Little Bear said with an angry tone in his voice.

Little Bear pulled Black Feather away from Jennie. He then smiled at the defenseless Jennie who was lying on her back. He felt her body trembling when he touched her and then backslapped her across the face. "Don't fight me!" he warned as he forced himself onto her.

When Little Bear was finished sexually abusing Jennie, he stood up and glared down at her. He wore an evil smile across his face and laughed out loud. His smile faded away quickly and his laughter suddenly ceased after he felt something penetrate deep into the middle of his back. He stumbled past Jennie then fell forward and landed on the ground, striking his head against a large rock. As his life faded away, he wondered who had just killed him.

After hearing a loud thump, Black Feather turned around and saw Little Bear lying on the ground with an arrow shaft sticking in the middle of his back. Black Feather pulled an arrow from his quiver, but before he had a chance to notch it, an arrow slammed into his chest. He dropped his bow and arrow as he lost control of his body. He then fell to his knees before falling on his side a few moments later.

Jennie heard someone running toward her but couldn't raise her head to look. She tried to move her hands and arms and then her feet and legs and felt her heart sink when she couldn't. She then realized she was paralyzed and defenseless as she heard someone kneel down next to her.

When Jennie heard White Buffalo's voice asking her if she was okay, she smiled knowing that God had answered her prayers, and she was now free from the two Comanche warriors who had been raping and beating her.

"I can't move my body, but I'm happy to see you. Thank you so much for killing those two Comanches."

"Where is Katherine?" White Buffalo asked.

"She's still free and running as fast as she can away from here. She was too fast for those two savages to catch her. Unfortunately, I wasn't."

"I'll stay here with you until you're rested up and ready to get on your feet again."

"Don't waste your time," Jennie said. "I won't be on this earth much longer. I can see the angels coming for me, and I don't want to keep them waiting any longer."

"What angels?" White Buffalo asked as he looked around.

"The two beautiful ones hovering over us!"

White Buffalo looked up at the night sky and then looked back down at Jennie and said, "I don't see any angels!"

"Believe me, they're here and want me to go with them." She then paused for a moment before saying, "Please find Katherine and help her get out of this canyon before Raven and his warriors find her."

"I will!" White Buffalo promised.

"Thank you," Jennie said before passing away. Her spirit then left her lifeless body and joined the two angels who had come for her to take her up to heaven.

White Buffalo stood up after he watched Jennie die. He walked over to where the two dead Comanche warriors lay and made sure both of them were dead. He then used his knife to slice both warriors' scalps off their heads. He placed those scalps into a leather pouch that White Sun had given him. He didn't know where his next lodge would be, but he intended to hang Little Bear and Black Feather's scalps outside of it.

*****

Katherine slowed down to catch her breath. She didn't know where she was but knew she was heading away from the Comanche village where she had been held captive. She held the knife she had stolen from Raven's lodge in her right hand, and she was determined to use it if she had to defend herself. Even though she was tired, she kept moving. She wanted to put the Comanche village as far behind her as she could before the night sky was replaced with daylight.

Katherine stayed alert while walking through the tall grass within Blanco Canyon. She came across a stream and stopped to get a drink of water. She placed her knife on the ground next to her then cupped her hands together. She dipped her hands into the stream, scooped up some water, and then drank it from her hands.

After Katherine quenched her thirst, she picked up her knife and stood up. She looked up at the sky and frowned when she saw the sun rising in the east. *I lost the cover of night*, she thought as she started walking through the tall grass. She frowned knowing it would be harder to hide from Raven and his warriors under a bright sunny sky.

When she heard a thundering sound in the distance, she turned and looked toward the direction the sound was coming from. To her horror, she saw a band of Comanche warriors riding toward her. She dove to the ground and hid herself in the tall grass hoping they had not spotted her. As the band of Comanches drew nearer and the sounds made from their horses' hooves grew louder, Katherine lay flat on her chest scared to death.

Katherine felt her body trembling with fear when she heard the band of Comanches halt their horses. *Did they see me?* she wondered to herself as she continued lying on her chest. The grass was tall that she was hiding in, but was it tall enough, she wondered when she heard the Comanche warriors talking among themselves. She understood some of the Comanche language but had problems putting sentences together using it.

Katherine lay still in the tall grass listening to the Comanche warriors and trying hard to understand what they were talking about. She heard White Buffalo's name mentioned often and Raven's a few times. She wondered if the warriors heard that she and Jennie had run away from the village. The warriors had not mentioned her and Jennie's names yet as they spoke with one another, so she started believing they hadn't heard that she and Jennie had escaped yet.

Katherine then wondered if Jennie was still alive. She hoped that Jennie was still alive and the two Comanche warriors that caught her just took her back to the village without harming her.

If the Comanche warriors killed Jennie, I could never forgive myself for leaving her, Katherine thought as she continued hiding from the nearby band of Comanche warriors.

Katherine lay still for ten minutes in the tall grass fearing for her life while the warriors sat on their horses nearby talking among themselves. She almost screamed when she saw a snake moving past her. She didn't know what species the snake was, but it looked ugly and poisonous to her. She was relieved after it slithered by her and then disappeared into the tall grass.

Katherine heard the Comanche warriors' voices growing louder as they spoke with one another and thought they might have spotted her. Just as she was thinking of trying to make a break for it, she heard the Comanche warriors leave. She was relieved, and her body stopped shaking with fear when she heard the Comanches ride their horses away. She pushed herself up onto her knees then looked over the tall grass to see what direction the Comanche warriors were riding in. She frowned when she saw the warriors riding their horses in the same direction she was heading.

Katherine knew she could not keep walking through the tall grass without being spotted by the Comanches. She had been lucky so far and knew her luck would run out soon if she kept traveling the same way she had been. She stood up after the Comanches were out of her sight and scanned the area. She saw some high cliff walls in the distance and decided to walk toward them hoping she could travel along the walls and keep herself hidden in the shadows of those walls.

Katherine bent over and picked her knife up off the ground. She held it in the palm of her right hand while she walked toward the cliffs. She never killed anyone before but was ready to if attacked. She had made up her mind that she would rather die defending herself with her knife than be caught alive and dragged back to the Comanche village she had escaped from. She was tired of being raped and beaten by Raven and would rather die than go back to being his squaw.

35

"Here comes Siringo!" General Fitzpatrick exclaimed as he ducked back down in the gully that he, Cooper, and Sergeant Black were hiding in.

"I hope he found the Comanche village," Sergeant Black said.

"Even if he did, we can't sneak into the village until that damn sun goes down!" a disappointed Cooper said while pointing toward the sun rising in the east.

Siringo jumped into the gully, caught his breath, and then said, "The Comanche village isn't where it was rumored to be," Siringo said.

"So where is it?" General Fitzpatrick asked.

"The Comanches must have moved it deeper into Blanco Canyon," Siringo replied.

"How much deeper?" Cooper asked.

"I'm not sure," Siringo answered.

"We need to keep looking for it!" General Fitzpatrick demanded.

"We'll be spotted by the Comanches if we do," Siringo warned.

"How do you know that we'll be spotted?" General Fitzpatrick asked.

"Because there's way too many Comanche warriors between us and that village we're looking for. I've never seen so many scattered throughout this canyon before. They're looking for something or someone," Siringo said.

"Maybe my son escaped, and they're looking for him," General Fitzpatrick said.

"The general could be right. White Buffalo could have escaped," Cooper said.

"If he did, he might be heading our way," Sergeant Black suggested.

"If my son has escaped, we need to go find him before the Comanches do!" General Fitzpatrick said in a stern voice.

"Siringo is right!" Cooper exclaimed. "If we go searching for your son now, the Comanches will probably find us."

"So what if they do!" General Fitzpatrick said angrily.

"If they find us in this canyon and we have to use our revolvers to defend ourselves, every Comanche warrior in this canyon that hears our gunfire will come after us. We're too few right now. We came here to try to sneak into the Comanche village where your son was being held with two to three female hostages, rescue them, and then sneak back out of this canyon. We can't do that now since we don't know where the village is and because this canyon is now swarming with Comanches looking for someone or something. The best thing we can do right now is stay hidden in this gully until night and then continue looking for the Comanche village where your son and those female hostages are supposed to be."

"Why can't we go back to that old trading post where we left Captain Josh Stephens and his company of Texas Rangers and bring them back here with us and then find that Comanche village and ambush it in daylight or night?" General Fitzpatrick suggested.

"I think the general wants to get us all killed looking for his son," Siringo said. "If we do what the general just suggested, we'll all lose our scalps for sure."

"I know we can take those Comanches with the help of those rangers!" General Fitzpatrick said confidently.

"No, we can't! Half the Texas Rangers you're talking about were killed or badly wounded since leaving Lubbock. Even with the rangers that are left, it's still not enough to ambush the Comanche village if we find it."

"You're a coward!" General Fitzpatrick exclaimed. "No wonder you were branded a coward! You did desert your men during the Battle of White River, didn't you?"

"Now settle down!" Cooper warned while glaring at the general.

"I'm going to find my son, and I'm going now!"

"No, you're not!" Cooper warned.

"Don't try to stop—"

Before the general could finish what he wanted to say, Cooper knocked the general out with his right fist.

"That's one way to shut him up," Sergeant Black said, wearing a smile on his face from to ear to ear.

"You might have just blown any chance you had of being reinstated into the cavalry," Siringo said. "But I'll vouch for you if we make it out of this canyon alive that he would have gotten us all killed."

"If we were him, we might have done the same thing. He's a father and we're not. He's been blaming himself for many years now that his son was kidnapped by the Comanches, and he couldn't rescue him. I don't blame him for getting mad at me," Cooper said.

"He might try to rescue his son all by himself again when he wakes up," Sergeant Black said.

"He might, but he won't be able to. "We're going to tie him up and gag his mouth."

"I like that idea," Sergeant Black said and then chuckled.

"After we finish tying him up, the three of us are going to decide what to do. But whatever we decide to do, we're not going to do it till nighttime," Cooper said.

"What are we going to do the rest of the day after we made our decision?" Sergeant Black asked.

"Sleep," Cooper said. "We've been up all night looking for the Comanche village, and we all need to get some rest before the sun goes down."

"I'm starving! Do we have anything to eat?" Siringo asked.

"I have some jerky," Sergeant Black said. He then asked, "Do you want some?"

"Sure," Siringo replied.

While Siringo and Sergeant Black ate the jerky, Cooper used some leather straps he had with him to tie the unconscious general's hands behind his back. He then tied the general's ankles together and used his handkerchief to gag the general's mouth. He felt no guilt after knocking out the general and then tying him up and gagging his mouth. He knew the general was obsessed with finding his son, White Buffalo. He also knew the general could care less if he got Cooper, Siringo, and Sergeant Black killed. All the general cared about was finding his son alive and then rescuing him no matter the consequences.

Cooper knew he just blew his chance of ever clearing his name and restoring his reputation. He would now be forever branded a coward and never be reinstated back into the United States Cavalry, which he dearly missed. He was still determined to find and rescue White Buffalo if he could but only on his terms without interference from General Fitzpatrick.

Cooper and Siringo knew the area inside and around Blanco Canyon better than most who were not part of the Comanche Nation. But neither man knew where the Comanche village currently was located. They both had a few ideas where it could be located, but finding it without losing their scalps wouldn't be easy, especially with Comanche warriors scattered.

Cooper knew the Comanches were searching for someone or something but didn't know who or what they were searching for. He then thought of a way to find out the answer and decided to consult Siringo and Sergeant Black about it before deciding whether or not to do it.

"We need to find out what those Comanches warriors are looking for," Cooper said.

"That sounds like a great idea, but how are we going to find out?" Sergeant Black asked.

"By capturing one of them and then forcing him to tell us," Cooper said.

"I was going to suggest that too," Siringo said.

"When are we going to try to capture one of them?" Sergeant Black asked.

"When the sun go down unless one falls into our laps," Cooper replied.

"No Comanche warrior will ever be taken prisoner easily," Siringo warned.

"That's a fact, and that's why we need to use the cover of night to give us the best chance of capturing one of them," Cooper said.

"Then we'll have to wait until the sun sets before we try to catch one," Siringo said. "Until then, I'm going to try to catch some shut-eye. I'm exhausted."

"So am I," Sergeant Black said.

"I'll take the first watch and then wake one of you up in a few hours to relieve me," Cooper said.

36

"Something is wrong. Cooper, Sergeant Black, the general, and Siringo should have been back by now," Captain Josh Stephens.

"The Comanches must have killed them," a Texas Ranger named Chester said.

"Or they could have taken them prisoner," a Texas Ranger named JT said.

"Comanches rarely take prisoners," Josh said. "And if they were taken prisoner, they won't be alive for long. The Comanches will torture them first then burn them alive."

"Should we go back to the old trading post and hold out there till we know what happened to them?" Chester asked.

"Not now," Josh replied. "There're too many Comanches in and around this canyon. If we're spotted riding our horses back to that trading post, we could be ambushed and massacred."

"What should we do then?" JT asked.

"We'll stay here for another day or two and give Cooper and his three companions more time. They might be still alive and looking for White Buffalo and those three women that we were sent here to rescue," Josh replied.

"Do you think we have enough men to defeat the Comanches if Cooper and the others with him find White Buffalo and those three women and make it back here alive?" Chester asked.

"The entrance to this canyon that we're occupying is a natural walled fortress, which can be defended easily," Josh responded. "We'll be able to drive back the Comanche attacks for a while from our position here, but when we run out of ammunition, those Comanches will swarm all over us."

"So this could be our Alamo?" a nervous-sounding JT asked.

"Only if Willie Doyle didn't get through to Fort Concho," Josh answered. "If Willie made it to the fort safely and brings back a company of cavalry to help us fight the Comanches, then we should be able to defeat any Comanches chasing after Cooper and everyone with him."

"So we'll lose our scalps if Willie didn't make it to Fort Concho and brings the cavalry back with him," JT said, wearing a concerned look on his face.

"Yes, we will, so let's hope he made it," Josh said as he checked his lever-action repeating rifle to make sure that it was fully loaded.

JT sat down with his back against a boulder and thought about his past. He was from Kentucky and grew up on his family's farm. From the moment he was born, he always yearned for adventure; so when he turned sixteen, he left his family's farm and went to Texas looking for excitement in the Wild West.

After JT tried ranching for a few years, he volunteered to become a Texas Ranger. Once he became a ranger, all his childhood dreams of adventure became reality. For the last few years, he fought outlaws, Mexican bandits, Comancheros, Kiowa, and Comanches. He loved the excitement, but now he was beginning to have second thoughts. This was the first time his gut was telling him that his death could be near, and he didn't like that feeling. He always felt a little nervous before a fight but never scared to death like he felt now.

JT closed his eyes and started praying to God. He hadn't prayed in years, but now he was praying harder than he had ever prayed before. He didn't want to die and asked God to protect him and his fellow Texas Rangers from the Comanche warriors they soon would be engaging. He didn't know Willie Doyle that well but asked God to protect Willie and help him get through to Fort Concho so he could bring back the cavalry to Blanco Canyon.

*****

Willie Doyle and the two buffalo hunters named Quill and Brody rode their horses as fast as they could. A small band of Kiowa warriors were hot on their tail. Fort Concho was less than two miles away, but Willie and his two companions horses were exhausted and wouldn't make it to the fort if they had to keep running as fast as they were. Quill looked over at Brody and signaled him to halt his horse then he called out to Willie, "Keep riding to the fort. We'll try to slow the Kiowas down!"

Wille continued riding his horse toward Fort Concho, knowing the two buffalo hunters were going to sacrifice their lives, so he stood a better chance of making it to the fort alive. Quill and Brody halted their horses and then dismounted. They drew their Sharps .50 caliber rifles from their saddle scabbards, knelt down on their knees, and then aimed their rifles at the fast-approaching band of Kiowa warriors. When they were both sure they wouldn't miss the Kiowa warriors they had targeted, they pulled their rifles' triggers. They watched their two bullets strike and kill two Kiowa warriors.

Quill and Brody reloaded their rifles and then aimed them at two more Kiowa warriors. They squeezed their triggers and watched their bullets strike and knock two Kiowas off their horses. They loaded their rifles again as the band of Kiowa warriors charged toward them. As Quill was pulling his rifle's trigger, he called out to Brody, "I think our time is about up!" He then watched his bullet slam into the right shoulder of the Kiowa warrior he was aiming his rifle at.

Brody pulled his trigger and watch his bullet slam into the Kiowa's chest he was aiming at. The Kiowa fell off his horse and landed on his back. As Brody was reloading his rifle, he felt a burning sensation in his right thigh. He looked down and saw blood seeping out of his trousers. He then felt a bullet slam into his chest. The impact of that bullet knocked Brody onto his back. He gasped for air as his life quickly faded away.

Quill looked over and saw Brody lying on his back after he fired his rifle. He frowned knowing Brody was dying. He reloaded his rifle quickly and then raised it up and aimed it at another Kiowa warrior. As he was pulling his trigger, he felt a bullet rip into his chest. As he was falling backward, he wondered if his bullet had struck and killed the warrior he was aiming his rifle at. He died a few moments later not knowing if Willie Doyle made it to Fort Concho alive.

*****

When Willie Doyle no longer heard gunfire behind him, he knew the Kiowas had killed Quill and Brody.

I have to make it to Fort Concho so those two buffalo hunters didn't die for nothing, Willie said to himself. His horse was exhausted, so he slowed it down when he didn't see any Kiowas chasing after him. He knew the Kiowas had stopped to celebrate killing the two buffalo hunters and take their scalps. But he also knew the Kiowas wouldn't celebrate that long and would be pursuing him again.

Willie halted his horse on top of a small hill and smiled when he saw Fort Concho.

I made it! he said to himself before gently kicking his horse into a walk. He then heard war cries behind him that sent chills up his spine. He looked back and saw the small band of Kiowas chasing after him. He used the heels of his boots and kicked his horse into a gallop hoping it had enough energy left to reach the fort before the Kiowas caught up with him.

*****

"There's a band of Kiowas heading toward us!" Private Halteman exclaimed.

"Does it look like they're attacking our fort?" Major Kevin Cooney called out.

"No, sir! They're chasing someone!"

"Who?"

"Not sure but he's not an Indian!"

Major Cooney turned to the bugler who was standing next to him and ordered him to use his bugle to sound the alarm so the fort's garrison would know to run to the walls' platforms and get ready to defend the fort. He then ran to a nearby ladder, climbed up it until he reached the platform, and then ran over to where Private

Halteman was standing. He then looked over the wooden palisades and saw a white man riding for his life toward the fort.

"He's wearing something shiny on his chest," Private Halteman said.

"He could be a lawman," Major Cooney responded. He paused for a moment before calling out to the soldiers occupying the two blockhouses on each corner of the wall. He shouted, "Aim your cannons at the band of Kiowas, but don't fire until I give the command!" He then heard "Yes, sir" coming from both blockhouses as he turned his attention back to the lawman and the band of Kiowas that was chasing after him.

When he saw the band of Kiowas come within range of his cannons, Major Cooney called out, "Fire your cannons!"

*****

Willie Doyle heard loud booms coming from the fort and then heard several explosions behind him as he rode his horse toward the front entrance of Fort Concho. He looked back over his left shoulder and saw several Kiowas and their horses lying on the ground. He then heard a loud squeal and knew his horse had been shot. He jumped off his horse while his horse stumbled forward. Miraculously, he landed on his feet and suffered no injuries.

Bullets whistled by him as he ran toward the fort's entrance. He was lucky to still be alive, but would his luck hold out? He saw rifles protruding over the fort's palisades and then puffs of smoke.

Thank God! he exclaimed to himself. *The soldiers are giving me cover fire!*

Bullets continued whizzing by Willie as he neared the fort's gate. His adrenaline grew stronger as he pushed himself faster. He closed the gap between himself and the fort's gate quickly and breathed a sigh of relief when he ran into the fort unscathed. He then heard someone yell, "Close the gate!"

37

Raven stood still and stayed quiet while staring down at Jennie Farmer's lifeless body. He was stunned when he and his warriors first spotted the three dead bodies lying on the ground. He recognized the two dead Comanche warriors right away even though the top of their heads were covered with blood from losing their scalps. He wondered who had killed and scalped Little Bear and Black Feather. It didn't take him long to conclude that it must have been White Buffalo and that Katherine White must be with him.

"Did White Buffalo kill Little Bear and Black Feather?" a warrior named Dark Hawk asked.

"He must have," Raven replied.

"He took their scalps to tell us that he has declared war on us," Dark Hawk said.

"He sure did, and I look forward to taking his scalp once we catch up with him," Raven said.

"What will happen to him after you slice his scalp off his head?" a curious Dark Hawk asked.

"We'll burn him alive!"

"You're not going to torture him a little first?"

"Not this time," Raven said. "I plan on setting fire to his body right after we catch him, and I'll take his scalp."

"Good," Dark Hawk said, wearing an evil-looking smile on his face. "I never liked your adopted brother."

"He's no brother of mine, and he's no longer a Comanche either. He's a white man who needs killing!" Raven took one last look at Jennie before he turned away and walked back to his horse. After he mounted his horse, he called out to his warriors, "Did anyone find foot or moccasins' prints leading away from here?"

Several warriors replied they found one set of prints on the ground left by someone wearing moccasins with small feet. Raven knew right away that Katherine made those moccasins' prints because White Buffalo was too smart to leave any of his foot or moccasins' prints on the ground.

"Where do those moccasins' prints lead?" Raven asked.

"In all directions," Dark Hawk replied.

"What do you mean in all directions?" Raven asked. "That can't be possible!"

"Look for yourself!" Dark Hawk called out.

Raven jumped off his horse and walked over to where Dark Hawk and a few other Comanche warriors were standing. Dark Hawk pointed out small moccasins prints going in four different directions from where Jennie and the two dead warriors' bodies lay.

"How far do those tracks go in each direction?" Raven asked.

"Just a few horse lengths in each direction and then they disappear," Dark Hawk replied.

"White Buffalo is playing games with us so we don't know which way they went," Raven said. He then paused for a few moments before saying, "My father trained him well."

"What direction should we look for White Buffalo and your squaw?" a warrior named Yellow Wolf asked.

"We'll split up and look everywhere for those two inside this canyon. And when some of us find them, we'll send up smoke signals to alert everyone else," Raven replied.

*****

Katherine White walked cautiously along the bottom of the tall cliffs of Blanco Canyon. She tried to stay in the shadows of the cliffs so the Comanche warriors looking for her would have difficulty spotting her. The bottoms of her feet were sore, and she was exhausted, but she knew she had to keep moving or risk being caught.

Katherine only had a knife to defend herself with but was ready to use it if attacked. She would rather die than go back to the Comanche village and be Raven's squaw again. She saw a few Comanche warriors since leaving Jennie but was able to avoid being seen by them. She moved slowly during the day and tried to keep herself hidden as best she could as she moved through Blanco Canyon.

As Katherine was walking next to a large boulder, she heard a familiar voice call out to her. She stopped dead in her tracks, turned around, and smiled when she saw White Buffalo walking toward her. She felt a calmness come over her when White Buffalo smiled at her.

"I'm glad I found you before Raven and his warriors did."

"I am too," Katherine said, wearing a smile from ear to ear. "I've been scared to death since Jennie and me fled the village."

"I found Jennie," White Buffalo said as his smile faded away. "She died wearing a smile on her face telling me that she saw two angels coming for her."

"Did those two Comanches—"

"Yes," White Buffalo answered.

A sad-looking Katherine asked, "What happened to those two Comanche warriors?"

"I killed them and sent their spirits to hell!" he replied.

"Good!" she exclaimed. "I hope they both rot there for eternity!"

White Buffalo quickly changed the subject and said, "We need to keep moving and get out of this canyon before Raven and his warriors find us."

"So you'll take me with you?"

"Of course I will!" White Buffalo said.

"Thank you," Katherine said, wearing a smile on her face. "I felt so scared out here all alone."

"You look tired."

"I am and the bottom of my feet are sore."

"I know of a place that's well hidden that's not too far from here where we can rest a little before moving on."

"That sounds great!"

"Follow me. It won't take long to get there," White Buffalo said as he began walking away from Katherine.

"I'll be right behind you," she said, wearing a smile on her face. She then looked up to the sky and said to herself, *Thank you, Lord, for guiding White Buffalo to me!*

38

White Buffalo led Katherine White into a narrow passageway though the tall cliffs of Blanco Canyon. The passageway led to a small open area surrounded by rock walls. Katherine smiled when she saw a few trees, shrubs, and a little waterhole within the open area that White Buffalo led her into.

"Is this your private little oasis?" Katherine asked.

"This was Sun Flower's and my special place when we wanted to be alone. We spent a lot of time here together."

"You miss her a lot, don't you?"

"I really do," he replied, wearing a frown on his face.

"You'll see her again one day I promise," Katherine said.

"How?"

"Up in heaven," Katherine said.

"She wasn't a Christian," White Buffalo said.

"Oh, but she was."

"No, she wasn't. I would have known if she was."

"She was too scared to tell you. She thought you and others would get mad at her and might even throw her out of the village for being a Christian."

White Buffalo paused for a few moments before responding. He then said, "You're right. I never talked with her about God or the Bible. She never knew that I was once a Christian. I never told her that I was."

"Have you rededicated your life to our Lord and Savior?" Katherine asked.

"Yes, I have."

"Then you will see Sun Flower again one day because she accepted Jesus as her Lord and Savior. I would read the Bible to her often at places throughout the village where no one would see us. We prayed often that you would become a Christian too. She was so excited about being a Christian. She always looked pleased and happy when we discussed verses in the Bible together. She wanted to tell you that she was a Christian, but she was too scared to. She loved you so much and never wanted to lose you."

White Buffalo kept quiet while Katherine continued telling him stories of her and Sun Flower becoming stronger in their love for Jesus in the short time they knew each other. He wished he would have known Sun Flower had accepted Jesus as her Lord and Savior and regretted never telling Sun Flower that he was a Christian too.

I was too scared to tell her too just like she was too scared to tell me, White Buffalo said to himself while listening to Katherine tell him stories of her and Sun Flower.

White Buffalo's frown faded away and turned into a smile as Katherine continued telling him how Sun Flower accepted Jesus as her Lord and Savior. He no longer was sad knowing that he would see Sun Flower again one day up in heaven. His broken heart had healed thanks to Katherine telling him that Sun Flower had become a Christian.

"Thank you for telling me that Sun Flower became a Christian. I never knew she had. I understand how she would have been too scared to tell me. It's my fault because I never told her that I was a Christian too. I was too scared to tell anyone that I was a Christian just like Sun Flower was. For a long time, I forgot about God and the love he has for me. But all that changed when I was tied up and spread-eagled on my back waiting to be tortured by Raven and his warriors."

"What happened?" a curious Katherine asked.

"After I felt abandoned by everyone else in the village, I turned to God hoping he would hear me call out to him," White Buffalo replied.

"Did he?"

"Yes, I truly believe that he did. I felt his presence the more I prayed to him. I didn't ask him for help right away. Instead, I thanked him for never giving up on me first and keeping me alive after the Comanches had kidnapped me. I knew the Comanches tortured and then killed most of their captives and wondered why they didn't torture and kill me.

"When Chief Black Hawk took a liking to me, adopted me as a son, and then raised me to become a Comanche warrior, I thought it was just luck that I wasn't killed like most of the other captives had been. As I continued praying to God, I realized that it wasn't luck that kept me alive all these years. Instead, it was my Lord and Savior. And once I realized that, I thanked God profusely, and that's when I felt his presence."

"What was it like feeling God's presence in you?" Katherine asked.

"I felt an overwhelming sense of peace and trust that I had never felt before. It's a feeling I will never forget," White Buffalo replied.

"Did he help you escape from the Comanche village?"

"Yes, he did," a confident-sounding White Buffalo replied. "When I felt God's presence, I asked him to help me escape, and that's when I felt the stakes that bound my wrists and ankles start loosening in the ground."

White Buffalo then stood up and motioned to Katherine to do the same. He then hugged her tightly and said to her, "Thank for telling me that Sun Flower became a Christian before she died. I now know that I will see her again one day when my time down here is over. I look forward to seeing her smiling face again, and my heart is no longer broken knowing I will be united with her again one day."

"You're welcome," Katherine said as she and White Buffalo gently pushed away from each other.

"Let's drink a little water and get a little rest here before we leave," White Buffalo suggested.

"That sounds good to me," Katherine said. "The bottoms of my feet are still a little sore."

"Let me see your feet," White Buffalo said as he and Katherine sat down next to each other. "I might be able to help them feel better."

Katherine slipped her moccasins off her feet and then lay her feet upon White Buffalo's knees not knowing what to expect. White Buffalo took Katherine's right foot and started massaging the bottom of her foot with both his hands. When he was finished massaging her right foot, he began massaging the bottom of her left foot.

"My feet are feeling much better," a grateful Katherine said.

"I knew this would help," White Buffalo said as he continued massaging Katherine's left foot. "Sun Flower did the same to my feet after I came back from hunting all day."

"I'm glad she—"

White Buffalo released Katherine's left foot and signaled her to be quiet. He thought he heard something. He raised his right index finger to his lips again so Katherine would know to remain silent. He listened closely and then heard the sound again. He then looked at Katherine and whispered, "We got company!"

White Buffalo told Katherine quietly to hide behind a large boulder and be ready to use her knife if she was found. White Buffalo knew at least one Comanche warrior was approaching if not more. He quietly pulled an arrow from his quiver and then notched it to his bowstring. He pulled back his bowstring and then pointed his arrow at the narrow passageway that led into the area where he and Katherine were.

Katherine stayed hidden behind the boulder holding her knife's grip tightly in her right hand. She felt her body shaking with fear as she hid. She had never killed anyone before, but she was ready to if she had to. She then quietly prayed to God asking him to give her and White Buffalo strength and courage to face their enemies.

39

As soon as White Buffalo saw the Comanche warrior walk into the opening, he let loose his bowstring. He watched his arrow fly through the air and strike the middle of the warrior's chest. The warrior fell backward and landed on his back. He died wearing a stunned expression on his face.

White Buffalo pulled another arrow out of his quiver and notched it to his bowstring. He didn't know how many warriors were coming through the passageway but knew there must be more than one. He pulled back his bowstring and aimed his arrow at the passageway. It didn't take long for White Buffalo to get his answer.

White Buffalo let go of his bowstring as soon as he saw the Comanche warrior. His arrow struck the warrior in his left shoulder. White Buffalo reached for another arrow and notched it quickly to his bowstring. He let loose the bowstring and watched his arrow slam into the warrior's chest. The warrior fell backward and landed on top of the deceased warrior's body White Buffalo had just killed.

"Did you get them all?" Katherine called out.

"I'm not sure!" White Buffalo said as he pulled another arrow from his quiver and then notched it. He then told Katherine to stay hidden behind the boulder.

White Buffalo felt an arrow whiz by him as he pulled back his bowstring. He saw a Comanche warrior pulling an arrow from his quiver as he let go of his bowstring. Before the warrior could notch his arrow, White Buffalo's arrow slammed into him. The warrior stumbled forward and then fell onto his chest.

White Buffalo drew another arrow from his quiver and notched it to his bowstring. He pulled it back and waited to see if another warrior showed himself. When one didn't after waiting for a minute, White Buffalo decided to go into the passageway and see if there were any more Comanche warriors.

White Buffalo stepped over the three dead Comanche warriors' bodies and then entered the passageway. He walked slowly and stayed alert as he proceeded through the passageway. When he reached the end of the passageway, he saw a Comanche warrior mounting his horse.

Before the Comanche warrior could use the heels of his moccasins and kick his horse into a gallop, White Buffalo's arrow penetrated deep into the warrior's stomach. The warrior slumped over his horse's neck and then slid off his horse. After he landed on the ground, he tried to push himself off the ground. As he was trying to, he felt something sharp sliced into the back of his neck. Just before his spirit left his body, the warrior realized that White Buffalo's tomahawk had just killed him.

*****

Katherine felt her body shaking as she waited to see if White Buffalo was still alive. When she heard someone approaching the boulder she was hiding behind, she gripped her knife's handle tightly. She never killed anyone before, but she was determined to try if the person approaching her was a Comanche warrior.

Please give me the courage to defend myself, she prayed quietly as she waited to see who was approaching the boulder she was hiding behind.

When she heard White Buffalo call out her name, Katherine's body stopped shaking with fear. She stood up and came out from behind the boulder and fell into his arms. They held each other tightly for a while before gently pushing each other away.

"I thought you were killed," Katherine said. "When I heard someone approaching this boulder, I thought it was a Comanche.

I felt my whole body trembling with fear until you called out my name. I'm so happy you're alive!"

"So am I," White Buffalo said, wearing a grin on his face.

"How many were there?"

"Four."

"Did they have horses?"

"Yes, but I chased them away."

"Why did you do that for?" Katherine asked. "We could have used two of them to ride out of this canyon."

"Raven and his warriors would have spotted us if we took two of those horses. It's a lot easier to avoid Raven and his warriors if we stay on our feet," White Buffalo said.

"You're right," Katherine admitted. She then said, "I'm sorry for questioning you."

"Don't worry about it," White Buffalo said while drawing his knife out of his decorative leather sheath.

After White Buffalo walked over and knelt down next to one of the dead Comanche warrior's bodies, Katherine asked, "What are you doing?"

"I'm going to get some trophies to hang on my next lodge," White Buffalo answered.

"Oh, no, you're not!" Katherine exclaimed as she approached White Buffalo.

"Why not?" he asked as he lowered his knife toward the warrior's head.

"Because you're no longer a Comanche warrior," Katherine replied. "You leaving the Comanche way for good, right?"

White Buffalo held his knife's blade against the warrior's forehead and thought about what Katherine just said. He wanted to slice the warrior's scalp off his head but knew Katherine was right. He slowly removed his knife from the dead warrior's forehead and then slid it back into its sheath. He then stood up and walked away from the dead warrior's body. He then walked up to Katherine and said, "You're right! I'm no longer a Comanche."

"That's right, you're not," a relieved Katherine concurred.

White Buffalo led Katherine back through the passageway, and when they came back into the vast area of Blanco Canyon, Katherine asked, "Where to?"

White Buffalo looked up into the sky and then looked back at Katherine. He then said, "There is not much daylight left, but we can't stay here. I know of another place not too far from here where we can hide until the skies turn dark."

"What happens once the sky turns dark?"

"Once nighttime hits, we'll start moving again. From here on out, we only move at night so it will make it harder for Raven and his warriors to find us."

"Do you think Raven and his warriors will ever give up looking for us?"

"As long as Raven is alive, he'll never give up looking for us," White Buffalo replied.

40

"I feel like we've been crawling on the ground forever," Siringo complained.

"We have no choice but to crawl right now," Cooper warned. "If the Comanches spot us out here alone, they'll catch us for sure. There's too many of them inside this canyon. They're everywhere!"

"You're right!" Siringo concurred and then said, "We should go back to the gully where we left Sergeant Black and General Fitzpatrick."

"You can but I can't. I need to capture a Comanche warrior and find out where their village is and if White Buffalo and those female captives are still being held there. If I leave this canyon without White Buffalo with me, I will forever be branded a coward and will never be able to rejoin the cavalry, which I dearly love."

"If you are determined to capture a Comanche warrior, then I'm going to help you capture one."

"Good," Cooper responded. "I sure could use your help." He paused for a few moments before saying, "Every Comanche warrior we come across is never traveling alone. We're going to have to kill some quietly to be able to capture one. So from this moment on, we can only use our knives. If we use our revolvers, the gunfire will alert every Comanche warrior nearby."

"You're right," Siringo said. "The last thing we need are a bunch of Comanches swarming down on us like yellowjackets. And if we use our revolvers to shoot some Comanches, other ones nearby will definitely hear the gunfire. So knives it is."

*****

"We've been spotted!" White Buffalo called out to Katherine White.

White Buffalo then told Katherine to duck behind some nearby shrubs. He pulled back his bowstring and aimed it toward three Comanche warriors galloping their horses toward him and Katherine. He aimed his arrow at one of the warriors as Katherine dove behind the shrubs. He then let go of his bowstring and watched his arrow slam into the warrior he was aiming at.

The arrowhead penetrated deep into the Comanche warrior's heart. The warrior fell off his horse and was dead before he hit the ground. White Buffalo quickly drew an arrow from his quiver and notched it to his bowstring. He pulled back his bowstring and targeted another Comanche warrior. When he was certain he wouldn't miss, he let go of his bowstring. He then watched his arrow rip into the warrior's throat. The warrior dropped his hatchet and fell off his horse while coughing up his own blood.

White Buffalo heard Katherine screaming while he was reaching for another arrow from his quiver. He dropped his bow and drew his tomahawk from his belt. He then ran toward the shrubs where he told Katherine to hide. When he reached the shrubs, he saw a Comanche warrior on top of Katherine.

"Get off me!" Katherine screamed as she struggled with the warrior.

While keeping Katherine pinned on her back, the warrior drew his knife from his sheath; but before he could use it on Katherine, a tomahawk slammed into his back. The warrior dropped his knife, fell forward, and landed on top of Katherine. Katherine tried to push the dead warrior off her, but he was too heavy. When Katherine felt the weight of the warrior being lifted off her and heard White Buffalo's voice, she was no longer frightened.

"Are you okay?" White Buffalo asked after he pulled the dead warrior off Katherine and then tossed him to the side.

"Thanks to you I am," Katherine said while White Buffalo helped her off the ground.

White Buffalo then walked over to the dead warrior, grabbed his tomahawk's handle, and then pulled its blade out of the dead warrior's back. He slid its handle underneath his belt before walking over to the two other Comanche warriors that were lying on the ground. After he was satisfied they were both dead, he returned his attention to Katherine who looked upset.

Katherine picked her knife up off the ground before saying, "I know I should have tried to kill that Comanche with my knife, but I froze when I should have lunged it at him. I'm so sorry. I promise you I won't be afraid to use it the next time I'm attack."

"I believe you," White Buffalo said while picking his bow up off the ground. He drew an arrow from his quiver and notched it to his bowstring before saying, "We need to keep moving."

"I'm ready when you are," Katherine responded.

"As long as it's dark out, we'll keep moving. And when the sun comes up, we'll find a good hiding place to hide out in until it gets dark again."

"How much farther till we get out of this canyon?"

"If we're lucky, we should get out of this canyon sometime tomorrow night."

"When we do, I never want to see this canyon again."

"Neither do I," White Buffalo concurred. "I want to put my Comanche life in my past and become civilized again."

White Buffalo hid the three dead Comanche warriors' bodies as best he could. He hoped Raven and his warriors wouldn't discover them. He then chased the horses away knowing they would go back to the Comanche village where they had come from. He then led Katherine toward the entrance to Blanco Canyon knowing they still had many miles to go until they reached it. White Buffalo knew even if they reach the canyon's entrance safely, Raven wouldn't give up chasing them until he captured them or was killed trying to.

41

Cooper McCaw and Siringo dove into a small gully when they heard a few Comanche warriors talking to each other. They quietly drew their knives out of their sheaths and then crawled up to the top of the gully. Sitting around a small campfire were four Comanche warriors, one of whom Cooper and Siringo intended to forcefully get information from that they had been seeking.

While the four Comanche warriors continued their conversations with each other, Siringo and Cooper quietly crawled toward them. When they drew nearer to the Comanches, they split up so they could attack the warriors from two different directions. Cooper crawled through the tall grass hoping the four warriors sitting around the campfire would not spot him. He knew he and Siringo had to kill three of the Comanche warriors quickly and as quietly as they could. The fourth warrior had to be restrained and then forced to give them the information they sought.

Siringo hated Comanches and looked forward to killing the ones sitting around the campfire. He held his knife in the palm of his right hand and was anxious to use it. When he came within striking distance of one of the Comanche warriors, he didn't hold back his hatred.

Siringo plunged his knife's blade deep into the warrior's back then pulled it out. He then slit the warrior's throat before throwing the warrior's body to the ground. The three remaining Comanche warriors reached for their weapons after they saw their fellow warrior getting slain. The three warriors reaction were too slow.

Cooper tackled one of the warriors and buried his knife's blade deep into the warrior's chest. He twisted his knife's blade before pulling it out. He heard the warrior gasping for air as he turned away from him.

Siringo threw his knife at a warrior who was charging toward him holding a tomahawk in his right hand. The warrior stopped dead in his tracks when Siringo's knife ripped into his stomach. He wore a stunned expression on his face while falling down onto his knees. He tried to defend himself when Siringo pulled the knife out of his stomach but was too weak to do so. He died moments later after Siringo's knife ripped into his chest.

The last remaining Comanche let out a Comanche war cry just before he attacked Cooper. He lunged his knife at Cooper but missed when Cooper quickly sidestepped out of the way. As the warrior stumbled by Cooper, he felt a burning sensation on his right shoulder and knew that Cooper's knife had just sliced him. After the warrior regained his balance, he attacked Cooper again.

As the warrior charged toward Cooper, he felt something penetrate deep into his lower back. He fell to his knees wearing a stunned expression on his face. He then felt someone pulling out the knife from his back before he was shoved forward. After he landed face-first on the ground, he tried to push himself up off the ground but couldn't.

"Is he still alive?" Siringo asked while sliding his knife back into its sheath.

"Yes," Cooper replied after he rolled the Comanche warrior over onto his back and saw the warrior gazing up at him.

"Good because the other three look dead," Siringo said.

Siringo and Cooper both knelt down next to the injured warrior. They both knew the warrior was mortally wounded and wouldn't be alive for long. Siringo knew the Comanche language fairly well and began talking to the mortally injured warrior. Siringo questioned the warrior, and to his surprise, the warrior answered his questions. Within a few minutes, the warrior died but not before Siringo got all the information that he and Cooper had sought before attacking the four warriors.

"What did he say?" Cooper asked.

"He said all the warriors from the village are out looking for White Buffalo and a female hostage that escaped from their village. He said his chief won't rest until they are both found."

"What about the other females that are being held hostage at his village?" Cooper asked.

"They're both dead," Siringo replied. "One was killed a few weeks ago, and the other was killed yesterday after she escaped from the Comanche village."

"Are White Buffalo and the surviving female hostage traveling together?"

"The warrior didn't know for sure, but he thought so. He said two warriors' bodies were found lying next to the female captive that was killed yesterday. He and the other Comanche warriors believe White Buffalo killed those two warriors since their scalps were sliced off their heads."

"Did you find out where their village is located?"

"He died before I could, but there's no reason to go there now since we know White Buffalo and the last remaining female hostage have both escaped from that village."

"Good point," Cooper said. "I wonder which entrance to the Canyon they're heading to?"

"I'm not sure, but I am hoping it's the one we used," Siringo said.

"Let's head back to the gully where we left Sergeant Black and General Fitzpatrick and tell them what we found out," Cooper suggested.

"The general won't be happy when he sees you," Siringo warned.

"You're right he won't be, but he'll be happy to hear that his son has escaped from the Comanche village and obviously no longer wants to be a Comanche warrior."

"Do you think the general will ever forgive us for tying him up?"

"He might if we find his son."

"Let's hide these four warriors' bodies and then see if we can find his son and the female captive he might be traveling with before we head back to that gully where we left Sergeant Black and the general," Siringo suggested.

"I like your suggestion better," Cooper responded.

"White Buffalo and that woman he's hopefully with will stand a better chance of escaping from this canyon with our help."

"They sure will." Cooper paused for a moment before asking, "Where should we look for them?"

"That Comanche I was talking to told me he didn't think they came this far yet. He told me neither one of them had horses."

"So they're on foot like us."

"Yes, and they're doing it because White Buffalo knows it's harder to track someone on foot. Plus, you can hide yourself a lot easier without worrying about hiding a horse too," Siringo said.

"So maybe we should take up a position halfway between us and the gully where we left Sergeant Black and the general," Cooper suggested. "The canyon gets a lot narrower there, and it will be a lot easier to spot them if they come that way."

"That sounds good to me," Siringo said. He then added, "I wish we would have brought our rifles with us."

"I do too," Cooper concurred.

"At least we have our revolvers with us," Siringo said. "And once we get back to where the sergeant and the general are waiting for us, we'll get our rifles back too."

"By the time we do get back there, I have a strong feeling we're going to need our rifles."

"So do I!" Siringo exclaimed. And then he repeated, "So do I!"

42

White Buffalo heard an arrow whiz by his left ear. He looked at Katherine and told her to take cover. He then spun around and looked for the Comanche who shot the arrow at him. When he saw the Comanche, he quickly raised his bow and aimed his arrow at him. He then released his bowstring and watched his arrow slam into the Comanche's chest. The Comanche dropped his bow and fell backward. He landed on his back with White Buffalo's arrow shaft sticking out of his chest.

"How many are there?" Katherine asked as she lay down in the tall grass.

"I'm not sure yet," White Buffalo answered as he pulled an arrow from his quiver.

Two more arrows flew past White Buffalo as he notched the arrow to his bowstring. He searched for more Comanches, and when he found one, he aimed his arrow at him and let go of his bowstring. His arrow penetrated deep into the warrior's right shoulder. The warriors dropped his bow and then tried to draw his hunting knife from its sheath with his left hand. Before he could draw his knife, another arrow ripped into his chest. He lost his balance, fell backward, and died moments later after he landed on his back.

"I think there's one more left," White Buffalo said while notching another arrow. He then urged Katherine to stay down while he searched for the remaining Comanche warrior. It didn't take him long for him to spot the Comanche warrior. The Comanche warrior shot another arrow at White Buffalo, but the arrow missed. White

Buffalo released his bowstring and frowned when his arrow missed hitting the Comanche.

White Buffalo reached for another arrow from his quiver. He felt his heart drop when he realized his quiver had no more arrows left in it. He dropped his bow and drew his tomahawk from his leather belt. He then ran as fast as he could toward the Comanche warrior who was aiming an arrow at him. When the Comanche warrior released his bowstring, White Buffalo dove to the ground and heard the arrow whiz over him.

After the arrow missed him, White Buffalo stood up and charged toward the Comanche warrior. Before the Comanche warrior could aim another arrow at him, White Buffalo threw his tomahawk as hard as he could at the Comanche. His tomahawk embedded deep into the warrior's chest knocking him backward. When White Buffalo reached the dying Comanche warrior, he pulled his tomahawk out of the warrior's chest. He then rolled the Comanche over and took all the arrows that were resting in the warrior's quiver.

White Buffalo ran over to the other two dead Comanche warriors and took arrows from their quivers too. Now White Buffalo's quiver was no longer empty. It was full of arrows so he could use his favorite weapon again to fight any Comanches he and Katherine came across. When he walked back toward to the area where he left Katherine, he saw her stand up and run toward him.

"Are they all dead?" Katherine asked when she drew near to him.

"Yes," White Buffalo said, wearing an expression of relief on his face.

"I was so worried about you," Katherine said. "I'm so glad you're alright!" She then hugged him and thanked him for saving her life once again.

White Buffalo pushed her away gently and then said to her, "We need to keep moving. There's a lot more Comanches looking for us. Some of them are searching for us now on foot just like those three dead Comanches were."

"How much further until we get to the entrance of this Canyon?" Katherine asked.

"We still have a ways to go, but we can reach it by tomorrow if we keep moving," White Buffalo replied. He then said, "We have at least four more hours of darkness until the sun rises. Once the sun comes out, we have to move slowly while hiding in the shadows of the tall cliff walls. Right now, we can walk much faster through this tall grass under the cover of the dark cloudy skies above us, so we need to take advantage of that."

"You're right, so we better get going again!" Katherine exclaimed, wearing a grin on her face.

"You just read my mind," White Buffalo responded, wearing a smile on his face.

"I sure did!"

Katherine was the first woman who made White Buffalo smile since his wife, Sun Flower, was killed. He still missed his deceased wife and never would quit missing her. But the farther he got away from the Comanche village he had lived in since being captured as a child, the more he thought he might be able to fall in love with another woman again one day.

White Buffalo and Katherine continued moving through the tall grass underneath the dark skies above them. They moved quickly but cautiously and hoped they wouldn't run into anymore Comanches. They both knew, however, that their chances of not running into anymore Comanches were very slim especially with Raven determined to catch both. And they both were aware that if Raven did catch them, he would drag them back to the Comanche village and then torture them before he burned them alive in front of the entire Comanche village.

43

Major Kevin Cooney raised his right hand high above him while pulling back on his horse's reins with his left hand. The large column of cavalry following the major halted their horses. The major took a pair of binoculars out of one of his saddlebags and raised them up to his eyes. He looked through the binoculars and didn't like what he saw. A band of Kiowa warriors were heading toward his column.

"What's wrong?" Willie Doyle asked after he halted his horse next to Major Cooney.

"There's a band of Kiowas up ahead, and they're heading our way," Major Cooney replied.

"Are we going to fight them?"

"You bet we are!" Major Cooney replied. He then returned his binoculars to his saddlebag before saying, "We're going to have to fight our way down Tomahawk Trail to Blanco Canyon so we can help your Texas Rangers, Cooper, and General Fitzpatrick. I thought we might run into some Kiowas along the way, so I brought some weapons that will terrify them and hopefully scare them away from us."

"What type of weapons would scare Kiowas?" a very curious Willie asked.

"Cannons," the major replied.

Major Cooney turned toward Lieutenant Miles Patterson and ordered him to bring up the cannons. The major then called out to his men to form a skirmish line. The column rode their horses past Major Cooney and Willie then dismounted their horses and formed a skirmish line. The soldiers checked their rifles to make sure they were loaded and then raised them up and aimed them at the approaching band of Kiowa warriors.

Lieutenant Patterson and the cannon crews brought four twelve-pounders up and placed them behind the skirmish line. The crews then loaded the twelve-pounders with canister and then aimed the cannons at the fast-approaching band of Kiowas.

"What are they loading into those cannons? Willie asked.

"Canister shot," Major Cooney replied.

"What's inside those cans?"

"Those canisters are filled with small metal balls and will have a devastating effect upon those Kiowas when they come within range of those twelve-pounders," Major Cooney replied confidently.

"I hope so because there's a lot of Kiowas charging toward us."

"Have the men back up and line up parallel to the canons!" Major Cooney called out to Lieutenant Patterson.

"Yes, sir!" Lieutenant Patterson called back. The lieutenant then issued the major's order and watched his men moved back in an orderly fashion to the twelve-pounders. When the lieutenant was satisfied that the major's order was carried out, he shouted back, "Waiting for your order to fire, sir!"

"Target the enemy!" Major Cooney called out to his men.

The column of soldiers and the four cannon crews obeyed the major's orders and aimed their rifles and canons at the Kiowas that were riding their horses at a fast gallop toward them. When the major thought the band of Kiowa warriors were within range of his soldiers' rifles and canon, he ordered his men to fire. The metal balls from the canisters that were loaded into the twelve-pounders ripped through the Kiowa warriors and their horses. The skirmish lines also fired their rifles when they heard their commanding officer's order.

The Kiowas retreated after they suffered horrific casualties from the canister shot and the deadly fire from the skirmish line. Bodies of Kiowa warriors and their horses lay scattered on the ground. The cries and moans coming from injured Kiowas were heartrending. Only a few soldiers were shot and killed by the Kiowa while a handful suffered minor injuries.

"They broke off the attack!" a joyful-sounding Willie exclaimed.

"Reload those twelve-pounders with more cannister!" Major Cooney ordered. "Those Kiowas may be regrouping for another charge."

"Do you think those Kiowas will attack again after seeing what those canister shots can do?" Willie asked.

"Kiowas don't scare easy," Major Cooney said. "We're crossing over their hunting grounds, and they don't want us here. They'll attack us again. I guarantee you they will.'"

Major Cooney, Willie, and the soldiers heard a loud thundering noise approaching. Some of the soldiers looked up into the sky wondering if a thunderstorm was forming. Major Cooney and many of the soldiers who had fought Indians before knew what that sound was.

"Get ready, men! That loud sound you're hearing is coming from the Kiowas' horses. They're going to be coming over that hill any second riding their horses toward us at a full gallop. Aim your rifles at their horses. They're the biggest target to aim at and will be easier to hit." He then turned his attention to the cannon crews and shouted, "Are the cannons loaded with canister and ready to fire?"

"Yes, sir," several soldiers from the cannon crews answered simultaneously.

Major Cooney then returned his attention to the hill where the band of Kiowas would be appearing on shortly. He was proud of his soldiers for turning back the first attack and hoped they could do it again. He knew if his cannons' canister shot hit the Kiowas again, it would kill and maim a lot of them and most likely break the Kiowas' will to continue their attack. But if the canister shot missed, the odds of him and his soldiers defeating the Kiowas would dramatically decrease.

The band of Kiowas swept over the top of the hill and rode their horses at a fast gallop straight toward Major Cooney and his soldiers. The soldiers on the skirmish line aimed their rifles at the Kiowa warriors and waited for Major Cooney to give them the command to fire. The cannon crews had their cannons loaded with canister shot and aimed at fast-approaching band of Kiowas.

"Are the Kiowas within range of our cannons yet?" Major Cooney called out to Lieutenant Patterson.

"Yes, sir!" the lieutenant replied.

The major waited a few more moments before yelling, "Fire!"

44

"The night sky is disappearing fast," Katherine said as she and White Buffalo walked through the tall grass inside Blanco Canyon.

"We need to get back to those cliff walls before we're spotted out here in the tall grass," White Buffalo warned. He then asked, "How are your feet holding up?"

"Good," Katherine replied.

"That's good news because we need to run to those tall cliff walls before the sun rises."

"I'll race you!" Katherine exclaimed and then took off running toward the cliff walls.

"Wait up!" White Buffalo called out and then took off chasing after her.

*****

Three Comanche warriors named Yellow Feather, Black Bear, and Four Bears smiled when they saw White Buffalo and Katherine running toward the area below the tall cliff walls where the three of them were hiding. Two of the warriors wanted to slice White Buffalo's scalp off his head and take it back as a trophy to hang outside their lodges. Even though Raven told every one of his warriors not to kill White Buffalo when they found him, these two warriors never like taking orders from Raven or his father. They also never liked White Buffalo and thought he should have been killed after being captured instead of being raised as a Comanche warrior. The other warrior was a friend of White Buffalo's but kept quiet so the other two warriors with him wouldn't know.

"After we kill White Buffalo, I plan on having some fun with that white woman," the Comanche warrior named Black Bear said.

"You can have her as long as you won't fight me over White Buffalo's scalp," a Comanche warrior named Yellow Feather said.

"I won't fight you over his scalp," Black Bear promised.

"You two are forgetting about me," the Comanche warrior named Four Bears said. "What do I get?"

"You can have the white woman's scalp after I'm done having fun with her," Black Bear said.

"Are you nuts?" a stunned Four Bears asked. "We can't kill her! We can't kill White Buffalo either!"

"Why not?" Black Bear asked.

"Because Raven will kill all three of us if we kill White Buffalo or the white woman with him," Four Bears replied. "He told us to capture them and then bring them back to the village where he will decide their punishment."

"Are you going to tell on me if I have some fun with the white woman?" Black Bear asked.

"I won't but she will," Four Bears replied.

"That's why we have to kill her after I'm done having fun with her so she won't tell Raven," Black Bear said.

"Black Bear is right," Yellow Feather said. "We need to kill her so she won't tell Raven on us. And we're going to kill White Buffalo too!"

"How are we going to explain killing both White Buffalo and the white woman to Raven?" Four Bears asked. "He told us all just to capture them."

"We can discuss this later," Yellow Feather said. "Here they come!"

When Four Bears saw Yellow Feather and Black Bear notching their arrows, he knew they were going to try to kill White Buffalo. He notched his own arrow to his bowstring and then aimed it at the two warriors. When he saw the two warriors aiming their arrows toward White Buffalo, he called out to both of them to drop their bows and arrows.

"No," Yellow Feather said. "I'm going to kill White Buffalo!"

"No, you're not," Four Bears said and then let loose his bowstring.

Yellow Feather felt an arrowhead penetrate deep into the middle of his back. He turned around and saw Four Bears notching another arrow. He couldn't believe a fellow warrior had just shot an arrow into his back. He then lost consciousness, fell down onto the ground, and died moments later.

When Black Bear saw Yellow Feather fall down next to him with an arrow shaft sticking out of the middle of his back, he turned toward Four Bears and saw him aiming an arrow at him.

"What are you doing?" Black Bear asked, wearing a shocked expression on his face.

"I warned the two of you, didn't I?"

Before Black Bear could answer, Four Bears let go of his bowstring and watched his arrow slam into Black Bear's left shoulder. He notched another arrow to his bowstring and then pulled his bowstring back as Black Bear stumbled forward wearing a stunned expression on his face. Four Bears aimed his arrow at the middle of Black Bear's chest and then let go of his bowstring. He watched his arrow rip into Black Bear's chest and then lowered his bow knowing Black Bear would be dead before his body hit the ground.

*****

White Buffalo called out to Katherine to stop running when he saw Four Bear waving at him underneath the tall canyon cliffs he and Katherine were running toward.

"What's wrong?" Katherine asked after she stopped running and walked back to him.

"You see that Comanche warrior waving at us?"

"Where?"

"Over there," White Buffalo replied, pointing at the Comanche warrior.

"Now I see him," Katherine responded. She then said, "We better get away from him before he tries to kill us."

"I don't think he's going to try to kill us," White Buffalo said. "It looks like he wants to talk to us."

"Isn't that one of your friends?"

"Yes, that's Four Bears waving at us."

"I know him," Kathrine said. "He was always kind to me and Jennie after you and Sun Flower took us into your lodge and took care of us.

"He's a good friend of mine," White Buffalo said. "He might be trying to warn us about something or have news to tell us."

"Let's go find out," Katherine suggested as she and White Buffalo started walking toward Four Bears.

*****

Four Bears and White Buffalo greeted each other wearing wide smiles on their faces.

"It's sure good to see you," White Buffalo said after he and Four Bears shook hands.

"It's good to see you too," Four Bears said and then nodded his head at Katherine.

Katherine smiled back at Four Bears and then said, "Hello, Four Bears."

"What happened here?" White Buffalo asked after he saw the lifeless bodies of Yellow Feather and Black Bear lying on the ground.

"I killed them," Four Bears said.

"Why?"

"They were getting ready to kill you and then they planned on having some fun with her and then kill her too when they were finished with her," Four Bears said as he pointed at Katherine.

"Thank you, Four Bears, for saving our lives," Katherine said.

Four Bears nodded his head again at Katherine and then turned his attention back to White Buffalo. He then said, "Raven is very angry with you. I've never seen him this upset before. He wants all the warriors in the village to hunt you two down and then bring you two back to the village so he can determine your punishments. He's already said what he's going to do to you after your captured."

"Let me guess," White Buffalo said. "He's going to torture me first and then burn me alive in the middle of the village where everybody can watch me die."

"That's right," Four Bears acknowledged.

"What does he plan to do with me?" Katherine asked.

"No one knows," Four Bears replied. "Some of us believe he'll torture you a little then take you back to be his squaw while others think he'll burn you alive with White Buffalo."

"It looks like I'll be in misery no matter what happens to me if I'm taken back to that village," Katherine said.

"Why are so many warriors trying to kill me if Raven wants me taken back to the village so he can torture me first and then burn me alive?" White Buffalo asked.

"Most warriors believe Raven will forgive them for killing you," Four Bears replied. "Plus, they all know you are too good of a warrior to be taken alive. Raven knows that too. He's just saying he wants you taken back to the village because he would love to burn you alive in front of the village. But if one of us kills you, he won't care as long as we give him your scalp so he can hang it up outside his lodge as a trophy."

"What are we going to run into if Katherine and I still head for the entrance to this canyon?" White Buffalo asked.

"A few more warriors," Four Bears replied.

"Only a few?"

"Yes because Raven and most of his warriors are still behind you," Four Bears replied. He then said, "You two have come far in a short time. You must have traveled all night."

"We did," Katherine said.

"You two need to keep traveling because Raven and his warriors are hot your trail. He sent Black Bear, Yellow Feather, and me ahead just in case you two got this far," Four Bears said.

"Can you help delay Raven and his warriors somehow for us?" Katherine begged.

"I'm planning on it," Four Bears said.

"Don't do it!" White Buffalo said with a stern voice. "You'll be killed if Raven catches you trying to help me and Katherine."

"I'm just going to try to delay him and the warriors with him for a little bit without him knowing I'm helping you. A lot of warriors with him are still loyal to you and don't want any harm coming to you. They'll help me figure out a way to delay him a little too. But whatever I decide to do, it won't delay Raven for long. He hates you so much that he won't let anything or anyone delay him for long," Four Bears warned.

Four Bears bade farewell to White Buffalo and Katherine and then mounted his horse. He then pointed to the two horses that belonged to Yellow Feather and Black Bear and encouraged both of them to mount the horses and ride them as fast as they could toward the entrance of Blanco Canyon. He then rode his horse away from White Buffalo and Katherine hoping both of them would make it safely out of Blanco Canyon.

"I think we should mount those horses and ride them as fast as we can out of his canyon just like Four Bears encouraged us to do," White Buffalo said.

"I agree, plus the bottom of my feet are killing me, and we don't have time for you to massage them again for me," Katherine said.

"No, we don't," White Buffalo concurred.

White Buffalo and Katherine mounted to two dead warrior's horses and rode them slowly away from the tall walls of Blanco Canyon. When they reached the tall grass, they each used the heels of their moccasins and kicked their horses into a fast trot. White Buffalo was grateful that his friend Four Bears was going to try to slow Raven and his warriors down. Four Bears was giving Katherine and him a chance to make it to the entrance of Blanco Canyon alive, and he would always be grateful to Four Bears doing that for them.

White Buffalo wondered quietly to himself what would happen to him and Katherine if they did make it out of Blanco Canyon alive. They still would have a far way to go to safely reach a town or fort and would have to cross Kiowa land to get to one. The Kiowas hated him for killing so many of them in the past. They would love to hang his scalp outside one of their lodges, and he knew it. He decided not to tell that fact to Katherine as they rode their horses toward the entrance of Blanco Canyon.

45

Cooper looked though his binoculars and couldn't believe what he was seeing. He didn't know what White Buffalo looked like, but he was pretty sure the young man he had been searching for was riding a horse toward him. A woman riding a horse that fit the description of one of the three females that Captain Josh Stephens and his company of Texas Rangers were looking for accompanied him. Cooper lowered his binoculars and looked over to Siringo wearing a smile on his face.

"What are you looking so happy about?" a curious Siringo asked.

"You won't believe who's riding one of those two horses approaching us."

"Who?"

"White Buffalo."

"No way!"

"Look for yourself," Cooper said and then handed Siringo his binoculars.

Siringo put the binoculars up to his eyes and zoomed in on the two riders galloping their horses toward the shrubs he and Cooper were hiding behind. He then said, "He sure fits the description of White Buffalo and that woman riding the horse next to him sure could be one of those young women that the Texas Rangers are looking for." He then paused for a moment when something caught his attention. He then zoomed the binoculars in on four Comanche warriors that were chasing after White Buffalo and the woman accompanying him.

He handed the binoculars back to Cooper and said, "There's four Comanches chasing after them."

"We have to help them," Cooper said.

"I wish we had our rifles with us," Siringo said as he drew his revolver from its holster.

"So do I, but since we don't, our revolvers will have to do," Cooper said as he too drew his revolver.

*****

"They're gaining on us!" Katherine warned.

"I know they are," White Buffalo said.

"We can't fight them," Katherine said. "There's too many of them."

"We're not going to fight them. Just I am."

"No, you're not! They'll kill you!"

"Keep riding your horse straight, and you'll reach the entrance to Blanco Canyon in a few miles."

"I'm not leaving you!"

"Yes, you are!"

White Buffalo pulled back on his horse's reins and then spun it around. He pulled an arrow from his quiver and then notched it to his bowstring. He looked back over his left shoulder and saw Katherine riding her horse away at a fast gallop. He then returned his attention to the four Comanche warriors riding their horses toward him.

White Buffalo targeted one of the warriors and then let loose of his bowstring. He watched his arrow fly through the air and slam into the Comanche warrior he had aimed at. He saw the Comanche warrior fall off his horse as he notched another arrow to his bowstring. He then saw muzzle flashes followed by the sounds of gunfire. He frowned when he heard his horse squeal. He knew at least one of the bullets the Comanche warriors had fired at him had hit his horse. He jumped off his horse when he felt his horse stumbling forward. He landed on his feet and ran over to where his horse lay. He knelt down next to his horse and saw blood pouring out of two bullet holes on his horse's neck.

More bullets whistled by White Buffalo as he pulled his bowstring back and aimed his arrow at one of the three Comanche warriors charging toward him. When he was confident he wouldn't miss the warrior he was aiming his arrow at, he let loose of his bowstring. His arrow flew through the air and hit the warrior he was aiming at. The arrow penetrated deep into the warrior's heart. The arrow's impact knocked the warrior off his horse. The warrior landed hard on his back and died a few seconds later.

The two remaining Comanche warriors closed the gap between them and White Buffalo quickly. White Buffalo thought he could kill one more of them but was doubtful he could kill both of them. As he was notching another arrow to his bowstring, he heard gunfire behind him. He looked back over his left shoulder and saw a white man wearing a tan buckskin shirt riding a horse that resembled the one that Katherine was riding. He then returned his attention to the two remaining warriors charging their horses at him.

White Buffalo aimed his arrow at a bare-chested warrior wearing red war paint on his chest. He let go of his bowstring and watched his arrow strike the warrior's chest. The warrior slumped over his horse's neck and then slid off his horse a few moments later. As White Buffalo was pulling another arrow out of his quiver, he saw the last Comanche warrior bearing down on him with a rifle pointed toward him. He then heard gunfire coming from behind him and saw the last remaining Comanche warrior fall off his horse just before the warrior could pull his rifle's trigger.

White Buffalo turned around and lowered his bow and arrow while the white man halted his horse not too far from him.

He is riding Katherine's horse, White Buffalo said to himself as watched the white man dismount his horse. As the white man approached him, White Buffalo heard him call out to him.

"Is your name White Buffalo?" the white man asked.

"Yes, it is," White Buffalo replied. He then asked, "What is your name?"

"My name is Cooper McCaw, and your father sent me here to bring you back to him."

"My father sent you?"

"Yes, your father, General Fitzpatrick sent me. He would have come himself, but we had to tie him up so he wouldn't get himself killed."

"You really tied my father up?"

"Yes. We had no choice," Cooper replied. He then pointed at one of the Comanche warriors' horses and said, "Grab that horse over there, and I'll take you to your father. He's not too far from here, and he'll be happy to see you."

"Are you going to untie him when we see him?"

"Yes," Cooper replied chuckling. "I'll untie him when we get to him."

"Good," White Buffalo said as he grabbed the reins of a horse's that belonged to one of the dead Comanche warriors that had just tried to kill him. He then mounted the horse and rode it up alongside Cooper who had just grabbed the reins of the three other horses that belonged to the other three dead Indians. He then asked, "Where's the woman who was riding with me?"

"She's back with my friend," Cooper replied. "We're going to take these horses to them so they can ride them back to the gully where your father is waiting for us with another friend of mine."

"Is your friend waiting with my father tied up too?" White Buffalo asked.

"No, he isn't," Cooper replied, wearing a grin on his face.

46

Sergeant Black grabbed his lever-action repeating rifle when he saw four people riding their horses at a fast trot toward him. He cocked the lever on his rifle and then aimed it toward them. As the horses drew nearer, he recognized the two of the four riders. He lowered his rifle, raised his right hand, and started waving it to let Cooper and Siringo know that it was safe to ride their horses into the gully.

"Is that who I think it is?" Sergeant Black asked after welcoming Cooper and Siringo back.

"Yes, that's White Buffalo you see dismounting his horse," Cooper replied.

"Who's the woman with him?" Sergeant Black asked.

"That's one of the young women that the Texas Rangers are looking for," Cooper replied.

"Does she have any news on the other two women that were being held hostage with her?"

"Yes. They're both dead."

Cooper then looked over General Fitzpatrick who was still tied up and gagged. He motioned for Siringo to cut the general loose and then turned his attention back to Sergeant Black. He then asked, "Did the general give you any problems since Siringo and I left?"

"He struggled to break free several times and yelled a lot, but I couldn't understand him since he was gagged," Sergeant Black replied, wearing a huge grin on his face. He then said, "You know he'll never let you back in the cavalry since you tied him up and gagged him. He'll probably have me court-martialed, so I hope you let me come with you wherever you decide to go."

"If you're court-martialed, I'll definitely let you come with me wherever I go."

"Good because here he comes!" Sergeant Black warned.

General Fitzpatrick's eyes were full of hate when he walked toward Cooper and Sergeant Black. He glared at both men as he walked by them and refused to talk to either one of them. Sergeant Black and Cooper watched the general walk up to his son, White Buffalo, and Katherine who was standing next to him. Siringo joined Cooper and Sergeant Black as they were watching the general talk to White Buffalo and Katherine.

"Is the general still mad at us?" Cooper asked.

"Wouldn't you be if you were tied up and gagged?"

"I guess I would," Cooper replied.

"Is there any chance he might forgive us?" Sergeant Black asked as they all watched General Fitzpatrick hug his son, White Buffalo.

"Doubtful," Siringo replied.

"I was hoping you wouldn't say that," a disappointed Sergeant Black said.

*****

General Fitzpatrick spent ten minutes talking with White Buffalo and Katherine before he came over to talk to Sergeant Black, Cooper, and Siringo. When he reached the three men, his eyes were no longer full of hate. He asked the three men to listen to what he had to say before making any comments and all three agreed to.

General Fitzpatrick cleared his voice and then said, "The whole time I was tied up I was planning on how to punish the three of you when you eventually freed me." He paused for a moment and then looked at Sergeant Black and said, "I was going to have you court-martialed." He then glanced at Siringo and said, "I was going to make sure you never worked as a scout in this state or any other state or territory as long as you lived." He then looked over at Cooper and said, "Your punishment was the easiest to decide. You would be forever branded a coward not only in this state but in all the states and territories that the United States control. I was also going to make sure the rest of the world knew that you were a coward too."

"It sounds like you might not be punishing us," a hopeful-sounding Sergeant Black said.

"Didn't I ask you to hear me out before you made any comments?" General Fitzpatrick asked while glaring at Sergeant Black.

"Yes, you did, sir. I'm very sorry, sir," a nervous-sounding Sergeant Black responded.

"Now shut up and let me finish what I want to say!" General Fitzpatrick said with anger in his voice.

"Yes, sir," Sergeant Black responded, now feeling terrible for interrupting the general.

The general took a few moments to calm down before saying, "When I saw my son, I was no longer angry with the three of you. I knew if you hadn't knocked me out, tied me up, and gagged me, I would have jeopardized our chances of ever finding my son. I never had to say this to anyone in my life, but I need to say it to the three of you. I'm very sorry for my behavior, and I now realized I deserve to be tied up and gagged."

General Fitzpatrick then looked at Cooper and said, "My son told me that if you hadn't come along when you did and killed that Comanche warrior that was about to shoot a bullet at him, he would have certainly been killed. I owe you for saving my son's life, and I owe you big time. Once we get back to Fort Concho, I promise you that I will have you reinstated into the cavalry with the rank of captain, and you will never be branded a coward again. I promise you that."

A stunned-looking Cooper then said, "Thank you, sir."

"You're very welcome, and thank you again for saving my son's life," General Fitzpatrick said before rejoining his son and Katherine.

"Weren't you a lieutenant before you were court-martialed and thrown out of the cavalry?" Sergeant Black said.

"I sure was," Cooper replied still wearing a shocked expression on his face.

"He promoted you to captain," Sergeant Black said, wearing a smile on his face.

"He sure did," Siringo concurred and patted Cooper on his back while wearing a huge smile on his face. He then said, "Congratulations."

"Thank you," Cooper said, now wearing a smile on his face too. He then said, "I never saw that coming."

Sergeant Black then asked, "Did the two of you hear him say whether I could keep my sergeant stripes?"

"No," Cooper and Siringo answered concurrently before breaking into laughter.

"I didn't either," Sergeant Black said and then tried to force his frown into a smile but couldn't.

*****

After getting reacquainted with his father a little longer, White Buffalo called everyone together and suggested they head toward the entrance of Blanco Canyon as soon as possible. He knew Raven and his warriors would keep looking for him and Katherine and wouldn't give up until they found them. He knew he and Katherine wouldn't be free of Raven until they both reached the safety of a large town or fort outside the lands belonging to the Comanches. He was also aware it wouldn't be easy getting through the lands belonging to the Kiowas since they all would love to hang his scalp outside one of their lodges.

White Buffalo, Katherine, General Fitzpatrick, Cooper, Siringo, and Sergeant Black mounted their horses and then rode their horses out of the large gully. They turned their horses toward the entrance of the canyon and then rode their horses at a fast trot toward it. They all hoped Raven and his warriors were far behind them but knew they probably weren't.

As White Buffalo rode with his companions, he quietly thanked God for allowing him to be reunited with his father. He was excited that God had given him another chance to be with his father. He started praying, but his prayer was quickly interrupted by loud Comanche war cries. He looked back over his right shoulder and dropped his lower jaw when he saw Raven with a huge war party chasing after him and his companions.

47

"One, two, three, four, five, and one more. That makes six, I count," a Texas Ranger named JT said as he looked through his binoculars.

"Do you recognize any of them?" Captain Josh Stephens asked.

"Not yet," JT replied as he continued looking through his binoculars. JT kept looking through his binoculars and finally recognized Cooper McCaw. He then lowered his binoculars, looked over at Josh, and said, "One of them is Cooper McCaw."

"Is General Fitzpatrick, Sergeant Black, and Siringo with them?"

JT raised his binoculars and looked through them again. He zoomed in on the other riders and then replied, "Yes."

"Who are the other two riding with them?"

"I'm not sure," JT said. "One is a woman, and the other is a white man with long hair and wearing Comanche clothes."

"Did you say he's wearing Comanche clothes?"

"Yes, sir."

"If he's white with long hair and wearing Indian clothes he must be General Fitzpatrick's son, White Buffalo. I wonder if that white woman with him is one of the three females I've we've been looking for."

"She fits the description of the one named Katherine White," JT said as he zoomed his binoculars on her.

"I hope it is her," Josh said. "If it is—"

"We got trouble heading our way," JT interrupted.

"What kind of trouble?"

"There's a huge war party of Comanches chasing Cooper and his companions," JT replied.

Josh turned around and then called out to his company of Texas Rangers, "Grab your rifles, men! We need to give Cooper, Sergeant Black, and their four companions cover fire! There's a lot of Comanches chasing after them!"

*****

Sounds of gunfire and Comanche war cries rang through the ears of Cooper McCaw, Siringo, Sergeant Black, General Fitzpatrick, White Buffalo, and Katherine as they rode their horses toward the entrance to Blanco Canyon. Bullets whistled by them and ricocheted off the tall cliff walls. When they all looked back over their shoulders, they were shocked by the size of the war party that Raven was leading.

All the Comanche tribes must have joined together to hunt for me and chose Raven as their leader, White Buffalo thought after seeing the size of the war party chasing after him and his companions.

"Keep riding your horses as fast as you can and head straight for that opening up ahead!" Cooper shouted out to the other riders.

"I hope Josh and his company of Texas Rangers are waiting for us at that entrance to give us cover fire!" Sergeant Black yelled back at Cooper.

"I do too!"

"What happens if they're not there?" Sergeant Black asked loudly.

"We'll all be caught, tortured, scalped, and then burned alive!" Cooper yelled back.

*****

"Don't fire until I say to!" Josh yelled out to his company of Texas Rangers. Josh waited until Cooper and his companions drew closer because he didn't want his men to risk hitting them. When he was certain Cooper and his companions would not be hit by his men's bullets, he yelled, "Fire!"

Josh and his Texas Rangers fired their lever-action repeating rifles as fast as they could. Their bullets ripped into the Comanche war party. Several Comanches were killed instantly while others were severely wounded. When Raven heard the gunfire and saw the muzzle flashes coming from the entrance of Blanco Canyon, he raised his right hand high into the air to signal his warriors to stop pursuing White Buffalo, Katherine, and their four companions. He spun his horse around and then led his war party away from the entrance of Blanco Canyon leaving several of his warriors lying on the ground dead or mortally wounded.

Raven didn't know who was waiting in ambush for him at the entrance of the canyon but assumed it was either soldiers or Texas Rangers. He had no clue how many there were of them but knew they couldn't outnumber all the warriors that were riding with him. When he and his warriors were out of range of the enemies' rifles, he halted his war party and then discussed strategy with the chiefs from the other Comanche tribes that had joined his war party. He and the other chiefs didn't like being ambush and wanted vengeance.

Raven vowed that he would capture White Buffalo and Katherine or die trying to. He hated White Buffalo and wanted to hang his scalp outside his lodge for everyone in his village to see. He also wanted to bring Katherine back to his village and keep her there as his squaw. He would torture her for a while so she would learn never to try to escape from him again.

Her body is going to have a lot of scars on it after I'm done torturing her, and every time she looks at one of her scars, she'll remember to never try escape from me again, Raven said to himself as he listened to the other war chiefs' strategies.

*****

Josh and his Texas Rangers lowered their rifles as Cooper, Sergeant Black, General Fitzpatrick, Siringo, and their two companions rode their horses into the rock formation that he and his rangers were defending at the entrance to Blanco Canyon.

"Welcome back," Josh said after Cooper and his companions dismounted their horses and walked up to him.

"We found my son!" a joyful-sounding General Fitzpatrick said. He then introduced White Buffalo to Josh and some of the rangers standing next to him.

After exchanging pleasantries, White Buffalo introduced Katherine to Josh. "I hear you and your men have been looking for her," White Buffalo said.

"Yes, we have," Josh responded. After shaking Katherine's hand, he asked, "What happened to the other two women that were with you? Are they still alive?"

"No," Katherine replied, wearing a frown on her face. "Jennie and Lillie were both killed."

"I'm sorry to hear that," Josh said.

"They both died trying to escape," Katherine said. "Neither one of them stood a chance. "The only reason I made it is because of White Buffalo and these four men standing here with me. I was the lucky one. Unfortunately, Lillie and Jennie were the unlucky ones."

"The Comanches are coming back!" the Texas Ranger named JT called out.

"Make sure your rifles are fully loaded!" Josh shouted to his men. "We need to fill those Comanche bodies with lead." He then returned his attention to Cooper and his companions and said while pointing at a boulder, "Your rifles are leaning against that boulder over there fully loaded and ready to fire."

"Thanks," Cooper said before he and the others ran to get their rifles.

Josh then looked at White Buffalo and asked, "Do you know how to shoot a rifle?"

"Yes, I do, but I prefer using my bow and arrows instead," White Buffalo replied.

"If you change your mind and want a rifle, we have a few extras one over where we'll be."

"Thanks, but I prefer my bow." He then paused and asked, "Where do you want me?"

"With your father."

"What about Katherine?"

"Keep her hidden behind you and your father."

"Okay," White Buffalo said before he and Katherine ran over to where General Fitzpatrick was.

As White Buffalo knelt next to his father, he heard Comanche war cries and gunfire erupting. He notched an arrow to his bowstring and then raised his bow. He aimed his arrow toward the large Comanche war party and waited patiently for it to draw closer. He heard his father cock the lever on his lever-action repeating rifle and then heard his father's voice say, "Don't shoot until you know you won't miss."

48

White Buffalo heard gunfire erupt all around him as the Texas Rangers, Cooper, Siringo, and his father fired their rifles at the fast-approaching Comanche war party. He watched a dozen Comanche warriors fall off their horses after bullets ripped into their bodies. He pulled back his bowstring and aimed his arrow at a Comanche warrior and then let loose of the string. He watched his arrow strike the Comanche's chest and saw the warrior fall off his horse.

While White Buffalo notched another arrow to his bowstring, he watched his father, General Fitzpatrick, shoot and kill a Comanche warrior that he once called a friend. White Buffalo picked out another Comanche to aim his arrow at, pulled back his bowstring, and then let loose of it. His arrow flew through the air until its arrowhead penetrated the warrior's lower chest. The warrior fell off his horse shocked that a Comanche arrow was about to kill him.

Cooper cocked the lever on his lever-action repeating rifle and then aimed it at a Comanche warrior. He squeezed his rifle's trigger when he was confident he wouldn't miss his target. He then watched his bullet strike and kill the warrior he was aiming at. Without hesitation, he cocked the lever on his rifle again, picked out a Comanche warrior to shoot at, and then pulled his rifle's trigger.

A bullet ricocheted off the boulder Siringo was kneeling behind. He cocked the lever on his rifle and aimed it at a Comanche warrior. As he was squeezing his rifle's trigger, he heard a bullet whistle by him. He watched his bullet hit and kill a Comanche warrior before he ducked down behind the boulder. He heard someone moaning as he cocked the lever on his rifle. Leaning up against the boulder next to him was a Texas Ranger named Clyde Jacobson. He had a bullet hole in the middle of his chest, and he was bleeding profusely.

Clyde noticed Siringo looking at him and asked, "How bad is it?"

"It doesn't look good," Siringo replied.

"My chest feels like it's on fire," Clyde said. He then started coughing up blood. He tried to tell Siringo something but couldn't get the words out. He died moments later.

Sergeant Black watched his bullet smash into a Comanche warrior he was aiming at. He grinned while watching the Comanche fall off his horse. As he was cocking the lever on his rifle, he felt an arrow fly by the right side of his head. *That was too close*, he said to himself as he targeted another Comanche warrior to shoot at.

Josh frowned when he heard a click after he pulled his rifle's trigger. He ducked back down behind the boulder he was defending and started reloading his rifle. As he reloaded it, he noticed several of his men lying on the ground. He knew they had been killed or mortally wounded by the Comanches attacking them.

We are too few. I hope Willie made it to Fort Concho and is bringing back a troop of cavalry with him. If he doesn't, we're all doomed, Josh thought to himself.

Katherine kept herself hidden behind the boulder that White Buffalo and General Fitzpatrick was defending. She heard White Buffalo and his father talking with one another as they killed the Comanches attacking them. She was happy the two were reunited and wondered if she would ever see her family again.

"They're breaking off the attack!" a jubilant-sounding JT shouted.

"Stop firing!" Josh ordered as he lowered his rifle. He then paused for a moment before shouting, "Make sure your rifles are fully loaded! Those Comanches aren't giving up! They'll be attacking us again!"

White Buffalo lowered his bow and then looked at his father and said, "We survived their first attack, but I'm not so sure we'll survive the next one if we stay here."

"What do you suggest we do, son?" General Fitzpatrick asked as he lowered his rifle and then started reloading it.

"If a few of us stay here and fight the Comanches, it would allow the others a chance to escape and give them a head start to try to make it back to civilization," White Buffalo said as he notched another arrow to his bowstring.

"That's not a bad idea," General Fitzpatrick said. "Let's go talk to Cooper, Josh, and the others about your suggestion and see what they say."

*****

"You don't have to stay," General Fitzpatrick said. "You've already proven to everyone that you're not a coward. I already told you that you earned the right to be reinstated back into the cavalry, and I gave you a promotion too. You'll no longer be branded a coward. I'll make sure of it."

"Thank you, General, but I volunteered to stay here to give you all a chance to escape not because I'm sick of people thinking I'm a coward but because I have no one to care for in my life like you do. You have your son back, and he's going to need your help re-adapting to civilization. Now if I get out of here alive, I plan on you keeping your word and reinstating me back into the cavalry."

"You'll be reinstated whether you live or die. I promise you that. I will also make sure your record is clear and any mention of you being court-martialed and branded a coward is erased."

"Thank you, General. I appreciate that."

"I see Sergeant Black decided to stay with you too."

"Yes, he did," Cooper said, wearing a grin on his face. "We've become close friends since leaving Fort Concho to hunt for your son."

"Josh and what's left of his Texas Rangers are staying here too," General Fitzpatrick said. "You all should buy us plenty of time to get far away from here without losing our scalps."

"We'll slow down the Comanches for you, White Buffalo, and Katherine, but you all still need to worry about the Kiowas."

"My son has been warning me about that too. Hopefully we won't run into any of them on the way back to the fort." The general paused for a moment to clear his throat and then said, "I don't want you all sacrificing your lives for us. As soon as you give the three of us a decent head start to Fort Concho, we want you to hightail it out of here and make a run for it to Fort Concho."

"We will, and by the way, there's going to be four of you in your group," Cooper said.

"Who's the fourth?" a very curious General Fitzpatrick asked.

"I am," Siringo replied as he came walking up to General Fitzpatrick and Cooper. He then said, "I thought you might need some help getting through Kiowa territory. The whole Kiowa Nation will be out looking for you when they hear White Buffalo is accompanying you. Every Kiowa warrior wants to hang your son's scalp outside their lodge."

"He's right they do," Cooper concurred. "You'll need Siringo's help to get you all through the lands belonging to the Kiowas. No one knows that area better than Siringo."

"We'll happily take you along with us," General Fitzpatrick said while looking at Siringo. "I've grown accustomed to your company and your advice too."

"Thank you, General," Siringo said.

"You all better get going. The Comanches will be attacking us soon," Cooper warned.

General Fitzpatrick, Siringo, White Buffalo, and Katherine took Cooper's advice and mounted their horses. They then rode their horses at a fast trot out of Blanco Canyon. They rode their horses toward the lands belonging to the Kiowas not knowing if they would ever see Cooper, Sergeant Black, Josh, and his few remaining Texas Rangers again.

49

"Are they ready?" Cooper asked.

"Yes," Sergeant Black replied. "Josh just signaled us."

"Good," Cooper replied. He cocked the lever on his lever-action repeating rifle before saying, "This is the only way out of this section of Blanco Canyon. The Comanches will have to ride their horses past this narrow passageway between these two tall cliff walls. With us on one side and Josh and his men on the other, we can draw the Comanches into a crossfire. We then can delay the Comanches for a while from passing through this passageway giving General Fitzpatrick and the others time to get away from here."

"The longer we give the general and the others time to get away from here, the better chance they have of getting through to Fort Concho."

"I agree. I just hope they don't run into any Kiowas along the way."

"If they do, we can help them fight them off if we all get out of this canyon alive."

"That's a big if, my friend," Cooper said as he watched Sergeant Black cock the lever on his rifle.

"You don't think we'll make it out of here alive, do you?"

"It will be a miracle if we do," Cooper said before he raised his binoculars and looked for Raven and his Comanche war party.

*****

"We left Lubbock with a whole company of Texas Rangers, and now there are only a few of us left," Josh said, wearing a frown on his face while talking to the few rangers that were still alive. "I don't know if we'll get out of this canyon alive, but if Katherine White makes it back to her family alive, we at least saved one of the three young women's lives that we were sent to this canyon to rescue."

"I never even heard of Blanco Canyon until we left Lubbock searching for the three women that were kidnapped by the Comanches," JT said. "Now we might all die in this canyon."

"We might, but if we do, we'll die heroes," a Texas Ranger named Percy said.

"Heroes?" JT asked.

"That's what I said," Percy replied. He then exclaimed, "We'll be in the history books!"

"I like the sound of that, but if I had my choice, I would rather live my life a little longer than die a hero inside this canyon today," JT said while making sure his revolver was fully loaded.

"Do you believe in the power of prayer?" Josh asked both men.

"Yes," both JT and Percy replied.

"Then start praying fast because the Comanches are heading straight for us," Josh said as he looked through his binoculars and watched Raven and his war party galloping their horses down the passageway. Josh was shocked by the size of the war party. He never saw so many Comanches before.

More Comanches must have joined Raven since the last attack, he thought as he continued watching the Comanche war party with his binoculars. He lowered his binoculars and then set them on the ground next to him. He then picked his rifle up and aimed it at the fast-approaching war party.

"Pick out a Comanche to shoot at, but don't pull your rifles' triggers until you hear gunfire coming from Cooper and Sergeant Black!" Josh shouted out to his men. "When you hear their gunfire, shoot your rifles as fast as you can. When your rifles are empty, shoot your revolvers and then reload your weapons and keep shooting them until you hear me say, 'Retreat.' When you hear me shout that word, run as fast as you can to your horses and then ride your horses away from this canyon as fast as you can because that Comanche war party coming toward us will be hot on your tail."

*****

"Hold it! Let them come just a little closer! We need to make sure our shots count!" Cooper shouted over the loud thundering sounds of the fast-approaching Comanche war party.

"Just let me know when!" Sergeant Black yelled back.

After a few more moments passed by, Cooper shouted, "Now!"

After Sergeant Black and Cooper started firing their rifles, Cooper heard gunfire coming from Josh and his rangers who were on top of cliff wall across from the one that he and Sergeant Black were positioned on. Cooper pointed his rifle's barrel down at the Comanche war party and picked out a warrior to shoot at. He then pulled his trigger and watched his bullet hit and kill the warrior he was aiming at. He fired his rifle as fast as he could and watched his bullets strike the warriors he was aiming at.

Cooper looked over at Sergeant Black while he was reloading his rifle and saw the sergeant firing his rifle as fast as he could. When he finished reloading his rifle, Cooper cocked its lever and then aimed it at a Comanche warrior. As he pulled his rifle's trigger, he wondered how Josh and his Texas Rangers were holding up on the top of the cliff wall that was across from the one he and Sergeant Black were on.

*****

"We've killed at least a dozen of them so far!" Percy exclaimed.

"Quit counting and keep firing your rifle!" Josh shouted. He then yelled out, "We need to kill a lot more than a dozen if we're going to get out of this canyon alive!"

JT pulled his rifle's trigger and watched his bullet rip through the Comanche's throat he was aiming at. He cocked the lever on his rifle again, aimed it at another warrior, and then pulled his trigger. He grinned when his bullet knocked the warrior he was aiming at off his horse. As he was cocking the lever on his rifle, he felt a burning sensation on the side of his left shoulder. He took a moment to look at the bullet wound and was relieved after he realized it was just a flesh wound. He then aimed his rifle at a Comanche warrior and squeezed its trigger. His bullet slammed into the warrior he was aiming at and killed him instantly.

A Texas Ranger named Elijah Ball fired his rifle. His bullet struck and killed the warrior he was aiming at. As he was cocking the lever on his rifle, he felt something penetrate deep into his chest. He looked down and saw an arrow shaft sticking out the middle of his chest. He fell backward awkwardly, landed on his back, and then died wearing a stunned expression on his face.

"They got Elijah!" Percy shouted as he cocked the lever on his rifle.

"Is he dead?" JT asked as he leaned his empty rifle against a boulder and drew his revolver from its holster.

"He ain't moving, so I think he is," Percy replied and then aimed his rifle at a Comanche warrior.

Josh saw dozens of dead Comanche warriors bodies lying on the ground beneath him. But he knew there were still many more warriors left willing and eager to kill him and take his scalp. He picked out a Comanche warrior to shoot at and then pulled his rifle's trigger. He watched his bullet hit the warrior's left shoulder. He cocked his rifle's lever quickly and aimed it again at the same warrior and then squeezed its trigger. This time his bullet smashed into the warrior chest knocking him off his horse.

As Josh was cocking the lever on his rifle again, he heard a loud moan next to him. He looked to his left and saw Percy lying on his back with two bullet wounds on his chest. His white shirt was covered with blood, and he began gasping for air. Josh knew Percy would die soon, so he kept firing at the Comanches beneath him instead of checking on his fellow Texas Ranger.

*****

"How you holding up on ammunition?" Cooper asked Sergeant Black.

"I'm almost out of cartridges for my rifle," Sergeant Black replied. He then asked Cooper, "How much ammo do you have left?"

"Not much," Cooper replied.

"What do we do when we run out?"

"Run to our horses and ride them away from here as fast as we can."

"Hey look, the Comanches are retreating!" a joyful-sounding Sergeant Black exclaimed. "They can't get past all dead bodies of the warriors and horses' carcasses piled up beneath us. The narrow passageway is blocked for now."

"It sure is blocked!" Cooper said with excitement in his voice. "Let's run to our horses and ride out of here while we have a chance to. It will take a while for the Comanches to clear away all those dead warriors and horses lying on the ground below us."

"We better signal Josh and his rangers to flee as well," Sergeant Black suggested.

"You're right. We need to," Cooper concurred. He then waved at Josh and signaled for him and his rangers to mount their horses and leave. He then returned his attention back to Sergeant Black and shouted, "Let's get out of here!"

*****

"Gather up your weapons! We're getting out of here!" Josh shouted at JT.

The two surviving Texas Rangers ran toward their horses and mounted them. They rode their horses slowly and cautiously down a steep narrow path to the bottom of the cliff wall. After reaching the bottom, they used the heels of their boots and kicked their horses into a fast trot and rode their horses away from the entrance to Blanco Canyon.

Within minutes, they saw Cooper and Sergeant Black and rode their horses toward them. When the four of them joined up, they all halted their horses and talked about the battle the four of them just fought with the Comanches.

"Are the rest of your rangers dead?" Cooper asked after Josh and JT rode their horses up alongside his and Sergeant Black's horses.

"JT and me are the only two rangers still alive," Josh replied.

"I'm so sorry to hear that," Cooper said.

"Don't be," Josh said. "They died the way a Texas Ranger would want to, fighting to help save others' lives."

"Do you think we bought General Fitzpatrick, his son, Siringo, and Katherine enough time to get away from Raven and his warriors?" JT asked.

"We bought them some time, but I doubt Raven and his warriors will ever give up until they find White Buffalo and Katherine," Cooper replied.

"Where to?" Sergeant Black asked.

"We're going to try to catch up with General Fitzpatrick and the others. I have a feeling they're going to need our help. Raven and his warriors will be tracking them soon, and they're bound to run into some Kiowas too," Cooper replied.

"Even if we catch up with them, we are too few to help them fight both the Comanches and Kiowas," Sergeant Black warned.

"Yes, we are, but we still might get some help," a hopeful-sounding Josh said.

"From who?" Sergeant Black asked.

"From Fort Concho if Willie Doyle made it there alive," Josh replied.

"For our sake, I hope he did," Sergeant Black said.

"We need to get moving," Cooper said. "Raven and his warriors will clear the pile of death blocking the narrow passageway soon. The farther we get away from here before they do, the better for us. Hopefully, we'll catch up to the others before they run into any Kiowas."

Cooper used the heels of his boots and kicked his horse into a fast gallop. He heard his three companions' horses galloping behind him as he rode his horse away from Blanco Canyon. He knew the odds of him and his companions escaping Raven and his warriors and then fighting their way through the lands belonging to the Kiowas were slim without the help of the soldiers from Fort Concho. He then wondered if the Texas Ranger named Willie Doyle got through to Fort Concho. And even if Willie got through, would the soldiers from the fort be able to get through Kiowa lands without being spotted and massacred in time to help him, General Fitzpatrick, Siringo, White Buffalo, Katherine, and the others? Cooper hoped so because if the soldiers didn't, he and his companions were sure to lose their scalps.

50

White Buffalo pulled back on his horse's reigns to halt it. He then motioned to his companions to do the same. He then pointed at ten Indians sitting tall on their horses riding slowing toward them.

"How did the Comanches get ahead of us?" an upset Katherine asked.

"Those aren't Comanches," White Buffalo said. "Those Indians are Kiowa."

"Should we try to talk to them?" General Fitzpatrick asked.

"They don't want to talk to us," Siringo replied. "All they want is your son's scalp so they can hang it outside one of their lodges. Your son's scalp would become big medicine to whomever possesses it."

Siringo drew his rifle from his saddle scabbard while looking for a place they could use for cover when the small band of Kiowa warriors attacked them. He saw a small group of Cottonwoods not too far from where they were and pointed at them. He then said, "Let's take cover over there."

Siringo, General Fitzpatrick, White Buffalo, and Katherine rode their horses at a fast gallop toward the cottonwoods. The Kiowas continued riding their horses at a slow walk but now headed for the cottonwoods where the renowned White Buffalo and his companions rode their horses. They were in no rush to attack since they all knew a larger band of their fellow tribesmen would be joining up with them shortly.

*****

White Buffalo jumped off his horse and tied its reigns around a nearby cottonwood. He pulled his bow off his right shoulder and drew an arrow from his quiver. He heard his father shouting at him as he ran toward the edge of the group of Cottonwoods. He saw several old dead fallen trees and knelt down behind one. He picked out a Kiowa warrior to shoot at and aimed his arrow at him.

When White Buffalo was confident he wouldn't miss hitting the Kiowa warrior, he let loose of his bowstring. He then watched his arrow fly through the sky and slam into the chest of the warrior he was aiming at. The warrior fell off his horse and landed on his back. He died shortly thereafter wearing a stunned expression on his face.

The nine other Kiowa warriors kicked their horses into a fast gallop and charged them toward the group of cottonwoods. They were angry and sought revenge for the death of their fellow warrior. White Buffalo drew another arrow from his quiver, notched it, and then aimed it at another Kiowa warrior. He then let loose of his bowstring and watched his arrow strike the warrior's stomach. The warrior slumped over his horse's neck for a few moments before he fell off and landed on the ground.

"How many have you killed?" General Fitzpatrick asked his son as he knelt down beside him.

"Two," White Buffalo replied as he notched another arrow to his bowstring.

"I'm going to help you kill some more of those Injuns," General Fitzpatrick said as he cocked the lever on his rifle. Before he pulled his trigger, he called out to Siringo who was kneeling behind a fallen tree next to them, "Take the ones on the right, and I'll concentrate on the ones on the right!"

"Will do!" Siringo shouted back.

General Fitzpatrick and Siringo aimed their rifles and then shot and killed the two Kiowa warriors they were aiming at. They both cocked the levers on their rifles, picked out two more warriors to shoot at before squeezing their rifle's triggers. Both their bullets struck and killed the two warriors they had targeted.

Siringo heard someone kneel down beside him as he was cocking the lever on his rifle. He glanced to his right and saw Katherine kneeling next to him. He told her to duck down after several bullets whistled past them. She obeyed and threw herself onto her chest and hid behind the fallen tree. She heard bullets slam into the fallen tree as she kept herself hidden behind it.

"There's only four of them left!" a jubilant-sounding General Fitzpatrick exclaimed. "Let's finish them off!"

"As soon as we do, let's mount our horses and ride away from here as fast as we can," White Buffalo said as he aimed his arrow at a fast-approaching Kiowa.

White Buffalo let loose of his bowstring and watched his arrow rip through the Kiowa's throat he was aiming at. The Kiowa fell off his horse, landed on his back, and died choking on his blood. General Fitzpatrick shot and killed the Kiowa warrior he was aiming at and then cocked the lever on his rifle. He targeted another Kiowa and shot and killed him. As he was cocking the lever on his rifle, he heard gunfire coming from Siringo's rifle. He then watched the last Kiowa warrior fall off his horse after Siringo's bullet slammed into the warrior's chest.

"We got them all!" General Fitzpatrick exclaimed. He then stood up and said, "Let's get out of here before more Kiowas find us here!"

Siringo and Katherine stood up and joined General Fitzpatrick and White Buffalo. As the four of them started walking back to their horses, they heard gunfire and loud war cries. They turned around and didn't like what they saw.

"More Injuns!" Katherine cried out as she felt her body trembling with fear.

"Take cover!" General Fitzpatrick yelled.

All four of them ran back to the two old dead fallen trees. General Fitzpatrick and Siringo dove behind one while White Buffalo and Katherine dove behind the other one.

"There's more of them this time," Siringo said as he peeked over the fallen tree.

"How many more do you think?" General Fitzpatrick asked.

"There must be at least twenty of them this time," Siringo warned.

General Fitzpatrick turned toward his son and Katherine yelled, "Get out of here! Siringo and I will stay here and give the two of you time to ride your horses away from here!"

"We're not going anywhere without the two of you!" White Buffalo shouted back as he notched an arrow to his bowstring.

As White Buffalo aimed his arrow toward the band of Kiowa warriors charging toward him, he told Katherine to stay down. Katherine refused and called out to Siringo to toss her his revolver. Siringo drew his revolver from his holster and tossed it toward Katherine. His revolver landed next to her. She picked it up off the ground and then aimed it at the fast-approaching Kiowas.

"Do you know how to shoot that revolver you're holding?" White Buffalo asked.

"Yes," Katherine replied. "My father taught me how to use one, and he had me practiced a lot just in case I was attack by outlaws or Injuns."

"Don't shoot it until you're sure you won't miss," White Buffalo said.

"That's what my father always told me to do," Katherine said.

*****

"Do you hear what I'm hearing?" Josh asked.

"I sure do," Cooper replied.

"Do you think it's Siringo, General Fitzpatrick, his son, and Katherine?" Sergeant Black asked.

"It has to be," JT answered.

"Let's ride our horses as fast as we can toward the sounds of that gunfire," Cooper said and then used the heels of his boots to kick his horse into a fast gallop.

Josh, Sergeant Black, and JT kicked their horses into a fast gallop and chased after Cooper. The four men rode their horses as fast as they could toward the sounds of gunfire. When they reached the top of a small hill covered with tall grass, they halted their horses. They sat tall in their saddles and saw a band of Kiowas attacking a few people pinned down inside a small group of cottonwoods.

"Are those Comanches or Kiowa?" Sergeant Black asked.

"Those are Kiowas," Cooper replied just before he reached into his saddlebag and pulled out his binoculars.

"Is it Siringo, General Fitzpatrick, his son, and Katherine White being attacked by those Injuns?" Josh asked.

"I can't tell, but whoever they are, they won't be alive for long unless we help them," Cooper replied. He then put his binoculars back into his saddlebag and drew his revolver from its holster. He then looked at his three companions and noticed they had drawn their revolvers too.

"We're ready when you are," JT said.

"Let's go help whoever is trapped in those trees down there before they lose their scalps," Cooper said.

51

Bullets ripped into the backs of the Kiowas as they were attacking White Buffalo and his companions who were pinned down in the cottonwoods. Several Kiowas were either killed or wounded before the rest of their fellow warriors realized they were being attacked from the rear. When the Kiowas spun their horses around, they saw Cooper and his three companions charging their horses toward them with their guns blazing away.

More bullets slammed into the Kiowa warriors as they broke away from attacking those pinned down in the cottonwoods and turned their attention to Cooper, Sergeant Black, Josh, and JT. The Kiowas tried to fire their old rifles and shoot their arrows at Cooper and his companions, but they were too slow. Bullets ripped into their bodies knocking them off their horses. The Kiowas lay on the ground dead or dying as Cooper, Josh, Sergeant Black, and JT rode their horses by them.

"It's Cooper and some of the men that we left back at Blanco Canyon!" General Fitzpatrick exclaimed.

"They saved our lives!" a jubilant-sounding Katherine said as she stood up from behind the fallen tree.

"They sure did," White Buffalo concurred.

"I see Sergeant Black and two Texas Rangers with them," General Fitzpatrick said as he looked through his binoculars at the four men riding their horses toward them.

"Who are the Texas Rangers riding with Cooper and the sergeant?" A curious Siringo asked as he started reloading his lever-action repeating rifle.

"One of them is Josh, but I'm not sure who the other one is," General Fitzpatrick said. He then handed his binoculars to Siringo and said, "See if you recognize him."

Siringo leaned his rifle against the fallen tree and then looked through the binoculars. He zoomed in on the riders and looked for the man General Fitzpatrick couldn't identify. He then spotted the man, lowered the binoculars, and said, "The other ranger is JT." He then handed the binoculars back to General Fitzpatrick.

"I guess the rest of the Texas Rangers were killed giving us a chance to escape Blanco Canyon," General Fitzpatrick said as he took his binoculars back from Siringo.

"They must have been," Siringo said. He then paused for a moment before saying, "I'm surprised those four escaped. I thought for sure they all would lose their scalps giving us a chance to escape Blanco Canyon."

*****

Cooper, Sergeant Black, Josh, and JT rode their horses up to the small group of cottonwoods. They halted their horses in front of the fallen trees that General Fitzpatrick, Siringo, White Buffalo, and Katherine were standing behind. They exchanged pleasantries for a few moments before General Fitzpatrick changed the subject.

"Are you four the only survivors?"

"I'm afraid we are," Cooper replied.

"All those rangers sacrificed their lives so we could escape Blanco Canyon," a sad-sounding General Fitzpatrick said.

"We might have escaped Blanco Canyon, but we haven't escaped Raven and his warriors," White Buffalo warned. He then said, "We need to get moving before Raven catches up with us."

"White Buffalo is right," Cooper said. "Raven won't give up looking for us until he's dead or White Buffalo is killed and Katherine is captured again."

"Stay where you're at so the four of us can grab our horses," General Fitzpatrick said. "Then the eight of us can ride our horses away from here."

"It's too late!" White Buffalo exclaimed. He then pointed toward the east before saying, "Raven and his warriors have found us!"

General Fitzpatrick and his seven companions were stunned after they all looked toward the direction that White Buffalo was pointing to and saw a large Comanche war party riding their horses slowly toward them. Siringo and General Fitzpatrick reached for their rifles while White Buffalo notched an arrow to his bow. Josh, Cooper, Sergeant Black, and JT rode their horses into the group of cottonwoods, dismounted, and secured their horses. They drew their rifles from their saddle scabbards and then joined the others behind the fallen trees.

"Nobody shoot until they draw close," Cooper warned. "We cannot afford to waste any ammunition."

Katherine tugged on White Buffalo's shoulder. When White Buffalo turned toward her, he saw her looking deep into his eyes with tears running down her cheeks.

"We're not going to survive their attack, are we?"

"You might," White Buffalo replied before saying, "I doubt the rest of us will."

"There must be a way we can beat Raven and his warriors," Katherine said.

White Buffalo put his hands on Katherine's shoulders and said, "There might be."

White Buffalo whispered something into her right ear, hugged her gently, and then walked away from her. She started crying when she watched him walk toward his horse knowing she may never see him alive again.

White Buffalo unwrapped his horse's reins from around the tree. He then mounted his horse and kicked it into a fast trot. He rode his horse out of the group of cottonwoods before anyone could stop him and rode it at a fast trot toward the large Comanche war party.

A very concerned General Fitzpatrick looked at a very upset-looking Katherine and asked, "Why is my son riding toward that war party?"

"He's going to try to talk to Raven in front of all the Comanche warriors riding with him. He didn't tell me what he was going to say, but he told me to tell you all not to try to stop him."

"Those Comanches will probably kill him before he ever gets a chance to talk to Raven," General Fitzpatrick said.

"He told me that they might, but if they didn't and Raven listened to what he had to say, it just might save all our lives."

Cooper, Josh, Sergeant Black, Siringo, and JT all came walking up to General Fitzpatrick and Katherine wondering why White Buffalo was riding his horse toward certain death. The general told them what Katherine had told him. They all shook their heads in disbelief.

"He's going to get himself killed," Josh said.

"We need to try to help him," JT said.

"If we chase after him, that Comanche war party will kill us all," Siringo warned.

"Siringo is right!" General Fitzpatrick exclaimed. "My son wants us all to stay here while he tries to talk his adopted brother out of killing us."

Katherine continued crying. She didn't like lying to everyone, but she knew if she told General Fitzpatrick and the others the truth they would have tried to stop White Buffalo from riding his horse out to Raven and his large Comanche war party. White Buffalo told Katherine that he was going to challenge Raven to a fight to the death hoping his adopted brother would accept his challenge. White Buffalo told Katherine if he could kill Raven, the Comanche war party might disband and return to Blanco Canyon.

White Buffalo knew the odds were stacked against him, but it was the only chance he and his companions had. He knew if Raven refused to fight him, he and his companions faced certain death. If, however, Raven agreed to fight him, then he and his companions stood a chance of keeping their scalps if White Buffalo killed Raven. He didn't know whether his adopted brother would accept his challenge, but he was going to try his best to encourage Raven to do so or die trying to.

52

"Where are you going?" Cooper asked when he saw General Fitzpatrick step over the fallen tree.

"I'm going to support my son," General Fitzpatrick replied.

"He asked us to stay here," Katherine reminded the general.

"If my son is going to risk his life for us, then I'm willing to risk my life for him."

"Let's all mount all horses and go chase after him," Cooper suggested.

General Fitzpatrick stopped dead in his tracks, turned around, and then asked, "You all would go with me to support my son?"

"Of course we would," Cooper replied.

General Fitzpatrick cracked a smile for a moment and then said, "That means a lot to me."

General Fitzpatrick stepped back over the fallen tree and walked back into the cottonwoods. He headed toward his horse. He looked back over his left shoulder and smiled when he saw everyone following him, including Katherine. General Fitzpatrick and the others unwrapped their horses' reins when they reached the trees their horses were secured to. They mounted their horses, spun them around, and then rode them slowly through the cottonwoods. When they reached the edge of the cottonwoods, they all heard someone shouting at them.

"Is that who I think it is?" Josh asked.

"Oh my god, it's Willie!" JT exclaimed.

"There's a column of cavalry siting tall on their saddles on top of the hill behind him!" Siringo said with excitement in his voice. "He must have made it to Fort Concho!"

"We need to get my son before Raven and his Comanche war party surrounds him," General Fitzpatrick said.

"It's too late!" Katherine cried out with tears running down her cheeks. She then pointed toward the Comanche war party and said, "Look."

*****

The large Comanche war party surrounded White Buffalo as he rode his horse slowly toward Raven. White Buffalo halted his horse twelve feet away from Raven who was sitting tall on his horse. Raven glared at White Buffalo for several seconds wondering what his adoptive brother wanted. He then broke his silence and asked White Buffalo, "Did you come here to die?"

"I came here to challenge you to a fight to the death," White Buffalo replied. "If I win, your warriors will return to Blanco Canyon."

"Why should I fight you when my warriors outnumber you and your friends by more than two hundred?" Raven asked.

Before White Buffalo could answer, a Comanche warrior rode his horse up to Raven and exclaimed, "Bluecoats are here!"

"How many?" Raven asked.

"At least a hundred, probably more," the Comanche warrior replied.

"Why risk losing half your warriors or even more fighting those bluecoats when the two of us can settle what angers you between ourselves?" White Buffalo asked.

Raven returned his attention to White Buffalo. He glared at his adoptive brother for a while before responding. He didn't want to fight White Buffalo by himself, but now he had no choice. He knew if he refused to fight White Buffalo, his warriors would think he was a coward. He wasn't scared of White Buffalo but knew his adoptive brother wouldn't be easy to kill.

"I'll fight you," Raven finally said.

"Good," White Buffalo said. He then asked, "What weapons do you prefer to use?"

"Tomahawks," Raven said.

White Buffalo took his bow and quiver full of arrows off his shoulder and dropped them to the ground. He dismounted his horse and gave his horse's reins to a Comanche warrior. He drew his hunting knife from its sheath and tossed it to another warrior. As he pulled out his tomahawk, he watched Raven dismount his horse. He knew Raven would be a fierce opponent and would be hard to kill, but he had a score to settle and was determined to kill Raven or die trying to.

*****

Willie Doyle pulled back on his horse's reins when he reached Josh and his companions. He told them how he, Major Cooney, and the column of cavalry fought a war party of Kiowas and suffered dozens of casualties. He then told them that Major Cooney had brought a few cannon with him and that those cannons were being positioned to fire upon the Comanches as they spoke.

"Cannons, you said?" General Fitzpatrick asked.

"That's right, sir," Willie replied. "Major Cooney and his soldiers have three with them. He had more, but the others were damaged beyond repair while fighting the Kiowas."

"Three should be enough," General Fitzpatrick said. He then looked at his companions and said, "Ride back with Willie to Major Cooney. You all will be much safer with the major and his soldiers."

"Where are you going?" Cooper asked.

"I'm going to ride my horse toward that Comanche war party and support my son," General Fitzpatrick replied.

"We're coming with you," Cooper said.

"Okay, but not Katherine," General Fitzpatrick said. "Her family must be waiting for her back in Lubbock, and we need to make sure she reunites with her family." He then looked at Willie and said, "Take her to Major Cooney and ask him to have a few of his men escort her back to Lubbock. We need to make—"

"I don't want to go back to Lubbock or anywhere else without your son. He rescued me, and I don't want to desert him when he's trying to save our lives," Katherine interrupted.

"Now listen here, young lady, you will—"

"No, I won't!" Katherine said with a stern voice.

The general stared at Katherine not knowing how to respond. He wasn't used to someone disobeying him. *That's one strong and determined woman*, he thought as he continued staring at Katherine. "Okay, I give up! You can come along with us!"

"I was going to come along with you whether you wanted me to or not!" she exclaimed.

"You made that quite clear," General Fitzpatrick said, wearing a grin on his face. "Now let's go support my son!"

General Fitzpatrick led Cooper, Sergeant Black, Josh, JT, Siringo, Willie, and Katherine toward the large Comanche war party where his son, White Buffalo, was getting ready to risk his life for them.

53

White Buffalo grasped the handle of his tomahawk tightly and waited for Raven to make the first move. He didn't have to wait long. Raven pulled out two tomahawks from his leather belt and charged toward White Buffalo.

Raven swung both his tomahawks at White Buffalo who quickly stepped back to avoid being hit. As he was backing up and ducking out of the way of Raven's tomahawks, he heard a familiar voice yell at him. He looked to his left and saw a Comanche warrior he knew and liked toss a tomahawk toward him. He caught the tomahawk with his left hand and then smiled knowing Raven could no longer overmatch him since they both now had two tomahawks to fight each other with.

Raven continued swinging his two tomahawks at White Buffalo. White Buffalo waited patiently and then saw an opportunity to go on the attack. He used both his tomahawks to block Raven's tomahawks and then started swinging his tomahawks at Raven. As White Buffalo went on the offensive, he heard some of the Comanche warriors start shouting his name.

Some of my Comanche friends are starting to cheer for me. That will make Raven want to kill me even more so he can silence them, White Buffalo thought as he swung his tomahawks at Raven.

Both White Buffalo and Raven were getting tired as their battle with each other continued. Neither one would quit because if one of them did, the other one would surely go for the kill. They continued swinging their tomahawks at each other, but their tomahawks either missed or were blocked.

Raven's frustration grew. He cried out a Comanche war cry then lunged toward White Buffalo. He stumbled forward and then fell face-first to the ground after White Buffalo quickly sidestepped out of the way. He pushed himself up off the ground then attacked White Buffalo with his two tomahawks.

*****

General Fitzpatrick, Cooper, Sergeant Black, Siringo, Josh, JT, Willie, and Katherine rode their horses up to the large Comanche war party. Not a single warrior paid attention to them when they rode their horses up and then halted them next to the warriors. All the warriors were watching White Buffalo and Raven fight while ignoring everything else around them. More and more warriors cheered for White Buffalo as the tomahawk fight between him and Raven continued. When Raven heard more of his warriors cheering for White Buffalo than for him, his hatred for White Buffalo reached its boiling point.

Raven threw one of his tomahawks at White Buffalo. The tomahawk sliced some flesh off White Buffalo's left shoulder and then fell to the ground. Normally, Raven would not have missed at such a close proximity, but he was getting tired and felt weak. White Buffalo felt a burning sensation on the top of his left shoulder but didn't let the pain divert his attention away from Raven. White Buffalo now had the advantage by having two tomahawks against Raven's one. He also heard Raven huffing and puffing and knew his adopted brother was extremely tired from swinging his tomahawks.

"Give up!" White Buffalo yelled.

"No," Raven shouted back. "This is a fight to the death! I'll never give up trying to kill you!"

"I have two tomahawks, and you now only have one!"

"I can still kill you with one tomahawk."

"Give up before I—"

Before White Buffalo could finish what he wanted to say, Raven attacked him. He held his tomahawk in his right hand and swung it several times at White Buffalo. Raven grew frustrated when his tomahawk kept missing. White Buffalo was too quick for him.

"Quit backing up and fight me!" Raven exclaimed.

"I'm giving you one last chance to give up! If you don't, I'm going to kill you!" White Buffalo warned.

"No white-eyes will ever kill me!" Raven stated and then swang his tomahawk at White Buffalo.

White Buffalo used his tomahawk he was holding with his left hand to block Raven's tomahawk. He then used his other tomahawk and sliced it across Raven's chest. Raven looked down and saw blood covering his chest. He then let out a Comanche war cry and swung his tomahawk again at White Buffalo.

White Buffalo blocked Raven's tomahawk again, but this time with the one he was holding in his left hand. He then swung his other tomahawk at Raven. White Buffalo heard Raven moan loudly when his tomahawk embedded in Raven's left shoulder. Raven stumbled forward before falling down onto his knees. He then looked up at White Buffalo, gripped the handle of his tomahawk tightly, and then raised his right arm up intending to throw his tomahawk at White Buffalo. But he never had the chance to.

White Buffalo used his other tomahawk and swung it at Raven. The tomahawk's blade sliced across Raven's throat. Raven wore a stunned expression on his face and stared up at White Buffalo for a few moments before falling down onto his left side. He died moments later lying in a fetal position choking on his own blood.

White Buffalo stood over Raven's lifeless body and stared at it for a few seconds. He then looked up and saw Raven's warriors staring at him. The cheering he heard during the fight had ceased. Would the Comanche warriors allow him and his companions to live since he had killed Raven in a fair fight? Or would they kill him, his father, and the rest of his companions? White Buffalo knew it wouldn't take long for the Comanches to decide his and his companions' fates. If the Comanches decided to kill him and his companions, White Buffalo was determined to kill as many Comanche warriors as he could before they killed him.

54

White Buffalo looked over his left shoulder when he heard a familiar voice yell, "The bluecoats are here!"

War cries erupted from the Comanche war party. Comanches hated the bluecoats and fought with them often but never without their chief. White Buffalo had just slain their chief and were without a leader. A young war chief named Quanah Parker rode his horse into the open area that the Comanche war party surrounded. He was chief of the Quahadi band of the Comanche Nation. He was known as a fierce warrior with great leadership skills. All the bands of the Comanche Nation respected him.

The war cries ceased when the Comanche warriors saw Quanah Parker signaling them to be quiet. Quanah knew the Comanche warriors wanted to fight the bluecoats, kill them all, and then take their scalps as trophies. He also knew the bluecoats brought their big cannons with them and those cannons would cause horrific casualties to the Comanches if they attacked the bluecoats.

Quanah saw White Buffalo walking toward seven white men and one white woman. He called out to White Buffalo and then rode his horse slowly toward him. When White Buffalo heard Quanah Parker calling his name, he stopped then turned around and saw the chief of the Quahadi band of the Comanche Nation sitting tall on his horse.

"Do you want to fight me too?" White Buffalo asked while looking up at Quanah.

"Not today, but if I catch you in Comanche territory again, I will," Quanah warned.

"What about my friends here?"

"They're free to go with you, but they better not step foot again in Blanco Canyon."

"We won't," General Fitzpatrick promised.

Quanah then pointed toward the column of cavalry and said, "Tell those bluecoats to stay away from Blanco Canyon."

"I'll tell them," General Fitzpatrick said. The general knew the bluecoats would be back one day to force the Comanches onto a reservation, but he knew this was not the time to tell Quanah that.

"You tell them if they come back here, they'll be wiped out!" Quanah said with confidence. He then pointed his rifle at White Buffalo and yelled, "Get out of here before I change my mind!" He then spun his horse around and led the large Comanche war party toward Blanco Canyon.

"Will Quanah be the next chief of the Comanche Nation?" a curious Cooper asked.

"I think—"

A loud thundering noise interrupted White Buffalo. He and the others turned toward the noise and saw Major Kevin Cooney leading his column of cavalry toward them. They stood still as the cavalry column approached and felt relieved that the Comanche war party was returning to Blanco Canyon. Major Kevin Cooney halted his column of cavalry and then rode his horse slowly up to Cooper, White Buffalo, General Fitzpatrick, and their companions.

"We have our canons in place and ready to fire when those Comanches decide to attack us," Major Cooney said after he halted his horse.

"They won't be attacking us today," Cooper said. "White Buffalo just killed their chief so they're going back to Blanco Canyon to elect a new leader."

"How long will it take for them to elect a new leader?" Major Cooney asked.

"A day or two, but maybe even sooner," White Buffalo replied.

"Will their new leader want war or peace with us?"

"War most likely."

"We better be a long way away from here when those Comanches come back out of Blanco Canyon," Major Cooney suggested. "We are too few right now and don't want to be caught out here in the open without more soldiers and cannon."

"I agree with the major," General Fitzpatrick said.

"We'll escort you all back to Fort Concho," Major Cooney said.

"Thank you, Major," General Fitzpatrick said. "We'll be ready to leave in a minute." The general waited for his son, White Buffalo, to mount his horse. He then turned toward Major Cooney and said, "We're ready to follow you and your men back to Fort Concho."

Katherine looked at White Buffalo and asked, "Will my parents be waiting for me at Fort Concho?"

Josh overheard Katherine and answered, "No. They will be waiting for you back in Lubbock."

"Will you take me there?" Katherine asked.

"I sure will," Josh replied.

"My father and I will visit you in Lubbock soon," White Buffalo promised.

"You better!"

"Don't worry! We will!" General Fitzpatrick also promised.

*****

Before Major Cooney ordered his men to ride their horses to Fort Concho, he made a loud announcement to them. "From this day forward, Cooper McCaw will no longer be branded a coward. He will be reinstated into the US Cavalry not at his former rank, which was a lieutenant, but at the higher rank of captain effective immediately." Major Cooney then looked at Cooper, smiled, and said, "Welcome back!"

"Thank you, sir," Cooper said.

"Thank General Fitzpatrick. He ordered it."

Cooper turned toward the general and said, "Thank you, sir."

"You owe me no thanks," General Fitzpatrick said. "You completed your mission and reunited me with my son. If anyone should be saying 'thank you,' it's me. The US Cavalry is lucky to have an officer like you. As soon as we get back to Fort Concho, we need to get you fitted for a new uniform. Those civilian clothes you're wearing are worn out and full of holes."

"Yes, they are, sir," Cooper concurred and then grinned.

Major Cooney rode his horse up to Cooper and then asked him, "Will you give the order to the column to ride to Fort Concho?"

"Yes, sir," Cooper responded, wearing a smile on his face. He then rode his horse slowly to the head of the cavalry column and halted his horse next to a proud-looking Sergeant Black.

Cooper smiled at Sergeant Black before raising his right hand above his head. He then commanded the column to move forward toward Fort Concho. As Cooper rode his horse toward Fort Concho, he was grateful he would no longer be branded a coward and could move forward in his life as an officer in the US Cavalry. He was anxious to wear a cavalry uniform again even though he knew he would most likely be ordered to return to Blanco Canyon one day to fight the hostile Comanches again.

55

Captain Josh Stephens smiled when he saw White Buffalo and General Fitzpatrick ride their horses into the town of Lubbock. It had been three long weeks since he last saw his two new friends, and he was anxious to visit with them. When White Buffalo and his father saw Josh waving at them, they rode their horses at a trot toward him. They both halted their horses a few yards from Josh, dismounted, and then exchanged pleasantries with the Texas Ranger. After a short conversation about their past exploits at Blanco Canyon, White Buffalo asked Josh if Katherine White reunited with her parents.

"No, she did not," Josh replied.

"Did they give up on her being rescued?" General Fitzpatrick asked.

"No, they did not," Josh answered.

"Then what happened?" the general asked.

"Both her parents died a month ago I was told after I returned to Lubbock," Josh replied.

"Died from what?" White Buffalo asked.

"Pneumonia," Josh answered while wearing a frown on his face.

"Is Katherine still here in Lubbock?" White Buffalo asked.

"Yes, she is," Josh responded.

"How is she handling her parents' deaths?" a concerned-looking White Buffalo asked.

"She's still mourning their deaths, but she's doing better every day," Josh replied. "I got her a job at a saloon here in town, which is keeping her busy. She speaks of you often, White Buffalo. I can tell she misses you."

"I want to see her," White Buffalo said. "Which saloon does she work at?"

"The one over there," Josh said while pointing at the saloon.

White Buffalo thanked Josh and then moved toward the saloon. His father, General Fitzpatrick, followed him. General Fitzpatrick knew his son cared for Katherine and had been concerned about her since they parted way back at Fort Concho.

*****

A gambler named Nolan Shep just won a large amount of greenbacks at the table he was gambling at. He was in a good mood and wanted to celebrate. He stood up, said goodbye to his fellow gamblers, and then walked over to the bar.

When Nolan saw Katherine White standing near the end of the bar, he walked toward her. He called out to the bartender to fetch him a bottle of whiskey and two shot glasses. When he reached the bar, he positioned himself next to Katherine and started flirting with her. Katherine was immediately turned off by Nolan's bad breath and had no interest in him or any other man. She was interested in only one man, and she doubted she would ever see him again.

"May I poor you a shot of whiskey?" Nolan asked Katherine after he introduced himself and flirted with her for a couple of minutes.

"No thanks," she replied.

"Why not?" Nolan asked with a stern voice. "Am I not good enough for you?"

"There's only one man good enough for me, and he's not here," she answered, wearing a frown on her face.

"What the hell are you working here for if you're in love with someone?"

"That's a good question," Katherine replied. Katherine then looked at the bartender named Sam, and said, "I quit!"

"You what?" a stunned-looking Sam said.

"I quit!" she said again. She then pushed her way through the crowded saloon and headed for its swinging doors.

"Wait a minute, you whore! You can't quit on me!" Sam exclaimed.

Katherine stopped, spun around, glared at Sam, and asked, "What did you just say?"

"You heard me," Sam responded with a stern voice.

Katherine continued glaring at Sam but kept her mouth shut this time. She tried to keep her anger under control but couldn't. No one ever called her a whore before. She was furious and wanted Sam to apologize publicly for calling her a whore.

"You better apologize for calling me a whore," she demanded.

"That will never happen!" Sam said with confidence. He then pointed at her and said, "Get back to work before I slap your beautiful face and keep slapping it until I make it look ugly."

"If you lay a hand on her, I'll kill you!"

Katherine's anger disappeared and was replaced with a joyous expression when she heard White Buffalo's voice. She turned around and saw the man she had fallen in love with facing her. She fell into his arms and held him tightly. She then said, "I was hoping you would come for me."

White Buffalo gently pushed Katherine away from him and told her to go outside and wait for him with his father, General Fitzpatrick. She looked deeply into his eyes with happy tears flowing down her face, nodded her head, and then walked toward the swinging doors of the saloon.

White Buffalo turned his attention toward Sam and walked calmly up to him. He stopped a few feet in front of the bartender and then asked, "What did you call Katherine?"

"I called her a whore," Sam replied.

"That's what I thought I heard you call her," White Buffalo said and then asked Sam, "Why did you call her that for?"

"Because—" Sam didn't finish his response because White Buffalo slammed his fist into Sam's face with such force that Sam was lifted off his feet and landed unconscious on the Saloon's wooden floor. Blood was coming out of Sam's mouth, his nose was broken, and three of his teeth lay on the wooden floor next to him.

*****

Katherine stood nervously next to General Fitzpatrick. She heard loud cheers coming from the saloon and worried about White Buffalo when she heard the sounds of celebration. Her concern for the man she loved quickly disappeared when she saw White Buffalo push through the swinging doors of the saloon.

Katherine ran toward White Buffalo as he walked toward her. She fell into his arms and held him tightly. She then whispered into his right ear, "I prayed every night to God to protect you and your father since we parted ways."

"God answered your prayers," White Buffalo said quietly as he and Katherine continued holding each other in their arms.

"Did you come to see me, or are you and your father just passing through this town?" Katherine asked.

"My father and I came here to take you away with us."

"Where are you two going?"

"We thought we head up to the Montana Territory and start a ranch."

"That's sounds interesting," an excited-sounding Katherine said. She then gently pushed herself away from White Buffalo and looked over at General Fitzpatrick. "Are you okay with me coming along with you and White Buffalo?"

In a stern voice, General Fitzpatrick said, "If you don't come with us, I will be very mad at you."

"I would hate to see you mad at me," Katherine said. She then turned her attention back to White Buffalo and asked, "Why do you want me to come with you?"

"How are you going to be my wife if you stay here and I'm up in Montana?" he replied.

"Your what?" Katherine asked, wearing a huge smile on her face.

"My wife!" White Buffalo exclaimed.

Katherine continued smiling as she looked deeply into White Buffalo's eyes. She then said, "Take me to Montana and please take me now!"

"Now wait a minute," General Fitzpatrick said as he approached Katherine and White Buffalo, "We're not going to Montana until you two get married."

"Is there a church in this town?" White Buffalo asked.

"There's one over there!" Captain Josh Stephens said as came walking up to White Buffalo, Katherine, and General Fitzpatrick.

"Is the preacher available?" White Buffalo asked.

"If he's not, I'll marry the two of you," Josh said. "Now let's get the two of you married."

"Yes, sir," White Buffalo and Katherine responded concurrently before falling into each other's arms again.

General Fitzpatrick smiled while watching his son and Katherine hug. He never thought he would be able to get his son out of Blanco Canyon alive. And he wouldn't have without the help of lots of very brave men. Now he could forget about Blanco Canyon and look forward to moving to the Montana Territory with his son and soon-to-be daughter-in-law.

THE END

ABOUT THE AUTHOR

David E. Waddell graduated from Revere High School in Richfield, Ohio. He then earned a BA in history from Oral Roberts University in Tulsa, Oklahoma, and a juris doctor from Thomas Cooley Law School in Lansing, Michigan. He currently splits time between Akron, Ohio, and Bonita Springs, Florida. He's married with two children.

Printed in the USA
CPSIA information can be obtained
at www.ICGtesting.com
LVHW091127021124
795328LV00002B/176

9 798894 270401